UNCORRECTED PROOF

Our Lady of Good Voyage

Our Lady of Good Voyage

Kevin Honold

ORISON
BOOKS

Our Lady of Good Voyage
Copyright © 2024 by Kevin Honold
All rights reserved.

Print ISBN: 978-1-949039-46-7
E-book ISBN: 978-1-949039-48-1

Orison Books
PO Box 8385
Asheville, NC 28814
www.orisonbooks.com

Cover art: collaged details from "Three Figures in a Moonlit Landscape" (1914) by Georges Rouault.
Cover design by Luke Hankins and Addison Skigen.

Manufactured in the U.S.A.

CONTENTS

Prologue	1
Chapter One	4
Chapter Two	13
Chapter Three	62
Chapter Four	69
Chapter Five	134
Chapter Six	138
Chapter Seven	179
Chapter Eight	185
Chapter Nine	193
Chapter Ten	211
Epilogue	220
About the Author	233
About Orison Books	234

When they sawe the starre, they were marveylously glad.

–Tyndale's *Newe Testament*, 1526

Prologue

Two shirtless boys sat on a curb with their bare feet flat in the gutter.

A blue car passed. A red car passed.

Kenny said, "Let's go to the burnt house and get that raccoon. I'm gonna make a pet of him."

"You'll never catch it," Joe said. His shorts, soaked with creek water, stained the pavement where he sat, and the stain crept down the gutter like a shadow. "That thing'll eat you alive." The noon sun stood in a cloudless sky. Its heat lulled him into dull watchfulness. As the sunshine crept through his damp hair, a brief shiver seized his shoulders.

The raccoon that lived in the burnt house was a mean and sober mama marked like a bandit. It was bigger than Billy Herlihi's raccoon too. Joe imagined her perched like a sailor's parrot on Kenny's shoulder. He imagined encountering the older boys who often sat on the loading dock behind the school smoking their mothers' cigarettes, and he anticipated the admiration that the raccoon would garner on Kenny's behalf. As Kenny's friend, Joe was certain to enjoy some collateral regard.

*

Armed with Wrist Rocket slingshots, they crouched in the weeds and observed the burnt house. Kenny fired a rock through a windowpane to see if anyone was home, but there was never anyone home no matter how many windowpanes they broke. The glass crashed with an outsize noise that shattered the noon calm. The boys squatted low and listened, but nothing stirred, and the stillness settled once more.

Bent low, they crossed the overgrown and littered yard on the double, scrambled through a window, and landed on a floor covered in familiar trash: splintered lathing and beer bottles and crockery, picture frames and magazines. Wide-eyed, ankle-deep in the startled dust, they listened to something scurry across the ceiling. A train sounded, compounding the sense of abandonment Joe felt whenever they visited this place, where silence called to silence from room to room. They set off down the hall.

In the drawers on prior visits, they had found photographs of people posing stiffly in cloaks and furs on the streets of alien, colorless cities where great spires adorned the sky. The words on the reverse sides of the photographs were written in a language that they could not read.

The previous winter, they had found a bill of currency worth one hundred thousand Reichsmarks, and they luxuriated for days in a surfeit of newfound wealth, beside themselves with good fortune. There it was, a real number, plain as day, printed in English on both sides of the bill: 100,000. The bill's Gothic script added to its legitimacy.

But they did not know what to do with the bill, and they were afraid to ask someone, so they placed the bill in a baby food jar and buried it down by the sewage treatment plant, preserving it against the day when they would learn the value of one Reichsmark and— of critical importance—whether one Reichsmark possessed the same value as one dollar. They had to find a bank that dealt in such matters or a moneychanger they could trust. With some misgiving, they admitted the necessity of taking Billy Herlihi into their confidence. Billy might know a moneychanger, but the kid himself was not above suspicion.

Whenever Joe entered the house, he wondered about these mysterious people who had arrived from grim and distant kingdoms. Why had they come here, and why had they departed this house in such a hurry leaving a fortune behind? Joe feared that one day he would turn a corner and encounter an elderly lady wearing a black-and-white checkered house dress like his grandma's, and she would turn away without a word. Or he would enter one of the trashed bedrooms on the upper floor and find an old man seated in a wooden chair at a wooden desk, turning from an unfinished letter to gaze out the window. In his mind, the couple never spoke, but neither were they malevolent. They lived, he imagined, like sovereign mice—hungry, sufficient unto themselves—in the undiscovered rooms of the house.

Kenny dragged a dresser beneath a hole in the ceiling. He climbed up and peered into the attic. "It's up there! The mama raccoon!" he said and jumped down.

He dashed into and out of rooms and returned carrying a butterfly net and wearing a German helmet, the oversize coal bucket sort with the bolts at the temples. He heaved himself through the hole, and his dangling legs kicked as he ascended, like a cat hoisted by the scruff.

Joe tracked the sound of footsteps across the ceiling, and he heard his friend's voice. "It's okay. I ain't gonna hurt you."

There occurred a racket and a cry. Kenny fell through the ceiling in a shower of plaster ten feet from the hole he'd entered by. He sat stunned, feet spread in the dust. Behind him, the empty helmet rocked on the boards.

Joe said, "Oh man, look at that!" A strip of lathing was fastened to the bottom of Kenny's sneaker and the nail was protruding, rusty and damp, through the shoe's upper canvas. Kenny looked in awe at his own foot, as from a great distance, and said, "There's no blood. And it doesn't hurt." Joe grabbed Kenny's ankle and pulled out the nail. Now it did hurt.

That afternoon, Kenny's mom took him to the clinic for tetanus and rabies shots, and the dream of acquiring a raccoon that would outshine Billy Herlihi's came to naught.

One

He drove slowly down Republic. On a few buildings—in faded letters high on the brick walls or engraved on the lintels—were the names of vanished proprietors printed in a disused script: *Lebensversicherung. Baptisten Kirche. Freie Presse. Apotheke.*

Many of the city's earlier residents had moved away to the suburbs in the surrounding hills. Now superimposed on the faded letters, were the watchwords of the new dispensation: *Smiling Sam's Used Furniture* and *Tip Top Barber Shop* and *Chickasaw Hill Chapel. Casa de Cambio, Sunshine China. Community Action Network. Catholic Worker Field Office.*

The residents of the neighborhood were the children of Black southerners who never made it north, Black northerners who never made it south, and a white remainder who never made it west.

More changes were afoot. Among the recent arrivals were Appalachians from the busted coal counties of eastern Kentucky and West Virginia. Guatemalans, Hondurans too. And college kids and artist types.

A few elderly Germans remained to haunt their disinheritance. They emerged now and then from some dim corner of the city's memory: an old man or woman in a woolen coat, shuffling down the sidewalk, making their relentless way to a produce shop. Like ghosts, they appeared always when Joe was thinking of something else. They seemed to be an incurious sort too, these deathless Germans, lacking the imagination to move on—which, he understood, is also true of ghosts.

*

Heavy, hot, windless weather. The people of the neighborhood were on the sidewalks, laughing, talking, sitting on chairs and buckets and stoops—anything to escape the stifling rooms. Two old men played cards at a makeshift table that was a wooden door set across cinder blocks. Mothers sat on folding metal chairs and trimmed and braided their daughters' hair. Young men lounged near radios and kept a careless watch over the passing cars.

On the sidewalk, a man led a woman by the arm. She walked beside him with her head down. When the man stopped, he placed a hand on her shoulder; when she tried to walk on, he pulled her back. Like a dance, the way he kept sidling in front of her, whichever way she turned. She recoiled from him as from a sweat bee but no longer tried to slip away. At last he stalked off, glancing over his shoulder at her as he departed, and she remained in her appointed place, posted to the sidewalk. Two men slowed as they brushed past her, spoke a few low words. They laughed and looked her down.

When Joe pulled in front of the woman, she began to walk away.

"You're not in trouble. Hang on. I just had a question is all."

She paused ten feet from the cruiser and bent to peer through the passenger-side window, keeping her arms folded around her waist. A six-inch scar ran obliquely down the side of her neck. Her short black hair was combed up straight.

"Pretty hot out," he said and had an impulse to suggest she find a cooler place, then he felt stupid, then said nothing.

"What?"

"Do you need anything?" he said and thought, God help me.

"What?"

"Look," he said. "I'm just asking. Are you in any trouble?"

"My feet hurt," she said, still bent at the waist. She glanced sidelong down the street. "My feet hurt from shopping. I been taking Tylenols for a sore throat, but they don't do nothing."

"What's the sore throat from? Allergies? Air pollution?"

"I don't know. Air pollution."

"Well, Tylenols are for pain, far as I know, but they ain't gonna do anything for a sore throat." He took out his wallet and handed her two dollar bills and suggested she buy lozenges. She took the bills and walked away muttering about having to shop all day.

As he drove off, it occurred to him that he'd exchanged words in a common language with another human being but had failed to trade a single piece of worthwhile information. It was laughable that the conversation had concluded with lozenges. I may as well be a goddamn German, he thought.

*

He parked the cruiser and walked across the street into the bar, where the bartender, the only person in the place, tucked the pencil behind her ear. He couldn't help smiling in the cool dark, knowing, as they both knew, that there was nothing he would ever be able to hide from her.

Vera opened an RC and set it on the bar top. "What time are you going to be home? Should we wait to eat?"

"No, I'm on till ten, but thanks. It's so damn hot out; there's nothin' shakin'. The murderers are watching television in their AC just like any sensible human." He took a long drink. The radio mike coughed. He turned the volume dial down to a hiss. "Ah, stuff it."

"Gosh. The heat is making you testy, isn't it?" she said. "I hope that wasn't for you."

"Of course it wasn't for me. So I'm a malingerer now?"

"Listen to you. So this is the big day, huh? Flying solo now? How is it?"

"I haven't shot myself yet." He handed the empty bottle to her and put his cap on. "Thanks. What do I owe?"

"Bring me a box of pasta, Officer Riley. See you tonight."

"Maybe. Maybe not."

There were things about this city and this work that everyone knew. The people on the street knew; the other cops knew. But when the people and the cops spoke about these things, they spoke in code, and when they decided not to speak about things, they were silent in code as well, and he knew that no matter how long he was among them, no one was ever going to tell him anything.

He cruised the uptown neighborhoods with the windows down, past the tall, narrow brick buildings. The weird lichen of graffiti spread across the walls in livid and iridescent colors.

*

The street narrowed. On the facades of buildings, he could see where the courses of mortar had deteriorated, how the limestone lintels were pitted, how the masonry had decayed over a century of winters and toxic rains.

A woman leaned from a window. A shirtless man straddled a sill with one leg hanging down the brick. A broken broom handle propped a dry-rotted sash.

Ahead, city workers were paving a lane, and traffic was stopped in both directions as a dump truck attempted to change direction. While the truck backed and filled in a nine-point turn, the workers raked asphalt in front of a creeping leveler. They wore stained orange vests and tar-smeared boots and hardhats pasted with American flag decals; they worked slowly, thoughtfully, like actors demonstrating the proper use of tools instead of road workers using them. The newly dropped asphalt smoked like fresh manure on a winter morning. One worker leaned on his rake with a pained expression, mouth open.

The drivers ahead of him waited in resigned postures, elbows on doors, supporting their heads with the heels of their hands. One man angrily wrenched his gearshift into park and threw himself back into his seat. Joe felt gratified by the outburst. "Get a grip, fuckface," he said out loud.

Through his window came the smell of boiling tar. Kitchen exhaust from a diner filled the street with a miasma of grill grease—a ropy, glutinous mix of stewed onions and pickles and scalded beef—with no breeze to carry it away. The odor collected dew-like on his neck and on the backs of his hands.

Gray crusty trash dammed the gutters. A smashed, half-eaten fish sandwich lay on the threshold of an entryway, as though it had been mightily hurled against the door.

He wound the window up. The flagger waved them through.

*

He parked the cruiser near the bus stop in front of the library, where a few dozen kids were shouting and laughing, bossing one another. The boys yanked on the girls' backpacks and hollered; the girls smoked expertly as they chatted and scorned the boys with curses.

He accosted two shouting students.

"Where you going?"

"We're waiting on the bus!"

"Which bus?"

"Seventy-seven."

"You know as well as I do that the seventy-seven picks up in front of the courthouse. Take your bags and go there. You're blocking the door here."

They wandered off laughing.

The city had mounted a speaker at the library entrance where the kids were wont to gather after school. It was the intention of the authorities to drive the kids away with loud classical music, confident that Beethoven, like a string of garlic, would ward off a teenager. Not so. In the middle of the sidewalk, six girls paired off into three couples, placed their hands on their partners' shoulders, and commenced with gracious smiles to dance a waltz by Schubert.

*

At Fourteenth and Bank, a woman wearing a black cocktail dress and carrying a faded backpack on her shoulder navigated the broken sidewalk in high heels. There was something significant, he thought, in the single-mindedness with which the woman hurried off, like a guest slipping away with a pocketful of spoons.

For a few hours, he accompanied a wrecker as it hauled broken cars off the street. Later at the scene of a house fire, he helped to cordon the streets for the ladder trucks. Flames snapped in the sultry air, and the fire roared as it fed on rafters and carpets and mice nests. People hugged and cried on the street, but there was nothing to do for it.

Toward the end of his shift, he pulled to a stop at a red light. People stood in clutches at the corners in front of barred and tinted shop windows.

Kids threaded bikes around garbage cans, their maneuvers choreographed to a trunk bass that caused the cruiser's mirrors to shiver.

*

In a basement bar he ordered a decaf and lit a cigarette. Inside was dark and cool, the solitude a relief. A row of windows high on the wall offered a view of the sidewalk where the disembodied feet of passersby hurried in both directions, constantly on the verge, it seemed, of breaking into a dead run. The door opened and a man walked in.

"What's new? I know you. I'm Fergus. Darryl's son. Kenny's cousin." The man took a seat and kept an empty stool between them. "You're Kenny's friend."

"I am. I remember you. You showed up for that roof job in Ashburn."

They shook hands. "Ashburn. That's right. First and last time I ever worked for him. I don't know how you and Kenny lasted so long."

"Me neither," Joe said. "He taught us some things, though. I can't see a work van without recalling how your dad threatened my life with a number ten wrench."

Fergus laughed. "You're a cop now."

"Working for the city, yep. Since about a year back I guess."

"What gave you the idea? If you don't mind my asking."

"There was an ad in the paper. What are you up to?"

"Painting. Started my own operation. Lots a yuppies moving downtown, rehabbing those old brownstones on Twelfth, Thirteenth. Shoot, I'm turning down jobs. I can't find nobody to work. What're you having?"

"Nothing. Thanks. Coffee."

"Quit drinking?"

"No."

"I hear you." He ordered a beer and a shot.

They smoked.

Joe watched the feet of the passersby. "Seen Kenny?"

"Not for years. You mean you haven't seen him? Where's he at?"

"I'm not for sure. He might be here in town. He'll turn up."

"You two were buddies."

"We were. We are. We got discharged at different times and never caught up again. You know, you stop talking to someone, and it just gets easier to continue not talking. It's been ten years, I think."

"Every so often I wonder about that guy. I don't see any family.

We ain't ones for reunions. My mom told me she heard he's living in a monastery in Egypt. I don't know who in the world told her that."

"Beats me. He'd like that, though," Joe said.

"He would too. My brother told me he thought he heard Kenny cracked up and was packed off to Longview."

"He'd like that even better."

"What else? Oh, yeah. I heard he's working for the DEA."

"That would just worry him."

"I might've made up that one. What a funny dude he was. Or is. My dad, as you know, wasn't the biggest fan of the human race, but he liked Kenny a lot." Fergus crushed his cigarette, set a five on the bar, handed his card to Joe. "Well, if you ever get tired of making a difference in the community, give me a ring. There's plenty of work. I'll sub you out and you can name your price. Tell Kenny I said *hey*. If you see him."

The card read *F.B.I. Fergus Building & Improvement*. Joe put it in his wallet, watched the feet of passersby in the window. The bartender sat on a stool on the drinking-side of the bar and read the sports pages. The radio, turned low, was tuned to the oldies station.

All summer long, Johnny Rivers sang, *we were groovin' in the sand*

Joe recalled long rides to job sites in an unmarked van, Uncle Darryl behind the wheel, singing along to the radio. Darryl kept the dial pegged to the same station that was playing right now. Kenny's uncle knew all the words to all those songs. As he sat at the bar, Joe recalled the old man mumbling along to a drowsy tune. A scent of scorched solder paste occurred to him just then, a trace in the air, and he sat up. But it was just a trick of the mind.

Yes, Kenny was in town. That was certain. I'll pop by his mom's house, Joe decided, someday soon, after my shift. She probably knows something. He might even be there, buried in his books in the basement. I should say *hello* to her anyway, he thought.

I have changed in the ten years since I last saw him. Maybe Kenny will notice a difference. I have done nothing significant, but I am not the same, and he will notice that. That's because I'm subject to the effects of time, like regular people. I fade a bit each day, get wearier by the year, and at some not-too-distant hour I'll stop breathing. But Kenny was never subject to time. He always was and would remain himself. He probably won't even die like the rest of us. He'll just vanish in a puff of smoke. He'll die different. That's how he is.

I will tell him these things when I find him, he thought.

A man's bare feet—conspicuous among the many shod feet—appeared in the window, stepping casually with the sidewalk traffic. Joe tracked the feet as they passed in and out of view, from pane to pane across the wall. He dropped the cigarette in the tray and ran to the door, past the startled bartender, up the stairs, and onto the street. He sprinted past the pedestrians in the direction the bare feet had taken. At the intersection he stopped, breathing hard as passersby stared at the man in the cop uniform who was behaving strangely.

He peered down each of the three blocks in turn. But everyone he saw wore shoes.

Two

The bus docked at the curb. He fed the ticket machine, sat down on the bench. Kenny, seated across the aisle, didn't look up but sat slouched in his flannel and jeans, reading a book whose title was printed in white type on the upper spine: *The Voyages of Captain James Cook*. When Kenny turned the page with the tips of his fingers, Joe felt his irritation rise.

"Cook was fearless," Kenny said, tapping the page. "Off he goes with a crew that believes in sea monsters, sailing clear down to where the sun never rises. The last place you want to bring a bunch of men who believe in sea monsters is Antarctica. Don't you agree? But that's just my opinion. Don't you agree, Joe?"

The other passengers read the bulkhead ads for cut-rate car insurance or observed the middle air with practiced dispassion. Joe picked at some dried joint compound on his trouser knee.

"Some of these guys had never left sight of the coast," Kenny said. "The world had only been round for two hundred years. And now they arrive at this place where mountains of ice are floating in the water! So Cook sends a boat out with four men to investigate. They break off a few chunks of ice, bring them back to the ship, and guess what: it's fresh water! That's how Cook solved the drinking-water problem. The sailors were probably thinking, what the heck? How can this be? How can gigantic ice cubes of fresh water be floating in a salt sea? I mean, put yourself in their shoes for a minute. Even with your fancy modern high school education, Joe, you wouldn't have a clue. But then, you never paid any attention in science class anyway. Honestly, I don't know how you earned a diploma."

Joe watched a man pedal a bicycle down the sidewalk. The man stopped at a newspaper machine, scanned the headlines, dug a few coins from his pocket, thumbed them into the slot and pulled out a paper. He read a bit more as he sat on his bike, folded the paper under his arm and pedaled off. One-handed. In no hurry. What a jerk, Joe thought. Where's that guy get off? He pulled the cord.

"I have something to tell you," Kenny said, as they walked down the street toward Darryl's place. "I had a visitor last night. I woke from a dream and sensed a presence in the room. It was a woman. She was barefoot and wearing a colorful robe, a kinda patchy, frayed, colorful robe. Like a milkmaid. Like an Incan milkmaid. There she was at the foot of the bed, watching me."

"I heard about them types."

"She wasn't malevolent. She had a smile, an old sad smile. She knew me. It was Mary. She had a crown of stars, Joe, and she wore a cloak of sunlight. I couldn't speak, then she vanished. Do you believe me? Of course you don't." He added worriedly, "I think I offended her. She had a message, but she didn't give it, because I was so frightened!" Kenny slowed to a stop. "It wasn't a dream, Joe. She'll be back. Don't you think?"

"They always come back. Now walk."

"You won't tell anyone, Joe, will you?"

"Of course not."

In the small gravel lot behind the house—beside the rear door of an unmarked Econoline van with ladder racks bolted to the roof—a man was waiting with his hands on his hips and an unlit cigar in his mouth. As they came down the driveway from the street, the man made a show of reading his watch. "There's honest, God-fearing citizens out there waiting to shit and shower and you two come wandering in without a care in the world like la-dee-fuckin-dah."

"We ain't late, Uncle Darryl!" Kenny said.

"Kenny saw a ghost, Darryl. Not a scary one. It was dressed up like an ancient milkmaid. It mighta been Mary, but we're not sure."

Darryl glanced at a slip of paper in his hand. "I don't want to hear a lot of silly shit today, Kenny. Now get in the van and check them fittings bins. Some of 'em are empty goddamnit. We're low on inch-and-a-half elbows and nineties, and we'll need a load cause it's gonna be a long goddam day. Get some wax rings and mud blades out of the garage. And the toilet auger. Wipe the poo off that auger before you put it in my truck, hear me? Sonsabitches."

*

"Hand tools," Darryl said as he pulled to a stop. Joe opened the rear double doors of the van and picked through a mess of tools and trash for a flashlight, screwdriver, Channellocks. He slipped them into his back trouser pocket and followed the others to the door of a four-family. The shades were drawn on the ground-floor windows.

The man who opened the door wore flip-flops. A ratty T-shirt fell halfway down his boxers. What remained of his thinning hair hung in damp spindles over his shoulders. "Are you the plumbers?"

"No, we're the I-team from channel seven," Darryl said. "I'm pullin' your leg, chief. You called about a toilet problem?"

The man turned without a word and Joe followed the spectral blue of Darryl's shirt through the dark room. As he stepped between knee-high stacks of magazines, his eyes adjusted sufficiently to read the titles on the covers. *Cherry. Hustler. Barely Legal.*

The three workers crowded into a bathroom to consider the shit-filled bowl. A fine gauze of body hair was lacquered onto the vanity countertop by a coat of Final Net. The miasma of Colgate and feces and peroxide stopped Joe's breath.

Darryl viewed the bowl with his mouth shut tight. "Didn't wait too long to call, did you? Another day and you could plant Old Glory on this mess." The man watched from the doorway, his back to the leaning shadows of the hall, and did not answer.

Darryl said to Kenny, "Run upstairs and tell the people above us to flush their toilet." They listened to footsteps, muffled talk, the silver rush of water in the pipes. Darryl flushed the tank and the waste rose, ebbed sluggishly, then stilled.

"Okay, we'll take it from here," Darryl said, and shut the door in the man's face. "Alright. Here's the lesson for the day, numbskull. You ready? Now, we know the stack is clear because the upstairs toilet flushed fine, right? That means the obstruction is in the bowl's trap—probably his panties or his Raggedy Ann doll, by the looks of him. So now we're faced with what's called a dilemma. We can get the auger and rod this toilet, in the process of which we'll splatter ourselves with this pervert's shit. If you're not keen on that, then I propose we move on to plan B."

He squatted and cracked the bowl's base with a sharp rap from the Channellocks.

Darryl opened the door and called the man back into the room. "Look here," he explained, pointing to the toilet's base. "The toilet's busted. See that crack? That crack'll migrate through the bowl and one day the fucking thing'll crack in half, probably while you're in the middle of one of your movements. We'll get you a new one. Forty bucks sound alright?"

The man turned away. They unbolted the toilet and tipped it free of the seal. "How'd I get to be so smart?" Darryl said to Joe. "Where's my idiot nephew at?"

"I think he's still upstairs."

"Jesus Christ. Kenny!"

As Joe and Darryl crab walked to the door, carrying the toilet between them, faces twisted from the bowl, Darryl said, "Be back in an hour," through the corner of his mouth. The man stood in silhouette against the window, backlit by the daylight burning through the drawn blinds.

Kevin Honold

They drove behind a McDonald's and heaved the toilet into the trash container. In the back of the van was another toilet salvaged from a recent tear-out job. They freed the thing from a tangle of debris, wiped it down with rags, drove it back to the house, installed it, and left with two twenties.

*

"Nephew, you read a lot of books, but do you know the first thing about practical matters?" Darryl asked as they sped down the state route. "I mean, like how to run a business? For instance, take the forty bucks I just peeled off that child molester. Where's that money go? Do you know? Tell me."

Kenny frowned at the road. "I don't know, Uncle Darryl. Taxes?"

"Taxes! I don't pay any dumbass taxes. Listen now. Five goes in the tank. Five goes to coffee and cigarillos—that's what they call overhead. Ten goes to pay off two poor incompetent children for doing nothing. And twenty goes to the landfill because I gotta pay to dispose of the junk that people pay me to remove. What's left over, Nephew? A lotto ticket and a corn dog if I'm lucky. It's a blessed miracle I make enough to drink."

Darryl turned onto the unpaved track that led to the top of the landfill. The low-slung sky above a moonscape of mud reminded Joe of pictures of a World War I battlefield he had seen in one of Kenny's books. Dark clouds scudded by, wrung to husks; crows lifted and settled on scattered heaps of trash. Here and there in the green stormlight, garbage trucks backed into position, arched their backs, and shat. Darryl pulled up beside a ditch of half-buried refuse, and they commenced to clean out the van.

Kenny winged a chunk of Sheetrock into the mud and paused to survey the scene. "She was wearing a crown of stars when she appeared to me," he said.

"Don't get all moony back there, Kenny," Darryl said from the driver's seat without a glance in the mirror. "It stinks on this hill." Smoke from his noon cigar drifted into the back of the van, where Kenny and Joe were pitching garbage. "Clear it out and let's go."

"Who?" Joe asked.

"The Star of the Sea. Mary. I knew you weren't listening to me. She's bringing a vision to everyone on earth. One person at a time. Now it's my turn."

Sea birds wheeled and screamed, three hundred miles from any open water; they pilfered the heaps, battled one another for scraps, carried off food-wrappers and sundry rot. Earthmovers assaulted the new piles with the relentlessness of insects. Black and white plastic garbage bags stuck like grit to the dozer blades.

Kenny picked up a five-gallon bucket filled with broken tile and slung it like so much dirty bathwater. "The earth will be renewed, and heaven will be renewed. That is the promise, and we all have a part to play. She's going to visit every one of us, one by one, and tell us all we need to know."

As he squatted at the open rear door of the van, shoving out waterlogged plaster and splintered lathing, Joe noticed household items uncovered by the earthmovers' tracks: a smashed highchair, a box of mason jars, a vinyl suitcase. "How does she know English?"

"She spoke Nahuatl to Juan Diego and French to Saint Bernadette. So she speaks English to English speakers. That's the nature of miracles. It's the ears of the heart that hear the words and understand, Joe. Not the ears of the head."

"Oh. I see."

The van was cleared except for the tools and three American flags on poles, which Darryl had taken from a flooded basement. Joe grasped them in his fist like a brace of javelins and was set to hurl them into the mud when Darryl shouted at him from the cab. "Fuckhead! Set those flags down."

"They're dirty, Darryl."

"I don't care if Tojo wiped his balls with them. They're American flags! Jesus, what is the matter with you idiots these days?"

*

They crossed and re-crossed the city, driving from call to call. From the truck stop on the southern rim of the business loop where the drains in the kitchen had backed up to cover the floor in three inches of greasy water, to the pricey developments north of town where half-million-dollar houses baked on treeless half-acre lots and homeowners fretted over dripping faucets and the dirt on Kenny's boots. From the industrial park office whose shoddy construction was a personal affront to Darryl—where a burst water line had turned the ceiling tiles to the consistency of oatmeal—to the restaurant downtown where a grease trap required periodic attention.

The trap was the size of a sea chest and Darryl knelt to unscrew the lid. The grease had coagulated in a three-inch-thick layer on top of the water. With a long knife, Darry cut the layer like a birthday cake into squares. Kenny and Joe lifted the squares with little red plastic shovels—the sort that kids bring to the beach—and dropped them into a bucket. They breathed shallowly through their noses and worked quickly as the rancid odor thickened. A dishwasher stepped up to observe the work. "God that's disgusting," he muttered and turned away.

The last call of the day brought them to a refurbished walk-up on a newly paved street uptown. The man who let them in wore a tight black T-shirt and shoulder-length bleached hair. The four of them stood in a high-ceilinged room filled with tapestries, sculptures of luxuriantly half-robed men and women, and framed cubic designs.

"Is this ancient Greek art?" Kenny asked the man.

"No."

All the sinks had lost pressure, the man explained to Darryl, who opened the faucet and observed the pencil-thin stream of water. He turned the faucet handle off and on, twice, three times and said, "Yep. Right you are," and turned to add something, but the man had disappeared. "Now where'd our beanhead scamper off to?"

Arms folded and head cocked, Kenny admired the place. "Look, Joe. It's modern art. You have to really think about it to understand it." A yellow-beaked bird mask gazed from the wall, beside a canvas bearing a study in red that hung above a tormented piece of wood. "Modern art is a reflection of the modern spirit. Self-divided. Melancholic. Reason at war with the beast. Hopeless? Maybe just honest. Honest—but not comforting. How does it make you feel, Joe?"

"Pretty good."

"Don't touch that crap, Kenny; it's worth more than you," Darryl said. He found the basement door and flipped the switch at the head of the stairs. The two helpers followed him down into a low, damp space with a packed-earth floor and a timbered ceiling. A single bare bulb, hanging by a length of bare wire, shed sulphur-yellow light.

Joe heard the hiss of the leak and saw the water jetting from a split in the water line. The water splattered against the creek rock wall of the foundation and ran in a zigzag rivulet across the floor to a moldy drain. His vision adjusted in tandem with his awareness of the space, and a scent of burnt hair came to him. Two chains of slightly unequal lengths were fastened to a timber in the center of the ceiling and hung halfway down to the floor. A three-legged stool sat beneath the chains. At the four corners of the room were lampstands, each bearing a black candle. Kenny stepped up to the chains and held a link between his thumb and finger, looked the chain up and down, grinned at some amusing thought, turned to Joe and asked, "Where's my uncle?"

Joe sprinted to the steps and collided with Darryl, who was returning at that moment with a tool bucket and an acetylene torch.

"Get back down there goddamnit and shut that main off," Darryl said, knocking Joe aside as he stormed down. While he unwound the hose from the tank, Darryl ordered Joe to cut the pipe twice. "Three inches from either side of the split. Don't wait for it to drain; just do it. Now give me what you cut." Joe tossed him the cut length and Darryl measured it and said, "Kenny, brush two couplings and paste 'em. Quickly now."

Darryl sanded and pasted the pipe ends, slipped the couplings on, fitted the repair piece, snapped the striker at the torch-tip. He ground the tips of his moustache with his molars as he heated the pipe, touched a claw of solder wire to the joint, turned the torch off, swiped a rag across the pipe, and threw tools into the bucket.

"Wrap that tank up," he said.

Darryl took the bucket and mounted the stairs two –at –a time. On the street, he opened the van's back doors, dumped the tools, caught his breath as he leaned on his fists. He wiped his forehead as he looked back at the building. "Nephew, do not tell your mother about that." He lit a cigar, composed himself, and frowned at the curtained windows. "I guess them sadistics got plumbing problems too," he surmised. "I'll be honest with you. When I was out here grabbing the torch, I was half tempted to drive off and leave you two in that psycho's torture chamber."

"Aw, Uncle Darryl," Kenny said. "You'd a never done that."

Darryl shook his head in sorrow. "Boy, it'll be a short, difficult life you'll lead."

*

Autumn arrived with snow and rain. On a gloomy afternoon, they drove into the farmland beyond the airport, past trailers and little gray houses and groves of bare black trees. The world looked to Joe like a job that had been subcontracted to a mob affiliation that used shoddy wallboard and spoiled paint, feigned six days of work, then skipped town.

They turned off the paved road onto a gravel one that curved to the top of a hill. Two mobile homes occupied the hilltop, each crowned with an arrangement of antennae and satellite dishes. The site resembled an armed compound of millenarians, or a listening-post in the Golan. Streaks of green snow lay in the black grass. The entire end of one of the trailers had burnt away, seemingly bitten-off by a fire, like a beer can chewed in half.

"I bet this is the one," Darryl said, knocking at the half-burnt trailer.

A sharp-faced teenager in Carhartt overalls and an orange knit cap opened the door with a bothered look.

Darryl said, "Veterans Fire and Water Maintenance and Repair. Had a fire, huh?"

"No it was built half burnt."

"No need to get uptight there. We're going to cover the thing up and start work in a few days, a week at the outside."

The kid leaned his face toward Darryl's. "You're gonna wait a week to start work? Dude, look at this shit!" He pointed with his index finger, thumb cocked, toward the burnt end. "Look at this shit! It's open to the sky!"

Darryl turned away, speaking over his shoulder as he stepped gingerly through the mud. "Yep, we'll get this thing covered up for you. Kenny, grab a tarp."

Inside the burnt end of the trailer, Darryl crunched thoughtfully through the debris. "Oh, it's all burnt up alright," he said.

Kenny waited unhappily in the mud outside, framed—from Joe's perspective—in the gaping mouth of the damage. He wore a fretful silence, holding the folded tarp in his hands like the novice butler bringing tea. Behind him, beneath the gray clouds, a bare tree worried about the six crows perched in it. A dog barked. A jet reversed thrust overhead and drew its nails down the sky.

Darryl addressed a mattress reduced to charred springs. "Good money says someone was smoking crack in bed," he said to Joe. "Go help dumbfuck now."

Joe set a ladder against the trailer and climbed topside with a drill. He fastened the edge of the tarp with sheet metal screws while Kenny secured the other edge from within. The result was proof against neither rain nor cold. The Kelly-green tarp bellied in the wind and cracked like a sail in a storm. Darryl subjected the work to a cursory inspection, then returned to the trailer's front door.

The teen sat on the couch, arms crossed, boot-shod feet splayed over the muddy carpet. A cord ran from the neighbor's trailer through the window and up to a television set that played a daytime serial with the volume off. The bitter odor of doused ash and burnt plastic permeated the place, a chemical taste that filled Joe's mouth with spit. Darryl retrieved a business card from his coat pocket and handed it to the teenager.

"So that's it," the kid said. "That's all you're gonna do?"

"I guess that's one a them rhetorical questions."

"A what?"

"Okay then. You're all set. We'll see you in a few weeks. Call the insurance people if you're unhappy about something."

They drove a few miles in silence. Kenny stared at the soaked fields.

Darryl said, "Remember that ratface kid?"

"Who?"

"The one in that burnt-up trailer."

"The one we just left?" Kenny asked.

"That's the one. I bet that ratface kid freezes his nuts off at night." It seemed to Joe that Darryl had puzzled at length on the matter.

"Hold your hand out," Darryl said, and dropped a gold molar into Kenny's palm. "I found this on the floor."

"Is that a gold tooth, Uncle Darryl?"

"Yes. It's also your wages for the day. Probably be enough for a haircut. We need to start looking respectable. I heard some of these new companies wear little booties so they don't track mud through people's houses. Did you know that, Nephew?"

"I think we should return the gold tooth. He might need it. I'm pretty sure he needs it, Uncle. Or, how about we cash it in and give him the money? I don't think we helped him much today."

Darryl frowned at the road. "You take that tooth, and you buy us all some booties, Nephew. The world's changing. Unfortunately, we got to change with it." He re-lit a half-smoked cigar and tossed the match out the window. "Find the best cheap ones," he said.

*

A light rain fell throughout the next morning. They drove down an empty state route between broad fields. The drowned furrows reflected the gray sky, so that the muddy acres appeared sluiced with mercury.

Twenty feet from the river's edge, a small house squatted on a concrete slab. A stain skirted the bottom half of the house, as though the structure had been steeped in tea. The contractor was waiting inside, leaning at a wall. The man did not greet Darryl but viewed him with dour satisfaction, for the arrival of this old run-down fix-it man and his unclean diggers confirmed what the contractor knew in his heart: though the rain might fall without cease, and though there be no hope of reprieve from another miserable day on this earth, this much at least was promised: the laborers will always be few, unqualified, and late.

The saturated carpet sucked at Darryl's boots, which left ghostly prints behind him as he walked about the room lightly as a man learning gravity, cocking his ear at his own spongey steps.

"Yep," he announced, having completed a circuit. "It's wet alright."

The contractor lit a cigarette and blew bullish streams of smoke through his nostrils. "They're keeping the place," he said with a flick. "You know how these river rats are. Me? I'd push the piece a shit into the water."

Joe stood at the window. The olive-drab river spanned the lips of the banks forming an unbroken surface plane with the level ground on either side. A car straddled the bank, its grill buried in the current like a pig at a trough. The water rushed through the rear window and roiled in the back seat. Garbage bobbed above the dash, trapped by the windshield. Beyond the car, black branches floated downstream. He wondered if anything of value remained inside the car and made a note to check the glove box.

"Take half a sheet off the bottom," the contractor said to Darryl, "then piece the new board in. Carpet: gone. Wiring: gone. The woman who lives here says she wants a bathroom. A proper one with pipes and shit." The man's cigarette hissed when he tossed it. "It seems the outhouse floated away with the flood," he said. "Ain't that something? But her insurance won't pay for a new bathroom, so we're putting the outhouse back. Ever build an outhouse, Darryl? It's like a little house but it's outside. Some folks like to carve a little half-moon on the door. I'll throw in an extra fifteen if you carve a little half-moon on the door, old timer."

"Old timer? I grew up in the Depression, son. People were lucky to have an outhouse. Only rich turds like you had bathrooms. But you wouldn't know real life from a hole in your head."

The contractor laughed. "When's it gonna get done?"

"It'll get done."

"You're still not bonded are you? What if the county comes poking around?"

"Bonded shmonded. My ex-son-in-law used to be an inspector. It's all covered. It'll be done when it's done, Carl."

"I need a time frame."

"It'll be done when it's done, I said. I got my A-team on it. All our work is warrantied: thirty minutes or until we hit the door, whichever comes first. Right, boys?"

The contractor departed, followed soon after by Darryl, and Kenny and Joe were left alone. They dragged out the carpet, removed the damaged panels, opened the windows, hung new drywall. They pried open a bucket of sealer and began to prime the ceiling.

Joe thought, Eight hours. Eight one-hour blocks of time. Always in his head was that dim awareness that each pass of the paint roller was one more stone dropped into the chasm between twelve o'clock and one o'clock. Between one and two. He drew comfort from the thought. Then he recalled the man on the bicycle, the man he'd seen from the bus last summer—the man with the wherewithal to purchase a newspaper on a workday. He wondered where that man was. Drinking a hot beverage, no doubt. Curled up on a futon, reading a magazine. Feeding his fish. Checking his ice cube trays. God only knows what that sort do all day.

An hour passed.

"Ever wonder why you weren't born in medieval times? Or in China?" Kenny asked.

"No."

"Yeah. What are the odds of being born at all? I mean," he lowered the brush, "of all the things that have to come together to create the precise conditions, over thousands of years, for you to be born. What are the odds? Think about it. Wars and hundred-year-floods, the odd fling behind the hayrick, miscarriages and arranged marriages. Consumption, pox, plague. Your immigrant ancestors somehow finding one another in a country none had been born in. Bone cancer and typhoid. Factory fires, boating accidents. Ferry capsizings. Drought and flood. The unlikeliness that ten thousand years of civilizations rising and falling, rising and falling, could somehow allow for all the pieces to fall into place, all the million happenstances to pan out into a You or a Me. And here we are spreading paint on Sheetrock. This is natural selection? This is evolution? This is how it all shakes out? You call this progress?"

"Stop."

"You know what this panel's made of? They call it gypsum board, because it's from calciferous materials, same as chalk and limestone. Chalk and limestone are the sedimentary layers of ancient seabeds. What happens is, over millions of years the shells of tiny aquatic organisms, mollusks and corals and plankton, die and sink and calcify, and that forms limestone, which we mine to make building materials. If you live in a building built in the last thirty years, you live within walls made of the skeletons of ancient sea creatures. See, what happens is—O! Good morning, ma'am!"

An elderly woman stood in the empty door frame leaning on a cane. She wore a gray house dress, Joe noticed, like his granny used to wear, and her gray hair tied up in a bun, just like his granny.

"Good morning, boys. I didn't mean to interrupt you."

"That's okay, ma'am. Are you the neighbor?"

"No, this is my house," she laughed. "Call me Anne. My sister lives up the road there. Not too far." Her eyes roamed the walls, and a look of fearful sorrow passed over her face. Only the muddy tip of the cane passed the threshold; she herself remained outside. "If you find anything, like a shoe or a picture, just set in on the windowsill, okay, child?"

"We will."

"Can I bring you boys some tea? Lemonade? My sister lives just up the road there. Not too far. I'd be happy—"

"No, thank you, we're fine."

"I'd show you where to answer nature's calls, but the flood took the outhouse. You can just use the woods for now. Did you bring your lunch? If not, my sister and I can fix you a little something."

"We brought our lunch," Kenny said. "But you are very kind. Thank you, ma'am."

"Call me Anne."

*

Joe spread the paint and glanced through the window to the gravel road, where the old woman made her way. She paused once and lifted her face to the bare trees and—though the distance made this uncertain—it seemed that she addressed a few words to them. He realized then that she wasn't wearing a coat.

Kenny sat on an overturned bucket and took a banana from his lunch box. "I need some fruit in my diet. Your body lets you know what you're missing. If you need fruit, you fall asleep on the couch a lot. If you lack vegetables, you get the stares. Last night I had a dream. Mary appeared to me. She wore a crown of stars and a robe that was all the colors of the sun," he said. "She acquainted me with my worst nightmares—coldness, darkness, falling—and showed me that they were powerless after all. She let me know that she was with me, no matter what, and I needn't fear anything in the world. She didn't speak, but I understood. She's bringing a message, Joe. You're not listening."

"Nah."

"You don't believe me. That's okay. I'm going to go look at the river. Want to go look at the river?" Kenny said.

"Don't drown."

Kenny ambled along the bank, planting the paint-pole like a shepherd's crook.

*

He returned an hour later. With a tape measure and a carpenter's pencil, Kenny plotted a series of points across the concrete subfloor, then, using a sharp stone, he drew lines connecting the points.

"Okay, I give up," Joe said. "What are you doing? We're supposed to be painting this hellhole. The longer you dick around the longer we're stuck out here."

"I was up the road. Anne and her sister made me lemon cake and hot tea. I brought some back for you. They're really nice. Maddy—that's Anne's sister—Maddy has a wonderful collection of watercolors she—"

"What are you doing."

Kenny wrote a number on the concrete and underscored it twice. "Anne would like a bathroom inside the house. It's getting tough for her to get around, you know, with that arthritis in both knees now. The insurance money doesn't add up to much, but they're going to use it to have a septic tank put in, so they can install indoor plumbing. I'm going to rough-in a bathroom. Then, when they scratch up the money to buy fixtures, I'll put those in. Meantime, Anne will stay with Maddy in—"

"Jesus, Kenny. Stop. First, you don't know how to install a bathroom."

"I'm doing it now. See? Watch."

"You plan to cut into the concrete. You're going to destroy what the flood couldn't. You're gonna be the end of this dump. Then they'll sue you."

Kenny frowned at the lines on the floor. "I've watched my uncle do it. It can be done. I believe I can do it."

"Good lord. Wait till Darryl hears. They're not paying you are they, them old ladies?"

"You're not listening. You don't listen." Kenny stood with his arms at his side and scrutinized the lines he'd drawn. "I believe I can do it. I could use some help."

An angry voice startled them. "Painting tends to go faster when you have a paintbrush in your hand." Darryl stood outside, arms resting on the sill of the open window. He leaned in and peered suspiciously around the room, and his eyes lit on the lines that Kenny had scratched on the floor.

"Please say something intelligent, Nephew," he said.

*

They stood at the bus stop in front of the tool rental shop.

"We look like idiots," Joe said.

When the bus pulled up, Joe shouldered the canvas bag that contained the concrete saw and helped his friend hoist the jackhammer into the bus.

Kenny paused to feed the fare machine. "Good morning!" he said. "Driver, can we take this jackhammer on the bus?"

"You gonna kill somebody with it?"

"Ha! No."

She shut her eyes and shook her head, not in refusal of the request but in refusal of the world and the men that dwelt therein.

Kenny sat with his hands steadying the jackhammer and read the bulkhead ads. "Look, Joe. Free Spanish classes at the Y. You got a pencil? It's like the universe is communicating to me."

The man across the aisle regarded the tools with grave dissatisfaction, but he could not settle on a legitimate complaint before he reached his stop.

"What is that?" a boy asked. His mother placed her hand on his head, but let the question stand. Joe averted his eyes from hers, which were not unkind.

"It's a jackhammer," Kenny said.

"Why do they call it a jackhammer?" the boy asked.

"Wow, great question! I don't know. I bet you're good at science."

"He loves science," the boy's mother said.

"Cool. Come here. I'll show you how it works."

"Do not be jackhammerin' on the bus," the driver said. "God help me."

*

They rode to the end of the bus route and set off on foot, Kenny dragging the jackhammer on its dolly, Joe shouldering the bag with the saw and blades. A two-mile walk brought them to the unpaved river road.

"Never again will I let you talk me into—what a miserable, stupid—"

"We should do this in the proper spirit. Or not at all."

"—dumb, fucking, asinine. A nice Saturday afternoon! Wasted. And for nothing!"

"Not for nothing, Joe. This is how we turn matter into spirit. This is how we transcend our earthly natures. Have you ever turned a solid into a gas? Of course not because your attendance in Mister Radermacher's chemistry class was awful. But that's okay because you're doing it now! Why else are we on this earth? Huh? Tell me! Why else are we here, man, but to turn matter into spirit?"

The sound of traffic receded, displaced by the rattle of the dolly being dragged over the gravel. Kenny hummed a few bars to "Greensleeves."

"What a beautiful day. It's so peaceful out here! Look, Joe. There's a woodpecker! I bet you wouldn't have seen that woodpecker if you were lying hungover on your couch watching *Scooby Doo*."

*

With the concrete saw, Joe cut two parallel lines across the floor; Kenny busted the strip between the cuts with the jackhammer. The van pulled up at the door.

"Holy Christ what a mess." Uncle Darryl stood outside, leaning inconsolably on the sill. "I told you not to do it. I was sitting at home, and then it hit me: I bet that dumbass is doing something stupid. Do you know I signed my name to this job? So when—not if—but when you fuck up this old lady's house, the lawyers are gonna take my truck, my house, and my first-born son."

Kenny leaned, elbows locked, on the hammer handles. "It's okay, Uncle Darryl. This is a whole separate job. It's all on me. Me and Anne and Maddy made an agreement."

"Anne and Maddy, is it? When the police show up, I never seen you before in my life. Got it?" Darryl viewed the work with disdain. "You have no idea what you're doing, Nephew. When you show up for work Monday, I'm not going to ask you about it, and I don't want to hear about it." Darryl turned away, muttering as he returned to the van. "Man alive. Anne and Maddy! Man alive."

*

Sunday morning was cold and clear, and the sidewalk seemed wider for the lack of traffic. Tinny music came from a transistor radio on a windowsill, a dry faraway sound like a voice from the bottom of a well. The doors were all closed and the shops were closed, and Joe felt kindly toward the world as though he might approach the next person he saw, and we'd have coffee and you'd come to know me for the good person I am and we'd be all friendly…

He felt that the people asleep in the rooms above the street were people he could please or impress, and he'd let them manipulate him if they wanted. He would smile and they'd smile because we'd all be in on it, and it would be okay. Then, as he was about to cross the street, a lone car sped through the red light, and he saw the jacketed torso bent over the wheel and his feet slowed and something collapsed under its own weight.

An issue of *People* lay on the pavement at the foot of a trash can. He picked it up as he passed, without breaking stride, leafing the pages as he walked, righteously resenting the photographs of bare-armed people seated in sidewalk cafes, people whose faces were partially hidden by outrageous plants. The people in the pictures ate with their sunglasses on, as though every last one of them had been raised without mothers. What miraculous lives they led, he thought. The resentment nearly brought his feet to a stop. He spit it from his mouth, dropped the magazine in a trash can, and walked on.

A flight of crows passed overhead. He wondered if crows banded in the autumn, or if their presence was merely more noticeable in colder seasons. They flew in loose formation, steady and low as they scoured the ground, bombers coming in under the radar. Their caws rang like a premonition of hard weather. He imagined winter grinding down from the Arctic like an immense blue leveler. He thought, If I put my ear to the pavement, I might even hear it coming. But he didn't put his ear to the pavement.

The apartment door stood open revealing Kenny seated by the window. He held a cup of coffee, tipped and near to spilling, in his fingers. An air-care helicopter landed on a hospital roof, near and out of sight, and the blades pulsed gently within the room.

"I don't know how you stand that racket," Joe said. "Why don't you move?" Joe picked up a book lying on the table. "This looks boring. You ready?" He let the book drop with a thud onto the table, but his friend didn't flinch.

"We're late for the next bus," Joe said. "Don't forget I'm doing this work for nothing, so let's get this job done and go. Okay, I give up. What's the problem?"

Kenny's face reflected the borrowed light of the pane. "She came to me; she talked to me; she wore a cloak embroidered with stars," he said, watching the sky as he spoke, like one speaking with clouds or with some unearthly auditors for whom one needn't raise one's voice.

"Love illuminates reality—the real reality—the place we inhabit but cannot see. We can't see it because it's concealed in the darkness men have created, the darkness of fear and anxiety, self-hatred and pride. These things have blinded us. But that real life is still with us; it's never gone away; it's been beside us all the while. To make that world visible to our eyes, we have only to open them and summon the courage to believe in what we see. The goodness of people. The beauty of the day." He wiped his face with his sleeve. "She told me all this, Joe, but not in words. She was there in the dark, and I heard it all clearly. The darkness spoke in her voice. It asked me: Do you know who I am? And I said, Mary. She said, Do you love me? And I said, Yes. Then she said, Do you love me? And I said, Yes. And once more she said, Do you love me, child? And I said, Yes, Mary. And she said, My son." His hands shook. "I asked her, Where are you?"

"Well? Don't stop now," Joe said. "You always blow your nose at the best part. Where's she at?"

"You'll never guess."

"Let me try. Is it an actual place?"

"It is."

"Oh, that's good. Is it bigger than a breadbox?"

"The center of the moon. That's what the darkness said to me: 'The center of the moon.' Do you know where that is?"

"We missed the bus."

"After she departed, I sat in this chair, wondering, waiting for the sun to rise. Then I remembered the book I brought home yesterday from the library, a book about Mexico. There it is on the table. The name Mexico in Nahuatl means—some people think—the center of the moon. And there were stars and moons embroidered on the cloak she wore when she visited the Blessed Juan Diego. And stars on the cloak she wore last night. See? That's how it all came together."

"What came together?"

"Now I've made a plan to find her. She's in the center of the moon, the Valley of Mexico. She's calling her children home, and I've got to go."

"I don't suppose you read a book about Mexico and then had a dream about Mexico. Because that would make too much sense."

"Exactly. You're being sarcastic, but you are exactly correct. Like Tom Sawyer said about Huck Finn's plan: it's too blame' simple, there ain't nothing to it. We're dealing with a whole other order of logic. Man's wisdom is heaven's foolishness. It's time to set aside the old habits of thinking. Mary is the end of this long sad separation between humanity and the earth. When she appears in hope to the world, human beings and animals and trees will be seen again for what they are: creatures of a loving creator. Only then will all things be restored to their proper status and be loved for what they are. When she appears, the sacredness of every living thing may no longer be denied. She herself will demonstrate the final proof of life's purpose. Now, I can't tell the world what I've heard and seen; I'm not eloquent. But I can walk. I'll go to her. I'll beg her to reveal the truth to everyone."

"Why does she need to be asked, if she's so wonderful?"

"That's the old way of thinking, Joe. We have to help in this work. Anyway, she cannot refuse me; it's not in her nature to refuse anyone or anything. It's unthinkable; it's impossible. And when Mary's star appears to the world, existence will be redirected from the ways of greed and fear to the ways of love and light, and the world will be saved from destruction."

"Hm. That's just crazy enough to work."

Kenny stood and wandered around the room. "The darkness is overtaking us. We all know it. She's the last defense against the darkness. When she was in the world, she was a light in the world, a rebuke to man's self-centeredness, a living indictment of human greed. That's why men banished her and anyone like her—so men could go on being selfish without consequence. But that's a delusion. Like Einstein said, nothing ever really goes away."

"The world is filled with milkmaids looking for fools."

"Now we've arrived at the fullness of time, and human existence hangs in the balance. Now we must undergo the cosmic course correction. It's time to start walking. The good news is, there is a part of each of us, buried deep down, which wants to rediscover that lost purpose, that lost world. Here's what else the darkness taught me: everyone I meet on my journey is going to help me, even if they don't realize they're helping me. And so I embark, with a light heart, a good stick, and a breeze from astern—bound for the center of the moon."

"Mexico, you mean."

"Mexico. Yes."

"Be sure to write."

"My whole life has been nothing more than a bad feeling that I've been left out of the joke. But now my eyes are open." He gathered the books into a neat pile. "I've been buried above ground, all this time, and I didn't even know I was alive."

"I hope it works out. I do. Now get your tools together. Did you pack your dumbass sandwich? Two buses went by while you gurgled."

"You probably think I'm crazy,"

"What gave you that idea?"

"Dreams are insights into the real world, glimpses of eternity. Think about it, Joe."

Against his will, he did think about it. He recalled a recent dream in all its sordid doom, and for the remainder of the day, he was troubled by the suspicion that he was condemned to spend eternity naked, lost, and late for his own hanging.

*

Over a month of weekends—in consultation with a few home repair manuals borrowed from the public library—Kenny roughed in the pipes for the new bathroom. He carried the tools and materials on the bus, to the annoyance of the drivers. On one occasion he was compelled to hire a taxi in order to transport several ten-foot lengths of plastic and copper pipe, which protruded from the passenger window like a brace of lances.

He asked Joe for a little money and for his help, both of which his friend tendered with a reluctance that was more apparent than real, for in truth, Joe derived a measure of gratification from the work, and though he burdened the hours with complaints, he did not miss a day. To run pipe square and plumb, to encounter difficulties and overcome them, to create something useful where there had been nothing, and to do these things without oversight, but according to their own creative lights: all of these generated a sense of pride in the work that outweighed the aggravation.

And each day, precisely at noon, Anne arrived with a thermos of coffee and sandwiches wrapped in linen napkins. She sat in a chair in the middle of the room, crocheting hot pads as the young men lunched. At these times, she told them about her childhood on the river, the floods of '38 and '72, and fishing from her father's duck boat. And when they finished eating, she gathered the napkins and departed with words of simple gratitude and a fussy embrace for each of them before setting off on the slow, painful walk back to her sister's house up the road.

One Saturday, a man drove up hauling a backhoe on a trailer and proceeded to install the septic tank; this was the work Kenny could not undertake, and for which the sisters paid most of their savings. At Kenny's request, the man climbed out of his machine and took a look over the work that had been done inside, for he was a local man, experienced in the ways of off-grid plumbing. The disdain inspired by the sight of Kenny's borrowed manuals and pencil sketches, and by the kid's apparent ignorance of even rudimentary pipe-work slang, gradually gave way to a reluctant admission that the work, overall, was not irremediably unsound. Kenny's enthusiastic report, in fact, and his humble solicitation of the backhoe operator's advice, even garnered promises of future assistance from the older man, whose grim reticence was, within the hour, transformed into a spirit of cheerful collaboration.

During the regular work week, Kenny was careful to arrive at his uncle's place on time, and he made no mention of the river job. Joe sensed that Kenny's uncle expected an update, or an admission of difficulty. Some intractable problem would surely compel Kenny, any day, to seek his uncle's counsel. But Kenny said not a word about the river job, and the work hours were shadowed by that weighty—

because unspoken—refusal. Once or twice, as they drove down the highway to some job, Kenny's uncle would cast a sidelong glance at his nephew, then turn his eyes back to the road with a scornful snort for this stubborn young fool. On Friday at lunch, Darryl drove to the river house and told them to get out.

"Don't worry," he said. "You'll get paid for a full day with me."

"Don't you need us this afternoon, Uncle?"

"Go finish your work, Kenny. Just don't destroy that poor old lady's house. Now beat it."

The next morning, Kenny and Joe rode the bus to the end of the line. On the long walk along the river, Kenny plodded through his calculations, and when they arrived, they found the backhoe man running electric lines, and Uncle Darryl framing a partition wall, and Ricky Nelson on the oldies station singing *oh my sweet fräulein down in Berlin town, makes my heart start to yearn...*

"Go out to the truck," Darryl said by way of greeting, "and start bringing that tile in. And the fixture boxes. What's the holdup? Me and Mike here got our own shit to do, and we don't plan to be here all day."

Kenny hurried to the truck without a word. The van doors were open, revealing a new sink, a shower kit, a toilet, and six boxes of ceramic tile, all in uncut boxes from the factory. Kenny did not speak.

"Holy crap, look at that," Joe said, and put a hand on his friend's shoulder. "What's the matter? Chrissake, what are you crying about now? Can't you just be glad?"

"Darryl was waiting for me to ask him for help. But I cut him out because I was proud, and I wanted to be self-sufficient. Yes, that is the original sin, the worst one of all: the belief that we don't need any help. Mary will never listen to me if I'm proud. I'm a selfish idiot! She won't suffer the sight of me, even if I walk ten thousand miles to find her."

"Jeez. C'mon, dummy, grab a box. And don't let your uncle see you blubbering. Or his new friend Mike. Ha! Your uncle has a friend. Don't that beat all?"

*

They walked up the narrow staircase of a burnt townhouse on Fifteenth. Kenny and Joe tacked plastic over the busted windows while Darryl wandered through the rooms.

Everything was in its place: the coat rack, the bookcase, the table and the chairs. All was intact but scorched, as though the place had been furnished with burnt things by burnt people. The writing desk and the wooden chair, flaked and blistered, waited by the window like wicked revenants of themselves, inseparable even in death.

During lunch, Kenny sat in the charred chair and gingerly arranged a thermos of coffee, a banana, and a cheese sandwich on the blackened tabletop. He ate in silence, observing the cold gray afternoon through the busted window.

The paintings on the walls, furred with tiny tabs of peeled pain, had been transformed by heat into abstract works—studies in charcoal and black ink, figures lost in cinder-storms. That afternoon, Kenny, like the curator at a gallery exhibition, pronounced the paintings' titles. "This one," he said, presenting a work to his uncle, "is *The Wood of the Suicides*. And over here we have *Crucifixion with Soldiers and Rain*." Darryl lit the dead cigar, partly unpersuaded.

*

Darryl inspected the china cabinet. Behind the glass doors the china was gone, but the shelves were sound and clean. Even the light coat of dust and the spherical absences of dust that marked the places of missing saucers and cups remained undisturbed. He said, "I wonder if we can't get this thing down to the street. Hell, I'll sand the burn off, slap a coat of varnish on it—good as new. I could get three hundred for this thing."

After gauging the cabinet's weight and the width of the staircase, Darryl determined that with four more hands he could do it. "There's a firehouse a block from here," he said. "Let's go see if they're busy."

They entered the firehouse through an open door and crossed the buffed, dully gleaming concrete to the center of the bay, where six firemen wearing pullovers were seated on metal folding chairs in a semicircle around a television. Beside the television was a livid space heater. The firemen sat slouched, boots splayed, arms crossed, in a little island of warmth and light. When Darryl stepped beside the television to address them, they stiffened in their slouches and viewed him with glum surprise.

Darryl began to speak, and all but one of the firemen returned their attention to the movie, in which a man was running along a river and waving a gun. Kenny and Joe watched the screen as though that were the reason they had come. The man on the screen stopped twice to peer desperately into the water below.

"I was wondering if two of you gentlemen might like to earn some extra cash. I got a china cabinet down the street in that building that caught fire," Darryl said. "I'll pay sixteen dollars per man. Shouldn't take more than a few minutes. And I'll throw in a couple bicycles."

The older fireman—the only one who wasn't slumped in his chair staring at the screen—lifted his hands, palms up, and looked around for a gentleman in a dark suit and slicked hair to emerge from a shadow with a lit cigarette and an explanation. "We're on duty," the man said, as though he himself couldn't believe it.

Darryl cast a flat glance over the firemen. "You don't look that busy."

"Look, who the hell are you anyway?" A few of the other firemen stared frankly at him now "Beat it. You got the wrong place."

Darryl remained. "Beat it? Who you think you're talking to? I thought all youse were supposed to help people."

"Beat it! This is a working firehouse."

"I wouldn't agree with that." Darryl started for the door but turned once more. His hands shook with anger. "You all seem pretty satisfied with yourselves. But this kid here," he said, his voice trembling, pointing at Kenny, who stood wide-eyed with the door handle in his hand, "This kid here's got more charity in his little finger than all you clowns put together. Heroes, huh? Balls."

As they walked back to the burnt building, Darryl said, "I thought for sure one of them would've given a hand, didn't you? What's three minutes for sixteen bucks and a bike? I never seen a lazier bunch a pricks." He cursed himself calm, then accosted a few teenagers on the sidewalk. The kids agreed to the offer at once and helped to carry the china cabinet to the van. Darryl paid them each fifteen dollars and a bicycle. "I'll give you forty more if you go and set that firehouse on fire," he said. But the kids walked off, counting the bills, no longer interested.

They picked through all the rooms in detail searching for anything to salvage. When Darryl held a camera to his ear and shook it, the thing rattled like a gourd full of seeds, and he said to himself, "Maybe I can fix it." He took a screwdriver from his back pocket and removed an old-time telephone, the kind with the speaking tube and the earpiece on a cord. The thing had blistered in places, tiny bubbles on the varnish like an ivy rash. He cut the phone wires with a utility knife saying, "I can refinish this thing." Meanwhile, Kenny and Joe scraped scorched wallpaper from the walls.

Late in the afternoon, Kenny stood back from his work and said, "I have to start an exercise regimen. And I have to learn how to build a fire. And how to sew patches. I have a Spanish lesson at the Y tonight. Do you want to learn Spanish with me? There's still a lot of seats, and

Missus Cortes wouldn't mind at all. I already asked her. I have to apply for a passport I guess. I was thinking of getting a dog to bring along. I think the name Rover would be appropriate and auspicious. Ironic too. Do you think you can bring a dog across international—oh, hi, Uncle Darryl!"

Darryl stood in the door frame. "What the hell are you doing?"

"Scraping these walls like you said, Uncle Darryl. Isn't that right? Is something wrong?"

Darryl's expression was strained, weary. His wonted exasperation had waned. "No, goddamnit, there's nothing wrong. Now put them hammers down. Let's call it a day."

*

"I'm off to a slow start," Darryl said when they knocked on his door in the morning. "Nephew, make me some coffee."

In the dim room that smelled of neat's-foot oil and newspaper ink, above the writing desk piled with bills and receipts, was a black-and-white framed picture of a young man dressed in a military jacket and tie, and wearing an overseas cap. The photograph bore the green shadows of smoke and years. There was a sort of reckless generosity in the young man's smile, the openhandedness of poorer years. Joe guessed the age of the man in the photo to be about his own age, and the photo must have been taken just before Darryl shipped out to join the fighting in Europe. Darryl walked outside without a word, and they followed.

They pulled to a stop at a red light. Beside Darryl's door, three sewer workers in muddy boots stood around a hole that had been dug into the shoulder of the road. The white men leaned on mud-scabbed shovels and kept a sullen watch over the traffic as the Black man, wedged in the hole, sought an angle for his spud bar.

Darryl leaned out the window, spit precisely, and spoke a single word to the sewer workers. "Figures," he said.

The workers, three above and one below ground, shared glances as they considered the various intimations of the word, and by the time they lighted on the most troublesome one, the light changed, and Darryl pulled away. "Goddamn union workers. Can't take a joke." His face was ashen and drawn.

"Are you sick, Uncle Darryl?"

"I got a flu."

They drove out to a development of new homes and chain outlets, all of it constructed in conformity to some inscrutable zoning regulation that seemed to mandate something Swiss, with steep roofs and false timbers set into white plaster facades. Improbably green strips of lawn bordered the street. The sidewalks appeared to have never been walked on.

"I'm gonna get a place out here," Darryl said. "Nice and quiet. It's a good place to die. Reminds me of the fatherland and I ain't even a Heini. What about you, Joe? What are you?"

"I don't know."

They walked back and forth across a sodden tract of grass in front of the new bank. Darryl paused once or twice to test the earth with his weight. He located the valve at the curb and stepped gingerly toward the building, listening as he walked. In the midst of the lawn, equidistant from the bank and the street, he stopped and cocked his ear. "Get the shovels," he said, and dropped his cigarette butt between his feet to mark the spot.

From the outset, stones obstructed the digging.

"What do you mean, you don't know?" Darryl asked as he stepped on the shovel head. "What do you mean? You don't know your own heritage? What's your last name? Riley? That's Irish ain't it? Boy, you grow up a McAdams and see if you ever forget where that name's from. To hear the old farts go on about it, you'd think the McAdams was one of the twelve lost tribes of Judah." Darryl handed the shovel to Joe and climbed out to watch him dig.

"You know, kid," he said to Joe, "you don't seem very curious. That'll keep you out of trouble I suppose, which might be a good thing. But if you never once stick your neck out—well, fuck it, nevermind. It's none a my business."

Joe was uncertain what the old man was talking about; it rankled nevertheless. To learn that at least one person in the world believed him to be uncurious caused him no little resentment. Well, I'm not curious, he thought. So what about it?

The three of them took turns with a maul and a spud bar. His shirt soaked, Darryl straightened from the work, lit a cigarette, stretched his back. "Understand," he began, orating from the deepening hole, "when they build these places nowadays, they scrape off the topsoil and replace it with debris and landfill. Then they sell the good soil to landscapers. That way they make money twice, and in the process break the backs of decrepit old laborers like me." He flicked the butt, grasped the spud bar, and hurled it at a spot between his toes like he was hurling lightning. "That's what you call a racket," he said, pushed the handle toward Kenny, and climbed out once again. An hour later they reached the broken line. Darryl repaired the split pipe while Joe bailed water with a plastic beer cup.

They filled in the hole, stowed the tools, and walked inside to use the bathroom. The teller peered over the counter as they made their way down the hall. "Don't you guys wear booties?" she asked.

Darryl said over his shoulder, "See what I mean."

On the drive to the next job, Darryl said, "Kenny, weren't you supposed to buy us booties? What did you do with that gold tooth?

You better not've bought some silly-ass books with it."

"I mailed it back to the ratface kid, Uncle Darryl!"

Darryl drank off the coffee, threw the cup over his shoulder into the back of the van, and spoke a holy name in vain.

*

In the parking garage beneath the Dixie Terminal Building in the late afternoon, they swept floodwater with push brooms into the floor drains. At five, they policed up the tools and buckets and departed through the deserted concourse, beneath the vaulted ceiling of ornate plaster and chandeliers.

"Once upon a time, this city wasn't an absolute hellhole," Darryl said as they stepped down the wide marble staircase. "In the old days, I used to ride the tram across the river to work, back when I was a young apprentice." They paused at the window overlooking the Ohio, where a limestone barge barely made way against the current. "The tram used to cross the bridge—over there—unload downstairs, and return to Newport. You step off the tram, walk up the stairs, and you're standing on Fourth Street. Then some thoughtful college graduates decided we didn't need shit like that anymore. God, it breaks my heart."

Across the ceiling, plaster cherubim played harps and lutes. Joe imagined the crowds of workers, women in silk headscarves knotted at the chin, laborers in blue dungarees, clerks and salesmen in flat caps and fedoras leaning at the counters, drinking coffee and smoking cigarettes, shoulder to shoulder, as commuters flocked up the wide marble staircase toward the exits and out into a sunlit racket of taxi cabs, trolley bells, jackhammers—into the postwar buzz of progress and commerce.

He imagined the Darryl of those days, whose likeness was captured in the photograph—a young man, like many young men, still wearing his summer service khakis months after VJ Day, smoking and laughing at the lunch counter with the other discharged soldiers, sharing stories whose entertainment value stood in inverse proportion to their veracity.

Did those men really believe, Joe wondered, that the world would wait for them to finish their coffees and their cigarettes and their jokes? There were no more crowds on the staircases, no one ordered coffee at the counter anymore. And the insurance company that now occupied the space, one of only a few surviving businesses in the terminal, was closed for the day.

Autumn rains had swollen the river, now bright with afternoon sunlight. A limestone barge pushed upstream through the golden water like an argosy plowing coins.

"Look at those miserable highway bridges," Darryl said. "Vandals built that garbage. Not a shred of humanity in them. They're falling apart after thirty years. Where's a Roebling bridge anymore? It's a lost science. Listen to me," he said, "talking like a bitter old coot. I sound like my dear old granny when she used to bounce me on her knee and tell me how she wished she was dead. You know, the world has a way of slowly but certainly turning its back on you, and there's nothing more pathetic than the geezer who can't take it." He laughed loud and deep, and slapped Kenny's shoulder. "How I go on! Let's beat it, weenies. If I don't get a drink soon I'm gonna slit my own throat. Right after I slit yours."

Kenny and Joe picked up the buckets. At the exit, Joe turned to see Darryl, alone on the wide marble floor, gazing up at the plaster angels playing psalteries. Darryl nodded to himself in his distraction, as if finally coming to terms with the sad fact of it all, as if his own presence in the midst of this grand solitude were the inevitable conclusion to all great effort, to everything executed with love.

*

Monday morning, Darryl was not waiting at the work van, and he did not answer the door. A neighbor leaned from a window to inform them that Darryl had been taken away during the night in an ambulance.

They took the bus to the VA hospital. Scattered near the entrance were old men in powder blue gowns, smoking cigarettes in their wheelchairs. Kenny and Joe asked directions at the front desk while, in the nearby waiting room, middle-aged and elderly couples waited. A college football game blared from a ceiling-mounted television. A few men leafed dourly through old numbers of *Bass Fisherman* or *Legion*.

Display cases lined the corridor. Inside the cases were mannequins dressed in uniforms from past wars. Infantry gear—canteens, compresses, trenching tools, grenades, bandoliers—was spread out neatly at the mannequins' feet.

An elderly man stood nearby, motionless, riveted to the display of a mannequin wearing mottled Marine camouflage and grasping a Thompson submachine gun. As the man and the mannequin gazed at one another through the glass, the man's lips parted briefly, then closed again.

Kenny and Joe found the appointed room on the eighth floor. One bed was empty; someone lay awake in the other.

"Do you have a roommate, sir?" Kenny asked.

The man grinned at the ceiling. His large black eyes were glossy with pain and drugs, and his big hands lay in a heap on his stomach. A soft pillow cradled his head and the black knit cap he wore.

"Yeah. He's next after me. We're off to the gas chamber." The man consoled them. "No need to fear, no need to fear. Just sit back," he closed his eyes, "and breathe deep." They left without another word.

Darryl lay in the next room by himself, wearing a white gown open at the neck. His chest was bandaged, and tubes ran under the gauze.

"You don't look so bad," Joe said. "Not as red as you used to be."

"Get me out of this place."

Kenny laid his hand on his uncle's shoulder. The man in the bed was smaller, more gray than the man they had seen just a week before.

"I feel like shit," Darryl said. "Stay a minute then get out."

"You want some water?"

"No. I want a drink and a cigarette. If I'm gonna die I'm gonna die doing the shit I like to do."

Joe said, "You're not gonna die."

"Oh, you're right. I forgot I was Jesus Christ." He pushed himself to a sitting position and Kenny and Joe edged closer, pleading caution as Darryl's face turned to shades of slush. He sank back again.

They stood over him, each to a side, looking for evil signs. Darryl's color slowly returned. "Listen." His voice was brittle, dry. "You see the white thing on that hill? Look out that window."

Across the avenue, scattered among the bare trees, a few houses clung to the hillside.

"What white thing?"

"You can't see that white thing? I know I ain't nuts. Maybe it's these drugs."

Joe scanned the hillside for the white thing. Confirming the presence of the white thing might bring the old man a measure of comfort.

"Do you know anything about the revolution, Nephew?"

"The American Revolution? Sure."

"Ever hear of Benedict Arnold?"

"Course, Uncle."

"Pick up that book on the desk. I brought it along when they took me away. Did you know Arnold led a thousand men through the Maine wilderness to take Quebec from the British? In the middle of winter? Almost took it too." The book's cover bore an illustration of men in buckskins and beaver hats paddling canoes up a river in flood. "They suffered on that trip. Hundreds deserted or died. When they reached the town, Arnold led a surprise attack during a snowstorm at night. But his men were exhausted and they couldn't pull it off. Almost. But not quite. And after all that, they passed him over for promotion cause they didn't like his attitude. Figures."

Joe took the book from Kenny and leafed through the pages. "Is it a true story?"

"Yeah it's true," Darryl said. "What do you mean?"

"I mean," Joe said, "is it true or is it a made-up story?"

"What do you mean, *made up*?"

"I mean, is it fiction or is it real?"

"What do you mean, *fiction*? Hell no it ain't fiction." He took back the book and leafed angrily through it, paused to read a passage, reassured himself on some point. "Fiction," he hissed, and set the book aside.

"I can draw, Nephew. Did you know that? I don't generally tell people." He picked up a sheet of notebook paper from the breakfast tray. It was a pencil sketch of a soldier wearing a rain cape and a tall miter cap with a pom-pom at the peak and a German inscription on the brow.

He held it for them to see. "It's a Hessian. I copied it from a book."

"That's a fine likeness, Uncle."

Darryl took it back and frowned at the Hessian.

"Time was, I could draw pretty well. I thought about doing something with it, but hell. What do you do with it?"

"Lots of things. You could take classes ..."

Darryl folded the sketch and slipped it into the book. "You don't understand. I can only draw Hessian mercenaries. What I wouldn't give to draw Benedict Arnold, sword in hand, leading his half-frozen men through the cobblestone lanes of Quebec City! If I had just one thing to show for this shitty life ..."

The thick silver whiskers did not match the pale and hungered face, Joe thought. Darryl wore the unwonted beard like a player acting the part of a mad old king.

Suddenly bewildered, catching his breath, Darryl said, "Listen. I remember one day, it was this time of year. We were walking along a high road. In Italy. There were hills all around us, snow on the higher ones. I'd never seen hills that big. Kraut spotters were on them hills too, watching us, you better believe. I swore that day, that if—"

A man knocked lightly on the jamb and waited at the open door. Darryl ignored the visitor and continued, a touch irritably, "I swore that if I survived, I would go back to that mountain valley, that very same one in north Italy, like any old dipshit American tourist. I'd visit one of them villages we kicked the Nazis out of, and I'd sit in one of them cafes, and I'd order a nice glass of red wine. Boy, I'd sip that wine, and look at those mountains, but without worry this time, you see. I'd have all day to just watch the light go out on the mountains, all peaceful and calm." Darryl sighed, and the dry Umbrian light departed from his eyes. "What is it, Father?"

"Guess what tonight is, Darryl." The priest entered and laid a hand on Darryl's shoulder.

"Oilers Browns, Padray, Monday Night Football. You shouldn't need to ask. If Houston wins, we got a shot at postseason."

"Well, that too I guess. I'm doing services. Thought maybe you'd like to take communion this evening."

"Father, this is my nephew and his friend." They shook hands. "This is Father Tom. He's chaplain here. We went to high school together. Tom was a hell of a football player. Then he became a priest, and I got a real job." Father Tom laughed and Darryl smiled unhappily. "I don't know, Tom. Maybe another time."

"I'll be out of town all this week," Father Tom said. "You could take it this afternoon if you like."

"Can't you just mail it?"

While they talked, Joe stood at the window and searched for the white thing. Darryl was going to die soon; that was a fact, and Joe thought about hell. All he knew about hell was what Sister Benedicta had told them in the fifth grade. She said it was not a lake of fire but a wind-blasted and barren place of dead trees and dried-up stream beds, where the solitary Damned shivered in rags. And years later, when he saw a picture of Scotland, he understood that Sister Benedicta's hell was not a vision of the afterlife but memories of a crappy vacation. Sister Benedicta had shared a vision of heaven too. In heaven there were no microwave ovens or TV dinners, she said, and nobody ever married. The Blessed sat on nice chairs and adored the face of God and enjoyed the songs of the angelic choirs, for forever. But when Tony Schweinfurt mentioned his sister who had cancer and asked the nun whether amputees got their arms and legs back in the by-and-bye, the spell was broken, and Sister Benedicta's illuminated visions vanished like the flowers of the field.

What waited on the other side, Joe wondered, for the likes of Darryl—who was not a bad person, really, but not a very good one either?

By an act of will—undertaken by the grace of heart disease—Darryl was going to check out. And he didn't seem terribly upset, just disappointed. All the gratuitous aggravations that made one lifetime enough—and more than enough—were going to end, here and now, without fanfare, flourish, or curtain call.

The priest left, the room was still, and Joe stood at the windowpane and searched the hillside across the avenue for the white thing whose presence Darryl suspected. But he saw nothing. And as he watched, all in spite of himself, a different scene resolved on the rain-streaked glass. An image of the room displaced the hillside, and there appeared—superimposed on the unclean pane—the pale reflection of two people behind him: a young man alive and an old man dying. Two shadows, two half-asleep and wordless specters, made visible on the pane by a common optical sleight.

But the image fled, and the rainy hillside resolved into sight once more.

"Uncle," Kenny said. "I never thanked you properly for helping us fix Miss Anne's bathroom."

"Don't mention it, Nephew."

"And I never apologized for being selfish and proud about it—"

"Forget it now. Listen," Darryl said. "Thanks for coming by. I just hate to be seen like this. But before you leave, I want to tell you something because I'm not going to see you again. You're not real smart, Nephew, so far as the world reckons smartness. But you know how to see good things. Now let me tell you, you'll be surprised how much the people of this world mislike that particular talent, but don't let nobody … Boy, I didn't teach you much, but I guess you didn't need to be taught after all. It's like what I said before, about that one day in Italy, about … Ah, forget it. You'll figure it out."

"I understand, Uncle." When Kenny leaned down and embraced him, Darryl patted his nephew's shoulder with his old inarticulate ferocity.

"I'm tired, boys. Come here, Riley." Darryl squeezed Joe's hand. "You're a good friend to my nephew." The old man looked at them, but his vision was trained inward, on the dark prospects of pain and the thunderlit places he was presently bound to pass through.

"Don't come back here again. Now beat it."

*

At the funeral service, on the following Saturday morning, a few old men sat at silent intervals in the pews. Light poured through the painted windows, steeped in the colors of the scenes depicted there:

green of pasture, silver fleece, bare and earth-brown feet, golden mane, the blue of still waters. Tipped bars of light fell across the casket lid.

Have mercy on us, said the congregants.

Lamb of God, you take away the sins of the world. Have mercy on us. Lamb of God, you take away the sins of the world. Grant us peace.

After the mass, they returned to Kenny's apartment and did not talk about the burial or the fact of their unemployment.

A package waited by the door. In the box was a pair of green mittens and an orange hat, from Anne and Maddy. Kenny sat beside the window and put the mittens on and held his hands to the light. He held the hat in both hands and spoke to it, and his voice was grave and small. "She put a little Mexican flag on it." He put the hat on and frowned. "How did she know?"

"There's an envelope in the box," Joe said.

"Open it."

"Three hundred forty dollars. No note."

Tears ran down his cheeks as Kenny sat with his green paws on his knees. "Uncle told them. But how did he know?"

"Dummy."

*

Joe drank Kenny's last beer and looked at pictures of Roman galleys in a picture book, *Naval Warfare in the Classical World*. In the ticking silence of the room, time came nearly to a stop.

Seated in the light, Kenny said, "You know what? When the Aborigines in Australia are out in the desert hunting and they get thirsty, they dig up frogs that live in the sand and hold them up over their mouths and squeeze, like so—" he held his fist over his upturned face. "And water shoots out the frogs' pee holes. But it doesn't hurt the frogs. The Aborigines just set the frogs back in their little homes and move on. That's living, man. That's the life that really is life. This skill might be useful when I'm crossing the great Chihuahuan Desert."

On the page in Joe's lap, Roman galleys cruised the Carthaginian coast, big eyes painted on the sails. Two banks of long oars lifted over the waves. *The oars that are the wings of ships*, the caption read. Whoever wrote that had a good eye, Joe thought. Oars like wings. So they are.

"Why don't you go with me to Mexico? You won't be an assistant," Kenny said. "You'll be a partner. Think of the adventures we'll have. It's a whole lot easier to get there than you think. Look at Sherlock Holmes. When London got too crazy for him, he'd just pick up and ship off to Tibet to think about life. No big deal. A few months later he's back, recharged, terrorizing the sociopaths, smoking his stuff."

"Have you ever stopped to ask yourself why Mary chose you of all people, in Ohio of all places?"

"I have. There's no good answer. It's just one a them mysteries."

Thumb-tacked to the wall was a *National Geographic* map of T. E. Lawrence's Arabia. There was a time, Joe thought, when a man might go out into the world and do great things. Not no more. The world was dirty and troublesome. Those pristine deserts from which you could lead a band of horsemen to raid the imperial mail or blow up a depot—those deserts are now fenced off by Gulf Oil and Texaco. The Syrian Desert? It no longer exists. No, these days, a man went out and worked for his family. If he's lucky he'll live on a bus line so he can get to work on those days when his car's not running, or the snow's too deep.

"Where are you getting the money for this? This is stupid because you're not gonna get far and then you'll come back and you won't have a pot to piss in and you'll be sleeping on my damn couch—"

"You should stay here then. That's best for you. But I'm going. Life has meaning now. For the first time, my life has a purpose. I've been selected. That happens once in a lifetime. You either accept or decline, but the offer will not be made again. The summons comes, and people say, *it's just the wind*, so they get up and close the window, and there's an end to it."

Joe drank the beer, bought more at the shop, and passed out in the chair with the picture book in his lap. He woke up next morning to an empty room and decided to return on foot to his apartment. A flock of pigeons swept by as he walked through an underpass. The sudden gust of birds startled him, and a stinging sweat broke out across his back. He cursed and spat from dumb anger.

The underpass smelled of piss and shadows. Pigeons looked down from shit-streaked, rusted girders and whortled, feathers ruffled against the cold.

He bought a takeaway coffee at a fast-food counter and paused at the edge of a skating rink that the city had set up in a corner park. He drank the coffee and smoked and watched the kids skate. The caffeine and nicotine set his blood spinning and he shivered in his jacket, comforted by the block weight of the sky low overhead, by the mothers and fathers holding their children's hands as they skated. His hand shook as he drank the coffee.

A man approached with one eyelid swollen shut and crusted with blood. "Look I'm not gonna bullshit you. I just need some money for a drink." Joe put the bills from his pocket into the man's hand.

A sign in a shop window read 100% HUMAN HAIR. The hair fell down seven faceless styrofoam heads arranged on the shelf like the heads of conspirators arrayed on London Bridge. Bottles of dye and tins of lotion were scattered about, and a handwritten sign read, SALE ON EXFOLIANTS. EXFOLIATE YOUR SKIN. He read the words a few times, turned away, vomited into a trash can, and arrived at his door without further event.

Kevin Honold

*

The apartment building was one of many narrow brick structures on a narrow street, so many cracker boxes set at right angles to the curb, each building representing a distinct point on the spectrum of disrepair.

He pulled some letters out of the mailbox, walked upstairs, unlocked his door, dropped the letters into the trash as he entered, and stood in the kitchenette, mulling.

On a back burner sat a dinted pan containing a days'-old dollop of pasta, now lacquered stiff and cold. An inch-high shoot had sprouted from the noodles, topped with a soft round spore, and he touched the spore with his fingertip, twice. He reached into the refrigerator for a beer, then set it back, ran water into a teakettle, lit the burner with a match, and listened to the pelting flame. An idea of cleaning occurred to him as a tolerable activity. He turned the burner off and reached into the sink for a coffee cup half-filled with yesterday's instant coffee and took a drink. It was okay.

For an hour he filled plastic garbage bags with aluminum cans, torn cartons, crumpled cigarette packs, newspapers, beer bottles. It was disheartening to see the furniture again: the end tables built with scrap pressboard and deck screws; the cassette holder that was too big and held, mostly, empty cassette cases; the lamp with the cord that had been chewed through, re-spliced, and bandaged with electrical tape.

Phone books propped the coffee table at one end. The table's top bore the painting of a pilgrim under a coat of polyurethane. Joe had purchased the table at a St. Vincent de Paul sale two summers back, on a hot August Saturday afternoon. The table was the last intact piece of furniture in the lot, and he'd pitied the old pilgrim standing bravely on a rock, clutching a fowling piece with a flared muzzle like a cartoon hunter's gun. The pilgrim gaped at the ocean like a man who had never seen one. Poor crazy pilgrim. Cost three dollars. Joe didn't know why someone would bother to paint a pilgrim on a coffee table, but they had applied great care, if not facility, into the execution. The artist had wanted to impart something to the world. Something spiritual—or patriotic, maybe. God only knows.

His furniture was all more or less garbage; nevertheless, he reasoned, you need things to set other things on. The carpet was matted with a thin gauze of dog hair. He dragged a vacuum from the closet and began sweeping, but the vacuum quickly choked. The belt seized and the air filled with the acrid stink of fried rubber. The vacuum clogged three more times before the belt finally broke. He cleaned the remaining few square feet on his knees, clawing the hair up with his fingernails. Someone knocked. Joe slipped a check off the table, opened the door, handed the payment to the man waiting there.

The landlord said, "Why must I here-come to receive the rent money? Why you sending it not before?" He craned over Joe's shoulder, peering into the room. "It gives no more hund here, oder?"

"No," Joe said, "no hoond gives here," and he shut the door, wishing he'd shut it harder.

He sat down with the coffee. On the television, a shiny sedan outmaneuvered giant rolling marbles in some ruined Roman pavilion. He turned the television off and sat beside the window.

Snowflakes fell singly and in pairs in the twilight of a winter day that seemed to have lasted no more than a few hours. In these short days, he thought, you must be watchful, or you'll miss the light, such as it is, altogether. The sky stood at two hundred feet and cast a gray shadow on the city. The cloud deck sagged with the weight of snow it carried, so much blue silk tacked to a ceiling.

He put on clean socks and a clean pair of corduroys because Vera would probably be at the party. It was good to dress nice for someone, though it was only a matter of time until she acquired a boyfriend—one with a job. That conclusion brought a measure of relief. What would people say if they saw him now, standing at the closet, discriminating among the three collared shirts that hung together, one inside the other, on a single wire hanger?

Snow covered the parked cars and settled in tiny piles on the gray housings of the streetlamps. It covered the pavement until only the black discs of steaming manhole covers remained. His vigil outlasted the afternoon till the snow was only visible in the cones of streetlight and in the headlights of slow cars.

Crows gathered from all points of the city to the roof. They paced across the copper sheeting filling the lamplit room with the clicking of claws and the rancorous caws of a winter hunger. There, in the ticking darkening evening, he heard their voices, wondering what the crows were telling one another, wondering why they were out past sundown in the snow and the cold. He took the remaining slices of bread from a sack, squeezed them in his fists, opened the window, and tossed the bread-balls, blindly and backward up onto the roof. Then he left for the party.

*

The music thrummed in his ribcage. Plastic Santas waved cheerily from corners. Cardboard reindeer were tacked to the panel walls. From beneath a neon Budweiser sign, an image of Rudolf transfixed the room with its gaze, its red nose pierced by a dart. The tables were pushed to the walls and people danced to a song. *O tell me why baby why baby why baby why you make me cry baby cry baby cry baby cry.*

Vera set out two beers and three shots of whiskey. "It's on me. Merry Christmas, guys."

"You look very nice tonight, Vera," Joe said, proud to have pulled it off without sounding silly. Finding him quite serious, she smiled and thanked him. "What're you doing on Christmas, Joe?"

"I donno. Get loaded," he said, but no one was amused. He wanted to make her laugh but did not know how.

"Everybody knows it's crass, but heck," Vera said, "it's the only time of year when people don't sniff each other like dogs and slink away. What're you doing, Kenny?"

"I won't be around, I'm afraid. I'm going to Mexico to find Mary."

Vera nodded, waited, turned to take an order.

"I'm nobody. I got nothin. No bills," Kenny said, counting off with his fingers. "No job. No possessions. Cancelled my subscription to *National Geographic*. Everything is ready. The stars are nearly aligned. Only, I forgot to return some library books, which I'm hoping you could do for me." He was drunk. "I hafta tell ya, I feel like dancing. Dancing like it's the last night of the world."

"What's that there?"

Kenny pulled a Greyhound ticket out of his shirt pocket and unfolded it. "I'm riding the bus to Arizona. Arizona's the point of no return, and that's where I'll cross the border. Don't give me grief. Today's a holy day."

"Arizona? Where at in Arizona? Moron, it's twice the size of Brazil. Let me see that dumbass ticket. Jesus. Tucson. Is that a real place?"

"It's a real place alright." Kenny folded his ticket and put it back into his shirt pocket. His glasses sat halfway down his nose as he slouched over the bottle. "There's still time," he said.

"Time for what? I told you a million times. You know what I think about it. What?"

Kenny spoke as if he hadn't spoken for days. "I'm afraid to go alone."

They sat together and drank without a word. Vera was relieved at two by the bar's owner. When a slow song came on, Joe asked her to dance, and they drifted awhile together. They talked about work and snow. He was tired and rested his head on her shoulder.

"They're closing up, Joe."

He leaned back to focus. He said the predictable thing, feeling compelled by some miserable convention to say it, despising himself even as he spoke. She understood all of this, of course, and, to his immense relief, took pity on him. "Maybe another time. I have to go to my mom's and pick up my youngsters. Do you need a ride home?"

He dropped his arms and pretended to stand straight. "No, I'll walk. It might clear my head enough to pack. I gotta go help fuckface find a milkmaid."

Three

The electronic traffic boards flashed SMOG ALERT at noon. A haze of exhaust hung above the highway like morning mist above a river. The channel of haze, rising to a hundred feet, betrayed the path of the highway far beyond the point where the pavement was lost to sight. A call came over the radio; he turned off at the next exit.

He entered the building and heard sobbing from a basement unit. When he knocked, the sobbing ended.

"Who is it."

"Police. Open the door, please."

Blood dripped from the woman's nose. She wiped it away with her wrist, smearing the blood across her cheek. Yellow knots stood out on her forehead. In a torn bra and blue jeans, she stood breathless in bare feet, and covered her eyes with her fingers. Mascara ran in gritty rills down her cheekbones.

"Is he still here?"

"No. He doesn't know what he's doing, I don't know where he is." She wrapped her arms tightly around herself, shivering. "It's stupid. He gets so crazy. Oh I'm sorry. I don't know where he is. I'm sorry."

"Don't be sorry. How do you feel? Are you okay?"

"I'm fine."

"Go ahead and put something on," he said as he followed her into the room. "Where'd he go? Does he got a warrant for anything?"

"I don't know." She wrapped a bath towel about her shoulders, sat on the couch, and trembled. "They put him on house arrest so he don't go anywhere, don't get a job or anything."

"Do you know where he is?" He walked down the short hallway into the bedroom, glanced into the closet and returned. "When's he gonna come back?"

"I don't know I swear."

"Alright. I'll call an ambulance. They'll be here in a few minutes so go ahead—"

"O no no no don't—"

"They're just gonna look at you—"

"No!"

"Okay okay. Sit and rest a minute." He went to the kitchen, put three cubes of ice in a dishrag. He pressed the rag to the welt on her temple and held it there until her hand took the rag from his hand.

"At least let me take a look at your head." In the hum of the window-mounted air conditioner, he placed his fingertip on the bridge of her nose; she closed her eyes, breathing in shallow starts. "Tell me how much this hurts," he said, applying only the weight of his finger.

"It hurts a little."

"Not too much? Not excruciating?"

"No."

"I don't think it's broken then. Still, I wish you'd get checked out. Getting beat on the head is bad."

"Thanks but don't."

"Your eye's gonna be black from it. Well, the one that's not black already."

She smiled once. He sat on the end of the couch, took off his cap; he retrieved his notepad, asked for a description, wrote some words.

They sat together, quietly for a moment. The air conditioner hummed.

"I am tired," she said.

The muffled unhappy voices of neighbors came through the walls.

Atop a bookshelf was a framed picture of a young woman in battle dress wearing a big smile and a field cap pulled low over her eyes. An American flag stood at her shoulder.

"You have a kid in the service?"

"That's my daughter. She's in the Marines. They just gave her embassy duty in Romania. She told me it's a big deal. She's so happy. She told me, 'They don't just give these jobs to anybody, Mom!'"

"That's neat. You oughta be proud."

Pots banged in the neighbor's unit. The small tremors of the woman's grief moved through him.

"I knew a person," he said, "I know a person. He used to say that all things—all living and nonliving things—are good and necessary. He used to say that there's a purpose to life, and the purpose is to help one another see the goodness of creation because it's often hidden and hard to see. He used to say we just have to open our eyes, and the world of goodness and beauty will appear because it's never *not* been there. He used to tell this to total strangers. Do you think that sounds crazy?"

"Who's this person?"

"He's a friend."

He rested his hand on hers and gave a small squeeze, and she closed her eyes. "The important thing, the most important thing," he said, "is to be kind to each other. It is of the utmost importance right now that we be kind to each other." He stood and put his hat on, set a scrap of paper with a phone number on the table. "But if you ever decided to murder that man," he said, "I wouldn't blame you."

Across the street in an empty lot, he parked the cruiser with a view of the apartment building. Visions filled the bleary windshield, fantasies of smashing the man's head with his nightstick until, in his mind's eye, he stood over a broken body on the sidewalk, blood pooling from the body's ear. His hands gripped the wheel like the handle of a club, his throat closed and his heart clenched, and he got out and paced around the cruiser, breathing hard, willing away the vision. But the vision of a beaten bloody man lying on the ground would not go away. And he saw that the man was himself.

The earth will open up, he thought, and I will sink into the earth. But the earth did not open up.

Then the trees, the buildings, the washed-out sky resolved once again in his vision, and resumed their proper modes and places. The noise of traffic faded in.

An hour passed with no sign of the man. He backed out of the space and drove to Kenny's mom's house, some miles out of his district.

*

The trees in his old neighborhood seemed scantier, listless, unfamiliar to him.

When no one answered the Stegemullers' door, he sat on the porch step beside a concrete goose that wore a yellow slicker and rain hat. The goose had maintained its post since Joe was a child. Its dress changed with the seasons—a scarf in the fall, rain gear in the spring—but its expression of faithful, emptyheaded watchfulness had not changed in thirty years.

He removed his cap and considered the house across the street where he had grown up. The youngest of his siblings had left; his parents had moved away. He did not know the new residents. How different the house was now, so trim and tidy, from the days when it was inhabited by nine human beings, not including his brothers' or his sisters' friends—at least one of whom, according to his recollection, was staying over at any given time.

Joe's mother made a point to put every young guest to work alongside her own children cleaning rooms and clearing tables and washing dishes and generally earning their bed and board. Every young visitor was spoken to like an adult who was expected to contribute to the upkeep of the household. After a few days, in most cases, the guest understood clearly the behavioral expectations of that place and the tasks allotted to each able body. Indeed, so it seemed to him now, those kids more often than not took ownership of their small duties with alacrity and soon enough began to shed their awkwardness, having earned by their own labor the right to second helpings of mashed potatoes and a warm place to sleep. His mom and dad, Joe thought, having themselves come from large families afflicted with desertion and drink and early mortality, believed that childhood, though good and proper in its season, was not to be overly indulged.

It was not always a comforting philosophy. Joe's younger sister brought a friend home, a girl who had lost her mother whose home was a shambles. He recalled the three of them seated at the kitchen table: his mom and dad, hands folded, and little Eileen Tarpey, whose feet did not touch the floor but swung nervously beneath the chair.

His mother said, "You have to be tough now, Eileen."

At these words, the girl's feet stopped swinging and she looked from Missus Riley to Mister Riley and back again. Joe recalled how they returned her gaze: not with authority but with a forgivingness born of long familiarity with trouble, which conveyed to the child an assurance that while they could not heal her hurt, they could provide a warm place to sleep and food to eat. Eileen sobbed then, only twice, and Joe's parents did not look away but let her finish. Then his mother rose and said, "Come with me, sweetie. You're going to help me make lunch. Are you hungry?"

On a shelf in the living room of his old house, he recalled, where the family pictures were arrayed, his mom had kept a little space for Jude. No figurine or image of the saint occupied the place at the end of the shelf, only a small candle in a baby food jar. Now and then, whenever there was some common trouble in the world or in their immediate lives, she set a few blades of grass and a glass of water beside the candle. The water was for Jude, the grass for his horse.

But there were other days—days when nothing had seemed amiss, at least to his mind—when she unaccountably set the blades of grass and the water on the shelf. He remembered now how he felt a little uneasy on those occasions, wondering what the trouble was—ominous because unspoken and unseen. But his mother would not share the matter that prompted the untimely offering, and he knew better than to ask.

As he sat on the porch step, it occurred to him that those offerings may not have been in response to some difficulty as he had once assumed. It was perhaps no more than a periodic gesture of gratitude, rendered according to some private liturgical calendar of remembrances, devised over a lifetime in accordance with her own calculations, which she alone observed and would not share. And he understood in that moment that his mother's life—and his father's life and his sisters' and brothers' lives—had been a great mystery to him.

As Joe sat on the Stegemuller's porch step and considered his old house, inhabited now by people he didn't know, he remembered that he must call his parents soon or visit them in their peaceful retirement to thank them for their generosity—the unquestioning generosity that never expected and rarely received the gratitude of its beneficiaries. But if he mentioned these things, his parents would probably be surprised and a little embarrassed, perhaps, and possibly a touch mystified. Today he would call them. Today is not too late.

*

There's an emptiness to certain streets on certain summer days, a mournful shadow filling the spaces between things when all the people are at work. At midday, a solitary cat will assume its regency over the neighborhood, and it will sink into intense studies—lasting hours—of incautious oblivious goldfinches.

He looked again toward the trees at the end of the street. Once, they had composed a forest of coverts and shadows, and he and Kenny were the woodsmen who ranged its paths in all seasons. But it was a narrow and disowned place now, and it seemed that even a squirrel could not hide in there for long.

Kenny was here in the city, Joe thought. He was right now in a room somewhere, sweating and shirtless in a third-floor efficiency scribbling notes at a battered desk piled with library books, making outlandish plans for adventures that would never come off.

He put his cap on and returned to the cruiser.

Four

The coach was quiet. People slept in their seats with their heads on pillows of rolled-up jackets. Dirty snow fringed the pavement. As Kenny munched a granola bar, the crumbs dropped on the page he was reading.

"Where we at?" Joe asked.

Kenny considered the sun, now scarfed in a pale haze, rising from the black trees. He held his thumb and forefinger in front of his right eye, closed his left eye, and peered through the gap of his fingers. "Eighty-two degrees, fifteen minutes west. Thirty-nine degrees, nine minutes north. Approximately." He turned back to the book.

"Where are we?"

"We're adrift in the uncharted soy fields of southern Indiana."

"Where we at."

"Southern Indiana."

"That's it? That's all?"

Joe recalled the pilgrim painted on the coffee table, who at this moment must be staring up at the ceiling of a deserted room. Someday soon, the fussy old German landlord will enter the apartment with his sons. He'll pester the two brothers as they incautiously carry the coffee table through the door and down the steps to the trash container that stands in the corner of the littered lot. Within a few hours, the garbage truck will back in, whining as it strains to heft the container over its mold-boltered maw to choke down Joe's earthly possessions. By noon, replete, the truck will set off for the landfill that rises like a boil on the western outskirts of the city, to the site where Darryl had once rescued three American flags from an ignominious interment in a landslip of waste.

No matter. Joe folded his hands on his lap and watched the trees, feeling comfortably trapped in the bus seat. Memories arrived from far away to reclaim their roosts. A boy, whom Joe recognized as himself, stands in the dim light of left field during a Saturday night little league game. There were not many adults in the bleachers; they were all gathered around the taps at the concession stand. The purpose of little league baseball was not baseball, he suddenly understood; the purpose was to bring all the children under a common supervision so that their parents could drink lukewarm draft out of plastic cups and tell dirty jokes about their bosses, spouses, neighbors, priests. One night a week, during Saturday baseball games, they became eloquent in good-natured obscenity, ridiculed the kings of the earth, spent all the cash in their wallets, and feared no man. No doubt, the ballplayers had to wait for hours, often past midnight, for their inebriated parents to drive them home in work vans and dented sedans.

He wondered, as he watched the black trees whirl by, whether he'd ever gain admittance into that fellowship—as a father, a taxpayer, a man with a job—certifying his fealty by standing rounds of beer on a few appointed summer evenings. The prospect of membership in the tribe troubled him only slightly less than the promise of his exclusion.

*

At Terre Haute, as Joe tended to baseball memories, an old man boarded with a suitcase, which he stowed in the rack above Kenny and Joe. As the man claimed the empty seat across the aisle, Joe realized that what he'd first believed to be a shadow or a botched haircut was in fact an enormous dent in the man's head. A smooth channel ran deep and wide across the skull—five, six inches in length, three wide and two deep, just right of center and parallel to the crown. It was the kind of damage incurred from the swing of a Louisville Slugger. Bristly hair grew in the dent, which made the damage seem organic. The sight of it made Joe's teeth ache. He was awed and appalled, and somehow unsurprised to discover that the dead do walk up and down in the earth.

The man stretched his legs beneath the seat in front of him. He arched, adjusted the crotch of his pants, pulled free the tails of his soiled blazer. Soon, his face collapsed onto his chin, and he began to snore.

Kenny woke from a doze, observed the man, and whispered to Joe, "Good lord! Did you see that? That guy's missing half his head!"

Presently the man woke up. "Boys thirsty?" He reached into the suitcase between his knees, produced a bottle of Old Crow, and brandished it at them like a severed head. He braced the bottle between his knees and twisted off the cap and took a drink.

Kenny took the proffered bottle. "Where you going, sir?"

The man retrieved a crumpled slip of paper from his shirt pocket and studied it. "California!" he said, as if he were laying claim to the place. "I'm going to California, where people'll kick you in the face soon as look at you. Ain't that right?"

"Hopefully it's not that bad," Kenny offered. "But I don't know." He handed the bottle to Joe. "We're going west too! Then south. We're going to Mexico to find Mary. I had a vision. She came to me when I was asleep…"

The old man took back the bottle. "You talk too much."

A woman seated four rows ahead had observed them with grave disappointment.

"Where in the hell we at, for godsakes?" the old man demanded of the bus.

"Illinois."

"This travellin' business is bullshit. You never know where the hell you are."

"Illinois."

"You gotta speak up," the man said. "I'm an old man. I shoulda made this trip when I was you boys' age. Sixty-eight years I never left Summit County except once to get shot in the head on Tarawa and twice to get that same hole plugged. But them weren't much a what people call vacations. My name's Ray."

Ray dug a wallet from his back pocket and opened it to a black-and-white picture of a woman who would not dream of smiling for a camera like some common fool. Rolling hills stretched away behind her. Her hair appeared to have been tied back in anger.

"That's my wife," he said. "She died."

Beside the picture was a white scrap of paper framed in laminated plastic, which read: *My name is Ray Seward. If lost, please contact...*

The man watched the land closely and drew their attention to unassuming things.

"Look!" he said, pointing to a howitzer parked outside a Legion Hall: "Cannon!"

Or, upon observing a man burning branches in an open pit: "Fire!"

He kept a journal too, which he also shared.

> 12.17 Rain for half hour. Snow mix
> 12.45 Factorys. coal and rock piles. kid said Illinois.
> 2. High quick water and muddy. half mile wide
> 3.50 Snow. woods. Elms Red Oaks not tall like home.

He said he wanted to remember these things to his brother in California. He perused all that he'd written to date and tapped the paper into his shirt pocket.

The offended passenger spoke like one who wants to be heard above the wind, "You're not supposed to be drinking on the bus."

Ray frowned. "Women always worryin' everbody," he said to himself.

Kenny asked about Ray's plans and tried to hold the old man to a conversation, but it was too late. The driver's eye watched them from a corner of the mirror. Next to the mirror was the sign that listed six rules—three of which they had violated.

At the next town, the driver got out to retrieve a passenger's bags. When he returned, he walked down the aisle and announced, "You three. Off the bus."

Joe pretended indignation, "What for?"

"Drinking, foul language. You're disturbing the other passengers. Let's go." He held his hand out. "Give me your tickets and step off."

Kenny carried Ray's suitcase down the aisle. The driver pulled a plastic garbage bag of Ray's clothing from the luggage compartment and dropped it on the pavement, then turned away to take tickets from two people waiting to board.

Kenny interrupted him, "Sir, I'll take the blame for the bottle. It was mine. But that old man's senile. He'll be lost and broke five minutes from now. Could you do him a favor—"

"Not my problem, chief," the driver said, handing a stub to a rider.

Ray watched a semi-trailer cross the overpass and spoke to it, "Where the hell is this?"

"Let's have a seat, Ray," Kenny said. They sat together on a bench outside the Greyhound ticket booth, which was a shed pieced together with pressboard, attached to a Sunoco station. Kenny knocked politely at the graffitied, padlocked, weather-warped door.

Ray said, "Good lord this travellin's wearin' me out."

The driver shut the bus's compartment doors, walked to the bench and returned Ray's ticket to him.

"Put this in your pocket where you won't lose it. There'll be another bus in about eight hours. It'll pull up right here. Alright?"

Kenny repeated the driver's instructions, in several iterations, until the man nodded.

"You boys live here?" Ray asked, in disapproval of the dead fields and the shabby houses of the town.

Kenny pulled some bills out of his wallet. "Here you go, Ray. This fell out of your pocket."

"That's not mine, son."

"It's not mine. You must've dropped it. You can buy a coffee and a corn dog inside the station. Okay, we'll be off now! Say hello to your brother for us!"

"Bless you, son," Ray said as they shouldered their packs and set off. "You listen to me now. Get out of this hellhole. There's nothing for you here."

*

On the shoulder of the on-ramp, Kenny lifted a thumb at a passing car, but the car roared by. He sat down beside Joe and glanced over the sodden fields.

"We can't buy the same bus ticket twice," he said. "That's not in the budget. We have to hitchhike. It won't be easy, but nothing worthwhile is easy. The point of pilgrimage is sacrifice, Joe. Mary will not deign to meet us if we arrive well-fed and on time. No, we have to arrive hungry and barefoot and smelling like gas station cheese." He spread the highway map on the asphalt. "So here we are: the interchange is here, not far. We shoot down this way, take this road, turn left here toward warmer weather, then pick up ten west in Louisiana. From there we bee-line to Nogales, where we'll cross the border." He traced the proposed route with his finger, lightly, down the Mississippi valley, across to Arizona.

Joe settled into his coat, loose and inebriate. He retrieved a whiskey bottle from his pack, took a drink, lit a cigarette, and reclined against a signpost in the cold sunlight. "I don't care."

"You took Ray's whiskey. That belonged to him."

"He shouldn't be drinking. He's real decrepit. What?"

"You didn't listen to my plan, neither. I'm worried."

"I heard your plan and it stinks. One person hitching is trouble enough. Two people might as well walk." He folded his hands in his armpits, drew his knees in, closed his eyes. "When I open my eyes, I will be sitting on my couch watching the playoffs and sipping a hot toddy." He opened his eyes. "Why in hell, by the way, did we head out in the middle of winter?"

"The weather's different down there."

"Yeah, but—ah, fuck it."

Kenny frowned at the gray sky. "Words like *hot toddy* don't belong on this journey. Don't say *hot toddy*. It's bad luck. You don't even know what a hot toddy is. I never want to hear that term again."

*

They ran to the pickup, climbed into the bed, and sat with their backs to the cab. The wind whipped up a minor cyclone of candy wrappers and straw. Kenny took off his glasses, grinned in the ripping air, and returned the wave of a small boy seated in the back seat of an overtaking Corolla.

The driver pulled onto the shoulder of an exit ramp. They climbed out and shouted *thanks*, but he drove off without a word. Kenny stuck out a thumb again.

A middle-aged woman pulled over. She informed them that her son was hitchhiking too, somewhere "out west," and she was hoping that a good turn on her part would transmit some good will his way. "Karma," she called it. Never in her life, she informed them, had she picked up a hitchhiker. She gave them ten dollars at the end of the ride, so relieved she was to be alive. A young couple in a Nissan pickup gave them a lift, a candy bar, a small sack of weed, and three and a half dollars.

The last ride of the day was a man who suggested that they keep to the Illinois state routes and bypass Missouri. "Missoura's wicked, man," he cautioned as they stood at the passenger door with their packs on their shoulders. The cab window behind the man's head bore a column of UAW stickers like emblems on a totem. The man chewed a toothpick and winced at some bad memory. "They'll snatch your ass up for nothing. Thumbing's against the law there, you know. You'll disappear and never be heard from again." He closed the window on them and sped away.

*

Out of sight of the road, beneath the trees, they spread their sleeping bags on the ground. The temperature fell. Joe emptied the tobacco from a cigarette and filled the paper tube with some of the weed. The trees edged closer as darkness fell. "Well, this is a lot of fun. I bet we'll freeze to death tonight. I bet the Virgin Mary's snug as a bug in her cave."

"She doesn't live in a cave."

"This is gonna be a bust. I can feel it. The only question is whether they hang us, electrocute us, or inject us with rat poison."

"It's not that funny. You shouldn't smoke that stuff. You don't have to smoke it just because someone gave it to you. Drugs are bad for you." He sat with his head bent, miffed. "I'm not going to hang."

"Yes you will. That's how the story ends. That's how the story always ends." He pictured Kenny, noosed and bewildered in sneakers and tube socks alone on a scaffold. The trapdoor drops; the mob howls.

"What's so funny?" Kenny asked.

*

Joe lay curled inside his bag, shivering through hours of semi-consciousness, until the branches resolved in a gray half-light. He crawled out, thumped his water bottle against the ground to break the ice, lit a cigarette.

Kenny woke with a start and sat up, the sleeping bag covering his head like a shawl of blue rayon. He pulled the map out of his bag. "That guy said Missouri was dangerous. According to this, though, there's only a little bitty stretch of Missouri before we get to Arkansas. Then it's a straight shot to sun and warmth. I say we go for it. Missouri'll be quicker. We won't have any problems. In a few days we'll be laughing in the sun."

Three rides and five hours brought them to the Mississippi. Joe felt a pang of consternation as he read the sign planted on the west side of the river, *Welcome To The State Of Missouri.*

They walked the buckled sidewalks of a town past mismatched houses skirted with empty porches, cars parked here and there, and found no place to fill their bottles. The wasted lawns were patched with gray snow.

In the gutters lay rivulets of rust-red powder. The powder coated the hoods of cars like so much pollen, and even the tops of the mailboxes bore thin maroon crests of dust. A factory wall loomed above the houses like untimely evening, and a faint rumble resolved in the air. Planted on a factory's roof was a pipe like the upturned barrel of a howitzer, and from the mouth of the barrel pelted a six-foot flame of waste gas. The flame feathered into so many black shrouds that drained into the sky, where the sun drowned face down in an umber puddle.

Kenny knelt in the gutter, pinched some powder, rolled it in his fingers and blew the dust away. "They're making night."

"Don't be so dramatic." Beneath a dead tree, a barefoot toddler dressed in a long T-shirt stood alone and stared. When a car passed,

Joe peered into the windshield but saw nothing for the weak glare of sunlight on the grime. The houses seemed precipitously vacated as though everyone had been called away on urgent and unpleasant business. On the boarded-up doorframes were the spray-painted characters of an apocalypse whose hour was known only to vandals.

At the convenience store, they bought bologna and filled their half-gallon milk jugs at the restroom tap. As they walked up the on-ramp, Joe felt a car engine idling behind him, and he told Kenny not to turn around. He looked into the trees that bordered the ramp and considered running or turning with conspicuous purpose back toward town. The car followed slowly, at a walking pace. The brief, inquisitive cry of a siren stopped them, and they turned to face the cruiser. The cop was slow to get out.

Kenny said, "Just act natural," in a breathy voice.

"Don't say anything stupid."

"How you boys doing?" the cop asked, settling his sky-blue smokey as he approached.

"Fine. Fine, Sir."

"Where you going?" The cop's voice was indulgent, cloying, as he tilted his head sideways to get a look at the packs on their backs.

"Arizona, Sir," Kenny said.

"Arizona, huh?" he said, sweetly curious, as to a child. The light and mincing timbre of the voice sounded more like a gas leak than human speech.

Joe had never seen arms as big as the cop's, except on television. They were hairless and stitched with vein, smooth as pistons on an old steam engine, and hung unnaturally from the ham-sized cranks of the man's shoulders.

"What's in Arizona?" the man asked.

Joe felt sick and wanted to look away from the cop's chin, which seemed to have been scraped of stubble with a pumice stone. "Looking for work there," he said. "Painting work."

"Where you from?"

"Ohio."

"Walking on the highway is illegal in the state of Missouri. Can I see some IDs?" He looked the cards over and said with careful enthusiasm, "Ohio, huh?" He reached up to the mic that was strapped to his shoulder and pressed the button. The voice was different now and matched the chin. "Two Forty-Four."

They waited for a voice to answer. *Yeah.*

"I'm going to need you down here."

I don't doubt that. But I don't know where you're at.

"Fifty-nine on-ramp." He looked around. "Southbound Penderton."

Be right there.

"Painting work, huh?" resumed the first voice. "There's a lot of painting work there, I guess?"

"We'll find out, I guess."

He squared himself to Kenny and spoke explicitly. "What about you. You looking for painting work too?"

"I'll tell you, Officer. It happened this way. Have you ever been somewhere, alone, and heard a voice call your name? And when you turn around, there's no one there?"

The cop leaned back as from a bowl of sour milk. "I'm sick of you jobless druggies coming through my state. You're the reason this country's falling apart. When I was your age I was serving my country overseas. Now listen to what I'm going to tell you. There's been a large flow of narcotics coming through this area recently. By your appearance; by the way you're acting, and by the answers you're giving me: I got reason to suspect you got something to hide."

"We got nothing to hide, Officer—"

"Then you won't mind if I look in your bags."

They shouldered off the packs as the second cruiser pulled up. "Walk towards that car," the cop said. He squatted on the sidewalk and began to pull clothes out of Kenny's pack. The other cop opened the rear door of his cruiser and smiled at them as they climbed in, then he shut the door and joined the other.

The air in the cruiser was close and chemical. The radio fluttered with red and green lights, squawked, squelched, fell silent. They overheard nothing as they watched the cops pull clothing and kit out of their packs and drop the items on the asphalt. The first cop extracted something of interest from Kenny's pack, but the man's back was to them, and they couldn't see what he held. The cops shared a few words. When the object was passed from hand to hand, they saw that it was a buck knife. Kenny said, with deep misgiving, "It's just my buck knife."

Joe concentrated on his breathing and furiously ticked through the items in his pack. Squatting in the mess of stuff, the cop clenched the small sack of weed in his fist, swiveled on his heel, and aimed his index finger through the windshield at Joe's face. The force of the gesture knocked the breath from him. "But I threw that shit away. How did—"

"I put it back in your pack," Kenny said.

"Why? I threw it away!"

"I thought you dropped it, so I put it back in your pack. I was just being considerate! Oh, no. I'm sorry. Dang it. Dang it all!"

"Quiet. Here they come."

They were removed from the car, handcuffed, positioned in turn for Polaroid pictures against a backdrop of black trees, and placed in the cruiser again. The cop climbed behind the wheel and said cheerfully, "Ready to go to jail, Picasso? A lot of walls need paint there. Too many walls."

"What for."

The man looked frankly through the mesh. "Boy, do you have any idea where you are? This is rural Missoura. You jumped in with both feet carrying drugs into this county." He wrenched the car into gear and gunned up the ramp and onto the highway. "The other one's being charged with carrying a concealed weapon," he added.

"But I would never hurt anyone, officer," Kenny said. So guileless were his words, the cop glanced in the mirror with an expression, it seemed to Joe, of puzzlement.

*

The county courthouse was a new three-story glass-and-brick structure that cast a block-long shadow over Main Street. The officer led Kenny and Joe through the street-level garage and sat them, cuffed, on a bench beside the processing desk. An hour passed before the desk officer uncuffed them and fingerprinted them. He led Joe into a small room and shut the door and told him to strip. Joe faced him, naked.

"Let me see the sole of your right foot. Left. Underarms. Lift your testicles. Turn around and spread. Not your legs, your butt cheeks. Put your socks back on."

"Underwear?"

"You don't get underwear. Put those on." Orange shirts and trousers lay folded in two stacks on the metal bench. The backs of the shirts bore black iron-on letters: LAFORGE CORRECTIONAL.

As Joe exited the room, Kenny searched his friend's face for a sign, looking up and down the orange suit, then toward the open door, from which a bodiless and ill-tempered voice called, "Next."

"It only hurts for a second," Joe said. Alone on the bench, he decided that the orange slippers on his feet were real, now.

When Kenny walked out and strayed bewildered toward the exit, the officer herded him angrily toward the desk, where each was issued a plastic cup, a blanket, a towel, a sawed-off toothbrush. The officer and a guard led them down ill-lit hallways to a steel door that opened of itself. The cop vanished, the door slammed behind them, and they stood facing a two-tiered semicircle of cells that overlooked a common area, where inmates in orange jumpsuits, seated on benches bolted to the concrete floor, sat playing cards at steel tables. Some of the men regarded the arrivals with sour curiosity. Kenny read the number printed in permanent marker on his cup and addressed the two inmates seated nearest.

"Excuse me. Can you tell me where I can find Twenty-two B?"

The men did not respond.

"This way," said another man, rising from a different table. "I'll show you."

Like a pair of servants bearing jewels, they carried the toothbrushes on folded GI blankets. Inside the second-tier cell were one stainless steel toilet and two bunks bolted to the cinder-block walls. When Kenny asked Joe, "Can I have the top bunk?" and Joe responded with a curse, the inmate smiled.

"I'm Billy Bogota, like pagoda with a B. What'd you do?"

Joe nicked his chin at Kenny. "He had a buck knife. I had a bit of weed."

"Where you from?"

"Ohio."

"Enough said. Being from Ohio is against the law here, boys. Well, don't worry about it. Just stick it out, be patient, you won't be here forever. I got some shampoo and toothpaste you can borrow. This bunk needs a mat too. I'll round one up."

"Thanks, Billy. I'm Kenny."

"Don't mention it. Kenny, I don't think you're in this cell—there's already some dude in here." He read the number on Kenny's cup and said, with a touch of regret, "Seems you're with me."

Kenny followed Billy out of the cell, glancing about like a rustic in the manor house.

"Like to read?" Billy said over his shoulder. "I got books you can borrow."

"Books?"

*

Joe washed his face, brushed his teeth without paste, lay back on his bunk. His muscles retained the high-speed ride in the cruiser, and the dip and swell of the highway rolled through his bones like the tide. He went to the common area where the inmates, about forty in all, played cards or sat in corners with paperbacks. Kenny was there, playing Scrabble with Billy and two men.

From a mess of paperbacks and pamphlets heaped in in a corner on the floor, Joe picked up a book called *Hollywood Kids* and sat at the end of the bench, within earshot of his friend. He flipped the pages, looked at the television, and thought about time, for there were no clocks and no windows and no one wore watches.

Kenny studied the words on the board. Billy said, "Don't worry, boys. The law says they can't hold you without charges for more than twenty-four hours, which means you should be out in a month."

The other players laughed unhappily.

"Oh, I'm not worried, Billy," Kenny said as he set down the letters S, E, R, F.

Ali reached for the dictionary.

"They'll rob you then see you to the state line. That's SOP for transients. Half the people in here got picked up on the interstate, driving with the wrong plates. The other half had the right plates and the wrong skin. We got a grade-A racket underway here in Saint Louis County, USA. Guess you didn't get the word. Listen. Don't bother nobody and nobody's gonna bother you. Don't butt in line. Don't whine and you'll be fine. Hey, Frank, did you hear what I just said? I'm a goddamn poet."

Kenny said, "Did you hear that, Joe? Just be yourself, and we'll be fine."

"Well, no," Billy said. "Don't just *be yourself*. On second thought, why not? Ali, just be yourself. Hear that? Ha! Just be yourself, the kid says."

"Being myself's how I got into this fucking place," Ali said. "Be yourself, huh? Shoot, I wouldn't mind being somebody else for just one goddamn day. Shit on being myself."

So they played Scrabble and discussed the advisability of Being Oneself, as opposed to Being Someone in the aspirational sense—or, alternatively, Being A Nobody, which struck Billy as a potential solution to a variety of troubles.

Joe listened to the talk and looked for a window to jump out of. The stark fluorescent light coagulated in the stale air. Everything was bolted, blunted, painted dull yellow. The act of thought nauseated him. At a signal Joe missed, everyone stood and formed a line at the door. The fire bell rang, the bolt shot, and the guard appeared in the entry and handed each man a tray of food from a cart. Conversation ended while the men fed.

"I can't eat this cat shit." Frank scraped the dollop of turkey salad onto his neighbor's tray and took a slice of white bread and a bruised pear in exchange. Joe sliced the mess with a limp plastic spoon and thought of hot scrambled eggs and hot coffee, certain he would not see such things again in this lifetime. After the trays were returned and the cart was wheeled away, the inmates resumed their card games or watched tv or stared at the walls, digesting, cogitating.

The guard entered the pod with the remote control and changed the station. Someone shouted, "Who the fuck told him to change that?" But the guard departed without a word, and Joe returned to his cell.

He lay on the bunk reading *Hollywood Kids*. His cellmate, napping below, awoke when the argument started and padded to the open door to listen, searching the noise with eyes wide. He was quiet, skinny, a teenager. He listened to the voices.

"Who told him to change the channel?" a voice from below demanded.

"I told him," came the reply. "We watch that stupid fucken shit every goddamn night."

"Motherfucker you got some fucken nerve, boy, you don't change that shit without my approval you hear me?"

"Fuck your approval—go fuck yourself."

"Motherfucker," the voice rose above the miasma of tv noise and boomed among the second-tier cells. "Do you *believe this shit?*"

Joe walked onto the catwalk and peered over the railing to the common area. "Stay back," the cellmate said. "Don't let them see you. Stay out of it."

The fight commenced. The men's slippers squeaked as their feet planted, and they cursed in breathless disbelief as bone tolled against metal. Inmates came out of their cells and leaned at the catwalk rail, shouting dispraise and encouragement, it seemed to Joe, according to skin color. The fire bell rang and the door's bolt shot; five guards entered the pod and cuffed both men. One man was hustled out. His shaved and bloody-mouthed head, bright with sweat, was stapled to his neck with a handlebar moustache. He gnashed over his shoulder, spitting vicious and incoherent words. His fury flooded the pod, a bowel-deep bawl that crashed through the place and made the metal sing.

When the door slammed and the crash faded, the only sound in the pod was the low and steady laughter of the man left behind, seated alone and cuffed to the table. It was a miserable laugh, Joe thought. It was the most miserable laugh in the world.

A voice from the intercom ordered all the inmates into their cells. The doors shut of themselves and each door's bolt shot home, successively down the line in a ragged fusillade. The clangor gave place to half-hearted profanity.

Joe slept deeply, did not dream, and awoke late in the night. Somewhere, a few cells away, a man was whistling. *You are my sunshine, my only sunshine.* The song seemed to rise from somewhere deep in the earth, from the bottom of a well, and Joe lay very still, singing along in his head. You make me happy, when skies are gray. You'll never know, dear, how much I love you. Please don't take my sunshine away.

*

The guard, posted behind a cart filled with trays, shouted *get up, get up* by way of reveille, and the inmates emerged from their cells wiping their necks and faces. Each took a tray and a plastic cup of grape juice, found a seat, and did not speak.

When the trays were returned to the cart, Billy set the Scrabble board on the table. Ali and Frank joined him without a word. Kenny watched alertly from the end of the table until Ali said "C'mon, Kenny. Play," and Kenny slid over. Joe resumed his seat at the end of the bench and read the book. He was sixty pages deep, often lost in it, but he could not recall a word or a name from one page to the next. The door opened and a guard shouted into the pod. "Books!"

Several men crowded the cart—a plastic tv stand on metal casters—and picked through the selection. For some, the choice took no time at all. Sci-fi was sci-fi, fantasy was fantasy. It was all spelled out on the cover. The only point to consider was whether you'd read the thing already.

Kenny and Joe shouldered to the front. Romances and Westerns. Religious tracts. Brochures on kicking the habit, be it alcohol or sex or cocaine. A book about German U-boats titled *The Admiral's Wolfpack*. A biography of Mario Andretti. James Michener's *Nebraska*.

"Make it quick," the guard said. At last, only four inmates remained standing over the books, rummaging, sifting. The other two inmates turned away empty-handed.

"You got any literature? Any history?" Kenny asked.

"What do you call this?"

"This is gerbil bedding."

"Don't like it? Don't read it."

"Can I get my books out of my belongings?" Kenny asked.

The guard turned the cart and aimed it down the hall. "No," he said. He pulled his walkie-talkie from his belt and said, "Close it."

"But I have books in—" The door slammed shut in his face.

For a time, Kenny didn't play Scrabble or read or talk but sat on the edge of the bench and stared at the cinder block wall like he was looking through it.

"I'll be done with my story in a few hours," Joe said. "It's a gripping tale." His friend's anger startled him, for it was a rare thing. "You can have it then."

"It's evil. Bad food, no air—so be it. I can take it. But this is evil," Kenny said. "It's evil to keep books from people. They'll pay for doing that. Someday, in some way, they'll pay for it." His eyes clenched at the pain of his fury.

"Now you're talkin'."

*

The door opened and the guards dragged in a long, lanky body by the arms and laid it in the middle of the pod. The body rolled over, moaning, clutching its stomach. The inmates glanced now and then from their cards or the tv screen to the young man on the ground, but no one made a move or said a word. The games went on as before. The young man crawled toward the door and reached a bony arm to the intercom and pressed the button. His sleeve dropped as he did so, revealing scabby bruises.

What's the emergency?

"I need ... I'm dying."

Speak up.

"My stomach."

Billy frowned at the Scrabble board. "This fucker's got a tummy ache. That's what you get for shooting that shit, dumbass."

The intercom rasped again, but no words could be heard at first, just the scrambled resonance of a television and scraps of background laughter. Then a voice said, *There'll be a med cart up after lunch. Talk to them.*

The man rolled onto his side and held his stomach and moaned.

Billy set a letter precisely in its square. "This ain't motherfuckin' daycare," he said to the board, but loudly. "Mommy ain't here to kiss your booboos. This is motherfuckin' jail goddamnit. Stop being a twat." The card players at the next table looked doggedly at their cards.

Kenny got up and stepped over the body and pressed the button and waited.

What's your emergency?

"This guy needs some help, I think. I think he really is sick."

Billy said, "Sit down, Kenny."

"I'm just, there isn't—"

"Sit down, I said. Them assholes ain't gonna help you."

Kenny took a seat.

"I know you're just trying to help but the jackass doesn't want your help; he wants your pity."

Billy tossed a bag of Scrabble letters in front of him. "Play the game, Kenny." The men subjected the board to a grim scrutiny. "I didn't mean to bark at you," Billy said. "You seem like a harmless kid.

I just can't tolerate cowards in this place. The only way to eradicate cowards from the face of the earth is to show no mercy to them."

"I understand, Billy," Kenny said in a small voice.

"I know you do, Kenny. Now play the game. It's your turn. You're killing us with suspense."

For an hour, the skinny man moaned and dry-heaved on the concrete. Then he crawled off to a corner and lay with his back to the pod.

Joe could not concentrate on the book. When a sentence remained nonsensical after three readings, he set the book down and sorted through his thoughts. He watched the Scrabble players, now glum and quiet; he searched for windows once again. Maybe the sun was shining out there.

He recalled waking beneath the trees, four days ago—was it Illinois? Four days ago, when the snow covered the ground, he lay wrapped in his sleeping bag watching the branches resolve against a lightening sky. Four days ago, he woke beneath a tree; high in the tree, a squirrel gripped the twig-end of a branch, and the branch bobbed gently under the squirrel's weight as the creature gnawed the stem of a desiccated walnut.

This trivial and no-account moment from the past returned now, revealing itself so vividly he could hear the trees sway and smell the cold ground once again, and the sordid circumstances of the present became, for just a moment, wholly unreal. His heart grew heavy in the memory. Four days ago, he assured himself, this thing happened: *a walnut dropped from a branch and landed nine feet from my head.* He recalled the walnut with ferocious clarity: a rough shell lying tipped in the leaf litter, paper-dry, fallen from the sky like a meteorite burnt to a cinder.

Our Lady of Good Voyage

*

The inmates ate Fruit Loops and drank black Sanka. They returned their trays to the cart and settled on the benches. Some ate spotted apples, some played Hucklebuck or Spades. Others sat off in corners with battered sci-fi novels or gazed at the wall-mounted tv. Three men paced the catwalk back and forth, back and forth, dressed in baggy orange trousers like Moorish caliphs strolling the battlements.

Joe took his apple, went to Kenny's cell, and rapped with two knuckles against the half-shut door.

"Who wants something?" It was Billy's voice.

"Stegemuller in there?"

The door opened and Joe found his friend seated cross-legged on the floor with his back against the wall. Two teenage inmates sat on either side of him, defensive seeming, a pair of unwashed and uncombed accomplices. Kenny smiled and said, "Don't worry, boys. He's alright."

Joe cursed his friend as he took a seat on the floor.

Billy, cross-legged on the bunk, retrieved a small paper packet from under his pillow. He opened it and scooted the loose tobacco into a pile with a fingertip, tore a slip of paper from the blank end page of a Bible, folded the slip in half, sifted the tobacco into the crease, twisted the ends, and plugged it in his mouth. A match appeared in his fingers; he struck it against the cinderblock wall and lit the cigarette with a glance at Joe.

"Don't mean to be inhospitable, but you can't trust anyone in this place. You youngsters don't understand. It could be so easy but everyone's too gutless to think straight." He blew smoke over them and spoke with his eyes closed as though reciting the company statutes to new hires. "It's no different than the East Germans. That's how they did it. Set up a snitch network, get people scared, no one trusts anyone.

Kevin Honold

Your neighbor'll sell your ass for six months' off his sentence, and so on and so on, until one in three sonsabitches is on probation and parole, afraid to turn around, afraid a speeding ticket's gonna land them back in the can. That's where the operation really kicks in. They give you seven years' probation on a penny-ante dope charge, and you got seven years to keep your shit straight, seven years of being in bed by nine, seven years of clean'n'sober because *if you don't*, if you slip up *just once*, it's back you go, and the whole process starts over again. Every now and then you'll hear a nice fairy tale about some company hiring felons. Don't believe it. That's just part of the lie. How many people do you know finish their probations? They spend their whole lives fighting to get out from under it, and the cops can stroll through their front door any time they like."

He tossed the butt underhand into the toilet and told Joe, who sat nearest, to flush it. "The best part is," Billy said when the noise subsided, "they keep you idiots out of circulation. Can't move to where the work is. Can't pay for night classes. Can't vote. They keep you stupid and broke. And that, my young friends, is what they call The System. It's a roach motel. You check in but you don't check out." There was a knock at the door. "What do you want."

A slim, clean-shaven man entered. He wore slick black hair parted to the side and a black moustache precisely trimmed. With a glance at the four sitting on the ground, he addressed Billy. "Wanna do some business?"

"Who with?"

"With me."

"What do you got?"

The man lifted his shirt and pulled two snack-size packs of Oreos from his trouser-band. He held one in each fist. "Got some Oreos. Got some stamps. Got two fingers." Again, he glanced at the seated young men, seeming to anticipate some objection to the offer. Joe was curious to know what sorts of objections were customarily raised in these situations.

"How much for a finger?" Billy asked.

"Four matches and a pear. Or an apple."

Billy spoke evenly. "Word to the wise, if there's any wisdom in that head of yours, Travis. When certain people conclude that you been fucking with them, they're gonna fuck with you back. Now beat it."

Travis turned out without a word. Billy lay back and stretched with a groan.

"That goes for the rest of you. Beat it and let me sleep."

Kenny picked two Bibles off the floor and handed one to Joe. "Take this. That Hollywood book you're reading is raising some questions amongst the boys." With these words, he stepped out of his laceless orange shoes and climbed into the top bunk with a Gideon's in his teeth.

*

Jarvis stood in the middle of the cell folding a white T-shirt. His eyes tracked his hands' business as he placed a folded shirt on the folded blanket that lay on his stripped mattress.

"Going home?"

"No. I'm going to federal," Jarvis said, preoccupied with stacking his linen. "I'll get it done with. Shoot, I been here four months already. I'll do seventeen there. You get your own cell there—no offense—and you can smoke, and you get outside for some fresh air every day. It'll be a lot better than this dungeon." He picked up his pile of linen. "I should've never tried to come back—that was my big mistake—but my girl didn't like it out there, and I couldn't find a job, and she was worried about the baby. That's why I came back and turned myself in. And now…"

He walked out.

Kevin Honold

*

Joe lay on the bunk and opened the Gideon's. He flipped a few pages and began at the beginning of the book called Samuel, and he read about Elkanah who had two wives—Peninnah who bore him many children, and Hannah who was barren. He read how Hannah prayed so hard for a son that Eli, the old priest who was lounging nearby, thought she was drunk. "How long will you make a drunken spectacle of yourself?" Eli asked the woman. He told her to pull herself together, the Lord would grant her petition.

Elkanah. Peninnah. Hannah. Joe did not recall these names from Sister Monica's eighth-grade religion class.

Out in the pod, the shouting did not abate; the laughter was not glad but derisive, bitter. He wondered when they would be let go. Or were they forgotten? What if their reports were lost, their cases misfiled under offenses they hadn't committed? What if their fingerprints were to be used to provide the missing puzzle piece of evidence in some other case that wanted resolution? Was this an election year? Maybe the prosecutor was hoping to boost his conviction rate. Who would come to the defense of two idiots in this shithole? What if the guards wouldn't let them out to make phone calls? They never let anyone out, it seemed, except to go to prison or another jail. He thought of the junkie lying on the ground, clutching his stomach.

He jumped to the floor and paced back and forth, fists balled. He wanted room to run, to sprint until his lungs heaved. He squatted and sprung up like a rabbit, squatted and sprung to kill the itch, then stood still in the middle of the cell, and felt miserable and foolish. *No, No, No,* he said out loud. *Get your act together, you ass.* He saw the apple lying on his bunk and picked it up. The skin of the apple was cool. He turned the apple in his hand, lay down again, opened the book, and regained his place in the story.

Wherefore it came to pass, when the time was come about after Hannah had conceived, that she bare a son, and called his name Samuel, saying, Because I have asked him of the Lord.

After years of misery, even Hannah's newfound joy was tainted. He pictured the woman, on her knees in the dust, the dark folds of her shawl falling over her head, hiding her face. Her words rose muted from the mound of dust that was her body, and he listened to the words, not a little worried on the boy's account. She was so desperately happy in the simple gift of her son, she made a poem of her gladness.

> The Lord killeth, and maketh alive. He
> bringeth down to the grave,
>   and bringeth up.
> The Lord maketh poor, and maketh rich.
>   He bringeth low, and lifteth up.
> He raiseth up the poor
>   out of the dust,
> and lifteth up the beggar from the dunghill,
>   to set them among princes

On reading the news, a thrill of satisfaction coursed through him. The words assured him that in some world, in some way, sooner or later, they'd get theirs. In his mind was only a vague notion of who *they* were, but that did not trouble him. The fact that, someday, someone was going to pack the bastards off to hell was enough, and this knowledge cooled his temper. He bit the stem of the apple with his incisors, feeling suddenly warm and very tired as the boy in the story grew into a man.

*

"Monarchies." The voice woke him out of a blank sleep. The man stood eye-level at Joe's bunk.

"Say again?"

"You're reading the Monarchies, the history of the Monarchies. Samuel, Judges, Kings, all that," the man said with cheerful irritation. "The book in your hands, man! I can tell," he nicked his chin at the Gideon's, "I can tell by where the book's opened, what part you're in." The man bent out of sight to arrange his mattress coverings.

He asked Joe where he came from, and Joe told him.

"What'd you do anyway?" the voice asked, and he told him that too.

"Hmm. Wicked state to get caught up in. When they let you out you best not look back."

When they let you out, Joe thought. The apple was still in his hand, and he resumed chewing on the stem. The man straightened with a groan and stood in the middle of the cell. Joe didn't want to talk but he couldn't find his place again in the book, and the words he read made no sense under the man's scrutiny. "Don't bite that stem off that apple," the man griped. "The stem's what keeps it cool."

"Have it," Joe said, annoyed.

"Alright," the man said. He took the apple and lay down.

The sound of cracking joints, a groan and a sigh, was the sound of the man settling into his bunk below. A sound like a branch breaking was the man taking a big bite of the apple. That apple is crisp, Joe thought. I should've kept it.

"Not a bad apple, Ohio." The man took another bite and spoke while he chewed. "Shoot, where was it? Virginia? No, New York. I made fifteen-dollars-a-bin picking apples. Picked sometimes fifteen bins a day. I ain't lyin." Joe could hear the man remember those bins of apples, and when he spoke again, his voice had grown softer, a step higher, as if spoken through a dream. "Yeah. I could be done some days by two o'clock in the afternoon, all washed up and sitting at the end of the lane waiting for my girls to get off the school bus. I ain't lyin'."

Joe pictured a man with the same bright eyes and the same furious brows—brows not yet gray. A young man shouldering a bin of apples between rows of trees in the sunlight.

"I wasn't smoking nothing back then neither. Boy, I was in good condition," the man said. "It would probably take me—" The metal bunk creaked as the man doubled with a deep cough that was like a wrenching of iron. Then the voice continued, breathless with pain. "Probably only take me two weeks to get back into shape like that if I had one a them jobs again." He sighed. "Yep. Apples in New York and Virginia, and them oranges down in Florida, boy, so heavy you didn't need no ladder, branches dipping right down to your shoulders. I ain't lyin'."

Wooden crates full of oranges arrayed themselves in unending rows, in sunshine, in Joe's mind. He turned from the thought because in that image of orange crates was a whirlpool that had the power to drag down planets and anybody with the bad sense to peer into it would be carried down without a sound, like a grain of rice down a drain. The man soon fell asleep and snored terribly.

> Then Eli called Samuel, and said, Samuel, my son. And he answered, Here Am I.
> And he said, What is the thing that the Lord hath said unto thee? I pray thee hide it not from me.
> And Samuel told him every whit, and hid nothing from him.

*

The man choked on a snore and rolled in his bunk. Joe could hear that the man was awake, so he asked the man a question.

"Oh, I do a little something. Work. Do a little something. Get by. You know. But I got a lucky number. You play the tickets, Ohio? Three-four-eight, that's my number. I got by for two months playing three-four-eight once. I holed up in a hotel room with a woman and only went out once a day. To buy tickets. No drinking. I don't drink. Just tickets and food. I kept them bills up in a ceiling tile. Three-four-eight, man. That was my daughters' ages then. When I get out I'm gonna play them numbers again. Even though the girls ain't that age anymore. You got a woman, Ohio?"

"Nah."

"Yeah. Women'll change your mental state a mind. Not all of them. You know. There's this one woman—huh, she really liked me." His voice brightened at a sudden inspiration. "You know what? I'm gonna give her a call when I get up out a here," and his voice trailed off. "I got her number somewheres."

The man rose from his bunk and walked the cell, three steps forth, three steps back, again and again. He dropped to the floor and knocked out thirty clean pushups, counting as he pushed, then stood and shook it off.

"Shit." He spoke lower as he rolled his broad shoulders. "I hate this fucking place. A carton a cigarettes and a bottle a vodka is all I took. Three hundred days for a bottle a motherfucken vodka." He dropped again and knocked out another set of thirty as quickly as the first, then stood, breathing deeply, eyes closed, practicing calm. When he spoke again, his eyes had acquired the same curious amusement as before. He held his hand out. "I'm Garreth," he said. "Listen to me, Ohio. You're quiet. That's a good way. Don't listen to these jackasses. Everybody in here, it's just talk talk talk. Don't believe a word of it. And stay out of Missoura. Go to New York, Virginia, anywhere but here. This place is wicked. I ain't lyin."

Our Lady of Good Voyage

*

After evening chow, Kenny entered Joe's cell to inform him that a preacher had arrived at the jail to speak with the inmates.

"No Christ crap today."

"It'll be something new! Anyway, Christmas is in two days. I bet you didn't know that, did you? Needless to say, I didn't get you anything. You know what? I don't think they're Catholics around here. I want to see what the big difference is, don't you?"

"Ain't no difference. More a the same bullshit."

"Jeesh. Your grammar's really gone to pot in the last three days. It must be something in the quote-unquote applesauce. Let's go," he said, shaking Joe's foot. "Bring your Gideons."

By the time the door buzzed open and the preacher walked in, most of the inmates had abandoned their card games and gone into hiding in their cells. The older men remained, Frank and Travis and Garreth and Ali, Billy and a few others. The preacher stood in the middle of the pod and remembered to remove his ball cap. He folded the cap's bill into his back trouser pocket, planted his feet, and looked frankly at the inmates. His demeanor betrayed a corn farmer's suspicion of crowds.

"Good evening, gentlemen. My name's Jim Tulliver, from the United Brethren Church in Alliance. I visit all the jails in the surrounding counties and a few of the state prisons, so maybe you've seen me before. I see a few familiar faces in here. Billy, good to see you. Mister Jones, good to see you, sir. Merry Christmas to you all. How many of you brought a Bible? That's alright."

"Merry Christmas, Mister Tulliver," Kenny said.

The man opened the book in his hand and flipped through the pages.

"Let's turn our books to First Kings chapter seventeen verse one." He watched sidelong as Travis flipped loudly to the correct page. Then he began. "Now Elijah the Tishbite, who was of the inhabitants of Gilead, said unto Ahab, As the Lord God of Israel liveth, before whom I stand, there shall not be dew nor rain these years, but according to my word. And the word of the Lord came unto him, saying, Get thee hence, and turn thee eastward, and hide thee by the brook Cherith, that is before Jordan. And it shall be, that thou shalt drink of the brook; and I have commanded the ravens to feed thee there."

Tulliver closed the book on his index finger and considered the inmates. "Now why would God send Elijah out to the wilderness? Where there's no food and nothing to drink?"

Travis sought the lost thread in his book, frowning as he rattled the pages.

"It's me speaking now, son," Tulliver said. Travis glanced up, sat back. "Thank you. Now, Elijah went to the wilderness with no food and nothing to drink, on the promise that he'd find a bit of water in that wasteland and that the birds would feed him. Why'd God do that?"

Kenny said, "Because birds are disinterested. They lose nothing by helping Elijah. And people are supposed to do the same. Nature is like the book of God, it's like the book God wrote that teaches us about ourselves and about the purpose of existence. The birds in the story, they teach us that we're supposed to act selflessly, without hope of reward. Is that it, Mister Tulliver?"

"What's your name, son?"

"Kenny, sir."

"Kenny, I think that's a real good answer, but maybe we don't need to think so hard about it. It's about faith. Not works. Just faith. You don't need to do anything but believe. Now, in the desert, everything is plain as day. God's grace, my own sinfulness: everything's revealed there. Do you understand, Kenny?"

"I understand, Mister Tulliver."

"Good. Now in those days, the people worshipped Ba'al. Ba'al was the god of rain and good harvests but God said to Elijah, No! I alone cause the rain to fall and I alone stop the rain from falling. You will find no nourishment in this world but by my Word. I will cause the ravens to feed you, even in a time of hunger, even in a place of desolation. Your idols, your treasures, your … fancy cars and women will avail you nothing in this place. Only in the Word will you find sustenance and life. You have to make yourself empty. Then you'll be nourished. The nourishment of salvation has to come from outside you. From above. That is to say, from God."

He opened the book again and read. "So he went and did according unto the word of the Lord; for he went and dwelt by the brook Cherith, that is before Jordan. And the ravens brought him bread and flesh in the morning, and bread and flesh in the evening; and he drank of the brook."

Tulliver took two steps forward and exhibited the book to them. He held it high, plumb and square, framed in his hands for all to see. The inmates watched his face or skimmed their books or looked at the yellow concrete floor.

"Now," he said, "when I say that this book has breadth, and length," he checked the book in his hands, "and width … What does that mean?" No one answered. "What's it mean when I say that?"

"Two-dimensional," Travis stated. "It's two-dimensional."

"Two-dimensional?" A trace of uncertainty crossed the preacher's face. "Well, no. Here's what I mean. Look at it, men." He held it at arm's-length, a touch higher. "It's got body. It's got substance. This ain't—this isn't an idea. It's a thing. The Word of God is real, as real as the water Elijah drank. As real as the benches you're sitting on. As real as this book."

One of the men spoke under his breath and another laughed. A hurt and angry look crossed Tulliver's face, and Joe felt sorry for the man. "Let me put it to you this way," Tulliver said. "What's your body made up of?"

"Bones and muscle," Travis answered—this time from the safe ground of fact. "And nerves."

"Water," the preacher corrected. "We're ninety-eight per cent water. How in the world do our bodies stay together when we're ninety-eight per cent water? What keeps the molecules from breaking apart and spilling over the ground?"

Travis wore a miffed expression.

Kenny sat up straight, squinting helpfully, alert for a pretext to agree with something—with anything—and when the silence became intolerable, he said, "Everything that is, proceeds from the Word, which isn't really a word like *cat* is a word. The Word's a symbol for the creative spirit. In a way, we're all echoes—reverberations, you could say—of God's one undivided thought. That's why we don't fall apart."

"That sounds a little Greek to me, Kenny, if I remember my seminary reading. Not sure where you got that from. But that's okay. You say *word*, but I say *grace*. Only by God's grace do we live and not spill over the ground. It's God's grace what keeps the planets in their orbits about the sun," Tulliver said, "just like the molecules in your bodies keep their orbits about your soul."

"I see!"

"This is all very interesting, Reverend," Billy said, "but it means nothing to the men in here now." He straddled the bench, one hand pressed palm-down on an open Bible. "Jim, I said it before and I'll say it again. I've known you for a while, and you know I don't mean nothing personal, but you got the wrong bunch a people. If you want to do some good, then go round and visit the judge's bigass house and the lawyers' bigass houses. The judge who goes to church—maybe *your* church—and doesn't think twice about taking years away from men's lives, taking them away from their families for some dumb shit they do, smoking crack or weed or whatnot—men who don't hurt nobody but themselves. The lawyers who take the life savings from people who ain't got nothing to begin with, then go and buy a nice new duck boat with the money or take their wives to the Bahamas. They're the ones who need to read that book in your hand. They're the ones who're gonna burn if there's any justice in this fucking world." Billy lifted his hand from the page and read the words he'd uncovered there. "Evil men do not understand justice. Proverbs twenty-eight."

Tulliver nodded sadly at his feet. "You got good reason to be angry, Billy. All you men do. But maybe there's another way to see things. We're all to blame for the evils in this world because we ourselves are hell, insofar as we don't do good and love one another. The lake of fire is in our hearts, and the man with the horns is in our heads. It don't do no good to spread blame. Anger's not the answer. We gotta start in here," he put a hand to his heart, "if we wanna make a change. If you can change what's in here, you change the world. With love and faith and hope—these three—all things are possible. That's the parable of the mustard seed. We can move that mountain out of its way if only we believe we can. And I'll finish the verse from Proverbs that you started: But those who seek God understand completely."

Billy smiled. "We're real glad you came to visit us again, Jim, but you'll never convince me you're not wasting your time."

"I'll thank you for the kind word, Billy, and I'll take the other words into consideration. You know I'm here because I love you, just as I love all you men. You know that. And so, for now, we'll just agree to disagree. I only ask you to keep looking into your hearts. If you do that, you will never go wrong. Now let's pray." He lowered his face and clenched his eyes. "Dear God, like your child Job we say, Behold, I am vile. What shall I answer thee? I will lay mine hand upon my mouth. We know we're all deserving of hell and wrath. Teach us to love one another and be patient with ourselves." He scanned the room. "Now who wants to come up here tonight and profess their weakness and ask Jesus Christ to enter into their hearts?"

The men looked away or read in silence. Garreth rubbed his neck. Travis peered at a page. Kenny stood and approached the preacher.

Mister Tulliver laid his hands on Kenny's head and said, "Know, my son, that flesh and blood cannot inherit the kingdom of God, nor does the perishable inherit the imperishable. Listen, child, here is a mystery: you will not sleep, but you will be changed, even in the twinkling of an eye. When the trumpet sounds, I say, all my sisters and brothers will be changed. Then what is written will come to pass, yea, that even death has been swallowed up in victory. And in that day all my brothers and sisters—even all of you, even this little one standing before us now—who have dwelt so long in darkness, will open their eyes and ask, Where, o death, is thy victory? Where, o grave, is thy sting?"

He turned Kenny by the shoulder, gently, so that he faced the inmates. "Give us a few words, son. Tell us what you see."

Kenny looked at the men as from a great distance, as if for the first time, and told them what he saw. "I see angels and demons flying above our heads. I see a woman clothed with the sun, wearing a crown of twelve stars, and the moon beneath her feet. And I see this whole rotten building at the bottom of the lake."

"Amen, little brother," Billy said.

*

The inmates took seats and poured milk from half-pint cartons onto their Fruit Loops. An undertone of dour mumbling was punctuated by the tapping of plastic cups on steel tables. The harsh light was suffused with the undifferentiated odor of scorched chicory coffee and Clorox and unwashed bodies.

No one looked up from his tray until an argument broke out over a piece of margarine-soaked white bread. Violent threats were traded, then the quiet descended again, broken only by muted bartering across tables: a jam packet for a sugar packet, a bruised pear for powdered eggs. Someone finished eating and set his empty tray by the door and looked up at the dead television.

"Them pricks need to turn something on," a man said aloud to no one.

That evening, Christmas Eve, the wind burred like a hornet through the air-exchange louvers, and the cold emanated from the yellow-painted cinder-block walls. Jim Tulliver arrived with printouts of holiday hymns. One inmate studied the sheets with an expression of mild perplexity, then set it aside. An old man held the page close to his eyes and mouthed words. Most of the men presented themselves for the service and quietly seated themselves on the benches.

As Joe scanned the hymns, a great sadness opened within him. This sadness spread to the corners of the pod and touched every living thing he set eyes on. Indeed, to set eyes on a man was to see him overshadowed, all unawares, in that same instant. Nor was the shadow merely a shade of dark, but darkness incandescent—a bright and living dark.

And it was not his mind that conferred this sorrow on the men around him; rather, it was that *their* sorrow, which had always been theirs, was suddenly revealed to *him*. All of them moved and spoke in a changed way: the inmates; the guards, one of whom had always shown them kindness; Tulliver too. All were quickened by what had come over them.

And Kenny, also, who sat chatting with an elderly inmate. Kenny held his printout for the man to see, indicating some notable line, scanning with his fingertip. Both of them, in that moment, were also transformed.

Now he understood. The fact that failure was predetermined was, to Kenny, no cause for disappointment; guaranteed failure, in truth, legitimized an undertaking. Anything else was not worth the time. Where that notion came from was a mystery to Joe.

It occurred to him now that Kenny's habit of seeing a world that was good and right—a world teeming with evidence of some universal purpose—was in truth not a gift at all, but a burden so onerous it would crush his friend eventually, and he cursed whomever or whatever it was that had cursed his friend with such a thing. And yet, Kenny did not seem burdened, not at all. On the contrary, it illuminated him. Yes, that too was a mystery.

What help had he ever given to Kenny, his only friend? He should have stayed home; he was worse than useless. It was his fault, after all, that they had landed in this hole.

The shadow that had fallen across them lingered only a moment, then dissolved, and the droning yellow light reasserted itself.

When all the men were gathered and seated, Tulliver recited an old story about a young woman who pondered heavy matters in her heart. How the doors of the town were all closed to her, though she was plainly weary and due to deliver at any moment. How the shepherds in the fields were sore afraid, in awe of a star they'd never seen before.

Tulliver began to sing.

> We three kings of Orient are
> Bearing gifts we traverse afar

An inmate took up the tune. And another joined in. Then more.

> Field and fountain moor and mountain
> Following yonder star

Soon all of the men were singing, and Joe picked up the sheet and sang too. It was good to feel the sound of his voice, like a live current in his chest. Good to hear the others' voices rising around him. Good to sing out loud, and along.

> O, star of wonder, star of night
> Star with royal beauty bright
> Westward leading, still proceeding
> Guide with thy perfect light

*

In the morning, Christmas Day, a delegation from a local church, along with several officers, filed into the pod, bearing armfuls of brown paper sacks, one for each of the inmates. Joe's sack contained a pen and a pocket notepad, three American flag postage stamps, three envelopes, a red apple with a waxy shine, a travel-size bar of soap in a motel wrapper, and a candy bar. He sat at the table looking at the small gifts and felt touched, then dejected.

Kenny sat beside him. "I got a Mister Goodbar," he said. "What'd you get?"

"New tie. Same thing every year."

"No you didn't!" Kenny said, peering into Joe's paper bag.

The people from the church fanned out around the space. The men wore cologne and smelled like wood smoke. The women wore holiday-print sweaters. They were gladdened to learn from the inmates that *It ain't so bad here* and *I'll be out pretty soon* and *Ma'am you won't catch me in this place next year!*

Joe noticed a small group of inmates attending a conversation between his friend and two men from the church. "There are such things as miracles," he heard Kenny say. The words brought an anticipation of unpleasantness.

Kenny sat on the edge of a table, legs dangling. His sockless feet, shod in orange canvas shoes, swung back and forth, measuring his words. "They happen all the time. But we lost the ability to see them. They're as common," he said, "as birdsong."

More church members approached to listen, and more inmates too, and one of the guards. They sat on benches or leaned against the tables or stood back—arms crossed, heads cocked, listening.

"The miracles of God are the miracles of the common day. Light is a miracle. A vulture is a miracle. So is the devil. So is wind and rain, and every stone and every stream. So is the fact that we are all forgiven, the devil included. Especially him."

Joe stood apart with a view of the inmates and the church people. Their eyes were on Kenny.

"The world wants me to keep the eyes and ears of my heart closed because it wants good citizens and good customers. But God doesn't want good citizens. He spits good citizens out of his mouth. If I go through life seeing only with the eyes in my head, I see clearly enough, and if I spend all my days this way, I might even die convinced I'd led a righteous life. I'll go to my grave, then, more or less mourned by my neighbors, more or less settled-up with the utility companies, having never experienced more than an inkling of the truth."

"What truth is that?" asked a man from the church.

"That I'm blind. Here's a great secret: the ability to see things in their true light is not only for prophets and saints. It belongs to all of us. It's a choice, though we choose not to see."

"We chose the light, young man," said a woman from the church, "probably since before you were born. We've followed the light of Jesus all our lives. We followed it to this place. We'll follow it after you're gone."

"I'm glad to hear that. I'm grateful too. But if people really saw this world in the light of their hearts, the world would be transfigured in an instant, and there would be no more mourning, nor crying, nor sorrow, just as John of Patmos said. We don't live in that world, needless to say. The forces that want to maintain the illusion are well-funded and well—"

"Where's Christ in this?" interrupted a man from the church. "You don't say anything about the redeeming power of Christ's blood. As if salvation were just, as you said, a simple choice, like between rye or white bread. That's dangerous and wrongheaded. To believe in one's own self-sufficiency, to believe you are in sole command of your destiny: that is original sin, son. It's called pride. Be careful where you stand, young man."

"But there is a choice. You mentioned redemption. What is redemption if it isn't freedom, in the old sense of the word—to purchase the liberty of a slave? Didn't the sacrifice of the cross purchase human freedom? And what is freedom if not choice? True freedom brings heavy obligations. Crushing responsibilities. True freedom has nothing to do with the freedom we usually hear about. It's the opposite of the things most valued—"

"You make no allowance for grace," a woman in a red sweater interjected, "without which nothing happens. You seem to be saying that the power to save ourselves lies completely with us. That's anti-scriptural. In your telling, there's no need of God."

"Do I honor God by waiting meekly for him to rescue me? Is that why we were created? Tied to the railroad tracks while the locomotive speeds towards us? We are here to help create the world. As for grace, God has set a compass in our hearts, and grace animates the lodestone, but the compass is just a piece of cold junk if we don't learn how to read it. That's up to us. There'll be storms and clouds for days, when no star is visible, and then what? Then we'll be on our own, and that's the bitter truth. But we're not helpless. We have minds and hands.

"So we have this to do: we have to prepare a little place, a dwelling place for the compass, to keep it safe and dry. The old sailors kept the ship's compass in a little box called a binnacle, and if they could keep the compass clean and level, there was a good chance they would reach port and see their homes again. So let's make a binnacle of our hearts, and keep it dusted and bright, and decorate it with beautiful designs."

A man in a green sweater squinted like one in pain. "If it was always in our power to save ourselves," he asked, "then what was the purpose of His sacrifice?"

"The Son of God suffers because the Son of God is a human being. His pain will endure for as long as pain endures. He's us, and we're him. We're bound together—to the bitter end. Inside—"

"You identify yourself with God?"

"Who was God identifying with when he wept at the death of a friend or said he had no place to lay his head? With himself? I have to act, not wait to be acted on. I have to see his pain, and your pain, and her pain—which is our pain and my pain—which is the pain of the world—which is precisely God's pain. It's not my business to wait to be saved by God; it's my business to save God."

Joe could hear the tremor in Kenny's voice, slight as a silver thread. The guard shifted from foot to foot.

"God is light and love," said the woman, "and all-powerful. Are you saying that God doesn't have the power to save us?"

"I'm saying that God can't even save himself. What is redemption, then? God's forgiveness is a gift freely given, but if we take it and keep it to ourselves, what have we done? God forgives and God loves—these are gifts. Who would take a gift and bury it in the ground? Only the frightened servant in the parable does that, and his descendants too—who are all around us today, even here in this room. The value of a gift lies in its being given. Hold it in your hands, and it is worthless. Give it away, and it shines like gold."

Travis smiled at a new thought. "Sometimes late at night," he said, "I hear someone call my name."

"The compass will guide me," Kenny said, his eyes on his canvas shoes, "if I can read it right. We're on our way now. But it's a difficult apprenticeship, this learning to navigate. I lack self-discipline, most days. I crack under pressure. Some days I wonder where I'm going, and these doubts make the needle go haywire. Like interference from a rogue planet. No, not from a rogue planet, from my own heart—"

"You say the devil is a miracle," said the man. "That's absurd. It's blasphemous."

Kenny lifted his head. "Is it? Doesn't the devil take on the appearance of the world? All the desert mothers and fathers say it's so. That's pretty miraculous, I think. The devil is the world we see when we look only with the eyes in our heads. We see what we want to see. Most of the time, I am my own primary point of reference: self-centeredness is the default setting of our waking days. But it's an illusion, an illusion more lovely—and more compelling—than the ceilings of a thousand Sistine Chapels. And in the middle of the illusion squats the devil. He pulls the strings, he draws the curtains, he directs the lighting, he feeds us our lines. The devil wants you to relax, take a deep breath, wait to be saved. But the truth is, if you're waiting to be saved by God, you'll be waiting a long while. And one day you'll find you've run out of time."

The women called to them from the door, and the men from the church turned away.

"It's hard, God knows, to change the way we see things," Kenny said to the inmates, of whom only Travis and Joe remained. "But I'm changing how I see. This journey is a means to that. Every day I see new things in new ways. And one day everything will be made new. If I don't believe it, I'll never find her."

He picked up the book and indifferently turned the pages. "Those nice people are wrong," he said. "The devil is a miracle. I know. I talk to him every single day."

"Me too," said Travis. "Every goddamn day."

*

In the afternoon, long after the church group had departed, the inmates were treated to a holiday dinner of green beans and ham slices, and the guards played a movie about some terrorists who never really had a chance.

The brevity of the day's bounty intensified the somberness of its aftermath, and the men withdrew into card games or into themselves. Three prisoners paced the catwalk, resuming their nightly patrol, somnambulists in outrageous pyjamas. In this manner, Christmas expired.

Joe picked over the pile of magazines and found a back issue of *People*, three years old, beneath the mess of pamphlets. He hesitated to pick it up, fearing ridicule, so he rolled it tight, carried it to his seat and opened it across his knees, out of sight beneath the table. No one noticed. The inmates lounged, digesting, and killed time through outright neglect of it. Kenny sat and slapped a paperback down on the table.

"Look what I got!" He leaned into Joe's shoulder, suspicious. "What're you doing down there? Find one of your movie star mags? I won't tell—"

"Shut the fuck up," Joe said, shamed and angry. He threw the magazine back to its corner and wanted to stand and go to his bunk to lie down, but a clutch of inmates was blocking the steps, and he couldn't bear the thought of shouldering past them. He feared the exchange that would have to take place before he'd be permitted to pass. The nod and the eye contact that had to be certain but not arrogant—or worse, timid—for one had to honor the customs of this place, as one would anywhere. To a visitor—to the church people, for example—the life of one of these men might appear as a grim and purposeless rummage, and that may have been true for some of the inmates. But for many of these men, beyond the resentment and rage, there was a dignity that attached to sticking it out and keeping alive on a tough road—whether undertaken as a result of unwise decisions or ineluctable circumstances—a road on which this jail was just a way station. And this dignity was the only sure possession many had; disrespect, therefore, was the only unpardonable sin. It demanded constant situational awareness to keep one's head above water—a lifetime spent carrying mercury in a spoon. Such a life, Joe thought, must be exhausting.

Again he thought about time. There were no clocks, no windows changing from blue to gray with the passage of hours, no sun or stars with which to synchronize one's sleeping and waking. No trees beneath which the evening shadows might gather.

This place, he thought, as he scanned the high walls, was where Time Itself was fabricated by inmates who earned seven cents for each discrete and functional minute that they fashioned. And at the end of the day, you see, the inmates gathered all the minutes that they had crafted with such painstaking care, and they shipped them to the four corners of the earth, where these minutes made some people late for work, and made other people irritable, and made everybody older. And the thing was, no matter how many minutes the inmates produced—reams of minutes, stooks and sheaves and bushels of them, pyramidal stacks of shipping containers filled with minutes—there were never enough to meet demand because once you spent a minute it was gone; it wasn't fungible like a dollar or a peso or a pound, and there were never enough of them. Even if you were inclined to gamble, with an eye to growing your little stash of time, well, there was nobody but yourself to bluff, and nobody but yourself to cheat.

A man took a seat at the table and said to Kenny, "What book you got?"

Love Conquers was tattooed in blue ink, like a botched suture, at an oblique angle beneath the man's ear. In black ink across his knuckles was printed *Hope*. It was the first time Joe had heard the man speak.

Kenny handed the book across the table. The man took it up and read the cover through the bottoms of his bifocals. "*The Odyssey*. Yep." He flipped through it. "Troy and all that."

"Did you read it before?"

"Long time ago. I like them old stories, when you can find them in here. Here there's nothing but garbage for the most part, but once in a while something good'll turn up. Yeah. This one's a keeper." He returned the book. "I named my daughter Cassandra."

"Cassandra." Kenny smiled at the sound of it. "That's a great name. She's in this one, right? What did she do?"

"I used to know. I guess I forgot."

The intercom burst with static: *Stegemuller and Riley.*

Kenny walked to the intercom and pressed the button. "Speaking."

Junk n bunk, boys. You're gettin' loosed.

Joe sorted the words in his head as blood rushed to his fingers and toes. He felt Kenny's hand slapping his back and he heard his friend say, "I told you it'd be alright, Mister Gloom and Doom!"

Downstairs at the desk, the duty cop handed their wallets across the counter. "How you like Missoura? You'll find your civvies in that room there. Change and put your orange gear in the proper bins. Wait a minute," he reached two forms and two pens across the counter. "Sign the register, please. Once you've done all that, leave the state and don't come back."

Outside on the street, the sun was shining. Cars passed at a uniformly slow, seemingly prearranged rate of speed, like it was all a put-on, Joe thought, or make-believe, and the drivers were driving back and forth from one wing of the stage to the other, just part of the show.

The county courthouse-and-jail was the largest, newest structure on Main Street. At three stories, with glass doors and ornate cornices, it dominated the road-level bail bond offices and pawnshops, the hair stylist and the diner and the bar. The building's shadow, at this hour of the day, fell across the roofs of the shops and across the stained, vinyl-sided houses of the townspeople.

Cars were double-parked along the potholed road, some with handwritten "for sale" signs taped to unwashed windshields.

"This state makes me want to die."

"We certainly didn't intend to stay this long, that's for sure!" Kenny said as they walked down the sidewalk. "This is what they call the scenic route."

The air was winter-bright, clean as grass. The sun, low above the roofs, flashed like a blade. The cold warmed quickly in his lungs, like glass cooling, like chilled gin. Joe bent to pick a half-smoked cigarette out of the gutter. He stopped a man in front of the diner and borrowed a match; his fingers shook when he lit up.

He hot-housed the smoke down to the filter, flicked the butt into the street. As he walked on, he whistled the bars to "If I Only Had a Brain," which was a strange thing to do. He hadn't whistled in years.

*

The elation of release, after eight days' confinement, subsided into an unaccountable despondence as they walked along the state route, and it mattered not at all to Joe whether he lay down in the trees to sleep or walked clear to Biloxi.

A pickup pulled onto the shoulder. The truck's body resembled a crumpled paper sack, with rust breeding in the creases.

"Where you boys headed?" the driver said. "There ain't a whole lot down this road."

Kenny told the man where they were from, where they were going, and why. Joe for once did not resent his talkative friend; he even added a few details, answering some unaccountable urge—an urge that had visited him the moment they had stepped out beneath the open skies—to share his mind with another soul.

The man listened and glanced at their shoes. "Tell you what. You can sleep on the floor at my place and I'll drop you off at the state line highway first thing in the morning. Get in. It's too late to be out walking. The dogs around here'll chew y'asses up. Not to mention the police." Kenny sat in the cab, and Joe climbed into the bed.

The truck rocked over manhole-sized depressions filled with black water. The road, washed out in places by rain and wind, was slowly vanishing into the earth. Passing a house that sat close to the shoulder, Joe felt a pang of shame to be caught gazing through a window into a woman's and a child's eyes as they sat at table for dinner.

As the truck lurched by, a dog shot from beneath a stripped car to contest its littered territory. The chain link clashed against the fence poles as the animal hurled itself against the fence, choking on snarls.

They drove for miles through heavy woods and sudden clearings, and Joe breathed deeply of the cold night and the pines, the standing water and dead leaves and hidden creatures. A winged shadow skimmed over the track and disappeared. The half-moon, low above the tree line, shed a dry chemical light on the fields.

In open country, clear of trees on both sides of the road, the truck nosed down hard on the gravel and rocked to a halt. The man opened the door, leaped into the truck-bed with one clean spring, pulled a rifle from beneath some sacks, planted his feet, leveled the rifle to his shoulder, and pulled the bolt handle back to chamber a round. His frame settled as he sighted. The moon held its breath. Joe looked downfield in the direction of the barrel and saw nothing. A cataract of white noise followed the first shot, and the spent casing rattled soundlessly between Joe's knees. The man fired again and the rifle's report rippled into darkness, muddled among the trees, and took its time in fading. He lowered the rifle and peered downfield.

"Didn't mean to startle you," he said. "I thought I saw some breakfast out there." He examined the rifle in his hands, pinched a mote from the rear sight. "But it might've been something in my eye."

He slipped the rifle back under the sacks, climbed behind the wheel and wrenched the truck into gear. They arrived at a tidy little cabin of rough pine planking. "You boys hungry?"

Suspended from a low branch just off the front door was a lantern that shed pale light on a mound of deer gut. The heap of entrails, two feet high, was gray at the bottom, but towards the top, where it was fresher, the guts gleamed in ultramarines and midnight-greens. A dog lay near the pile, stretched but awake. A second dog licked at the offal. They were too well-fed to trouble strangers.

A gutted deer hung from the porch awning. Two short lengths of chain connected the hooves of the hind legs to a joist, and the deer stretched groundward, frozen in the widest extension of its flight. The forelegs strained down, forever three inches from the earth.

"Can we look at that deer?" Kenny said. "I never saw a dead one close up!"

There was no trace of gore beneath the head. Joe drew his palm along the hide, smooth as oil to the touch. The carcass had been drained of blood, the blue cavity gleamed. Kenny reached his hand through the cleft in the animal's chest. Joe almost expected his friend to flinch on account of the terrible chill inside.

But he didn't flinch. With sacramental care, Kenny held one hand inside the body, as though the carcass were a sort of Choctaw healing tackle whose medicine was volatile, capricious, capable of wonders.

*

The man invited them to sit at the table and served them bowls of white beans with chunks of venison bacon. Kenny examined the compound bow that hung on the wall. He asked how someone goes about killing a deer with a bow and arrow. "Do you wait by their watering hole?" he asked. "Do you put out a salt block? Do you make mating calls?"

"You could do those things, I suppose. Or you might just sit in a tree stand with a mug of coffee and wait till something walks by. That's what I did anyway."

As Joe helped himself to a second bowl, the man asked. "Where'd you say you were headed?"

"Mexico," Kenny said. "To find Mary."

"Who's where now?"

"Mary. We're on a search, Mister Jackson. Mary asked me to come to her. She has a message. This message has explosive power. It has the power to destroy the world and to remake the world."

"You're not out to hurt somebody, are you, son?"

"Oh, no."

"Boy, you said a mouthful tonight," he said, rising from the chair. "I got to lay down now. There's a sink through that door there. Outhouse out back. Got blankets? Good. There's water in the pitcher if you get thirsty."

"Thank you."

"Don't mention it, son. I done my share of walking, believe me. Now get some rest. Even boys your age need rest."

In the morning, Mister Jackson dropped them at the state line highway and they set off beneath cold blue clouds. In the afternoon they came to a halt beneath a sign that thanked them for visiting the state of Missouri.

Kenny turned about, thumbs hitched in his pack straps, and rued the road they had traveled. "It sure was a big state," he said, like a man compelled to eulogize a miser. "We met some nice people there, though, didn't we? Like Mister Jackson. All in all, I have mixed feelings," he said.

Joe unzipped. "What a shithole," he said, pissing on the sign's post.

They began to walk.

*

Lucky with lifts, they reached the Memphis outskirts within two days. Kenny found, in a waterlogged phone book, the address for a Salvation Army shelter, and they arrived at the place an hour too late for dinner. As they sat in the corridor, a woman brought two bowls of rice and beans and took a seat on the bench. While they ate, she recited the rules: no fighting, no drinking, no weapons, no cussing. "Hungry, huh? Where you boys from?"

"Ohio."

"Looking for work or what?"

"No," Kenny said, talking around his food. "We're heading for Mexico."

"Is that in Tennessee?"

"No, it's the country. We're seeking an audience with the mother of the lamb."

"That's enough." She shut her eyes and waved away the words. "I don't even want to know about it." She turned to shout at the wall, "Russ Garrity! Got two more for you!"

"Thanks for the meal, ma'am."

"You're welcome, baby."

A gray man turned the corner, viewed them unhappily for a moment, turned away. They followed him down a yellow hallway to a room where five double bunks lined opposite walls. The man pointed at a bunk and said, "Wake-up's at five."

They sat on the bottom bed, in the fluorescent haze. The dull ache in Joe's feet spread up his calves, his thighs, and into his lower back as Russ Garrity talked. "You'll get some breakfast, then you'll get turned out. They'll let you back in at six in the evening. You can look for work in the meantime or do whatever the hell you want. Can't stay here more than two nights running, or three nights in a week, like I say, long as they ain't in a row. Got blankets? Good. Don't stray too far from your things, and watch out for that one." He indicated a man seated in a chair beside the window at the far side of the room. "He may just proposition you tonight."

"Why?" Kenny asked. "Do you mean he's gay, Mister Garrity?"

"Gay? Did you say *gay*? Gay! Ha! If he ain't gay—if *he ain't gay*, boy, he sure as hell got some esplainin to do. Ha! Gay!" Russ Garrity called out to the man, "Choo Choo be good now," and climbed chuckling into his bunk. "*Gay*. Good Lord. For all I know, he may be gay. Then again, he may not be gay. Maybe he sucks dicks just to piss off the rest of us."

Kenny unrolled his sleeping bag and spoke to himself in a miffed undertone. "Can't get a straight answer out of these people."

Joe tied his pack to the bunk's rail with a length of twine and climbed into his sleeping bag. Since their arrival, Choo Choo had maintained a still and silent watch at the windowpane. From across the floor, Joe could plainly see the purple and yellow welts on the man's temples, and the unhealed cut across the bridge of his nose.

The man gazed through the window into a brightly-lit room across the courtyard, where the women and children stayed. He gained the attention of a woman and waved to her, childlike, with the cup of his hand. When the woman waved back, Choo Choo emitted a small, wounded sound and buried his face in his hands. Russ Garrity flipped the lights off.

Joe thought about the man. He wondered if Choo Choo would suffer the term of his dismal life to run its natural course, or if someday he'd find a rope or a cliff and put period to an existence that was likely of little consequence to anyone in the world. Perhaps the man had a mother who was herself accustomed to sit alone beside a window with a cup of coffee on winter evenings in some faraway place and remember the boy who never quite fit in, who wasn't very good at school, who one day left home and never returned. Maybe as she sat beside the window, she would revisit the terrible truth that during his entire childhood, her son had never had even one good and lasting friendship and had lived under perpetual suspicion and in perpetual isolation for those habits of simple affection—unforgivable in a boy—which certified his otherness and confirmed his loneliness. There must be nothing in the world more agonizing, Joe thought, than to be the mother of a friendless child, and he concluded once again that it was better to never bring a life into this miserable fucking world.

Kenny whispered in the darkness. "Joe, I was thinking. We might easily get separated, traveling in this manner. So I got a plan. If we get separated, we'll leave a sign, either scratched on a rock or written in the dirt—somewhere prominent—for the other to find. If you see it, you'll know to remain in the vicinity. So I was thinking: our secret code word will be *Croatoan*."

"Crowatowan."

"Aren't you going to ask what it means?"

"No."

"It's from the lost colony at Roanoke. The ships dropped off the colonists and went back to England. When they returned a year later with more supplies, there was nothing there. Not a soul. Everyone had vanished. The only sign was a word scratched into a tree trunk: *Croatoan*. *Croatoan* happened to be the name of a nearby tribe, but still, the relief party wasn't sure what it meant."

"Mm."

"They asked the Indians. They even asked the Spaniards. Nobody knew nothing."

"Incredible."

"Lights out means quiet," Russ Garrity said.

Now and again, a cough disturbed the stillness of a room sour with body odor and unwashed blankets. A column of roaches filed up the wall beside Joe's head. They broke into squads, then individuals, as they fanned out across the cinderblock. Their wings shone in the dark. He marked their progress over the walls and desperately wished them good footing, that they might not fall onto him as he slept.

*

The ceiling lights buzzed and flickered. "Time to get up," Russ Garrity said. "Get up get up get up. You got thirty minutes to bunk shit wash eat and beat it."

In the bathroom, Kenny and Joe stood with the other men, three to a sink, and washed their faces. Stainless steel dinner trays screwed to the wall served as mirrors. The man between them, leaning over the drain to brush his teeth, shuddered and foamed like a broken washing machine.

"We should wash our ears," Kenny said. "Your ears are really dirty."

"Fuck my ears."

In the cafeteria, the sulfur-colored light was laced with ammonia. A hundred and fifty men sat at long tables, eating bowls of rice and beans with cardboard spoons. They talked little as they ate and washed the rice down with half-pint cartons of lukewarm white milk.

"There's an eyelash in mine," Kenny said.

"You got an eyelash?" Joe asked, seated beside him. "I'll trade you your eyelash for this ass hair."

"You gonna eat that food or make fun of it?" demanded the man seated across the table. He spoke without looking up. "If you got something better to eat, go eat it."

At five-thirty they were turned out. Kenny and Joe stood outside the shelter with paper cups of black coffee. Joe bummed a match for a cigarette. Bundled figures set off down the sidewalk and dissolved in the freezing darkness. Two men stood over a fire hydrant and argued about money. Others sat on the steps or squatted on the pavement, paired in desultory conversation. Kenny and Joe sat on the curb and waited for the sky to lighten, then walked toward the interstate, southbound I-55, and caught a ride in a pickup bound for Mississippi.

That day and over the days that followed, by long and short lifts, they made their way south. There were drivers who talked to themselves, drivers who offered food or money, some who said nothing at all, one who offered cash if they would agree to get blown. A man wearing a cowboy hat picked them up in a Corolla. At the end of the lift the man gave them two cans of pop, two singles, and a farewell in Spanish that chimed like a blessing.

South of Winona, three days after leaving Memphis, they climbed into the bed of a pickup. Three men wearing ballcaps sat shoulder-to-shoulder in the cab and drank beer from cans. When the driver abruptly exited the highway onto a state route, Joe rapped on the glass, but the men ignored him. They drove a mile, braked sharply, turned off the road and gunned the truck down a dirt path. Joe threw both packs over the tailgate, jumped after them, and hit the ground rolling. On hands and knees, he saw Kenny wobble in the truck-bed, stagger to the tailgate and tumble out. When Kenny stopped rolling, he clambered to his feet and followed Joe at a run. As they hurried back to the interstate, the truck passed and slowed down long enough for the driver to yell, "We just had to piss, you stupid assholes," and throw an empty beer can at them.

"Oh," Kenny said. "They just had to pee."

"You can never tell with these rednecks, Kenny," Joe said, unstrung, his hands shaking. "Don't ever take chances. God knows what kind of sick shit they'd do to you. They'd probably make me watch the whole thing too. That's how they are."

"Okay, Joe. Okay."

*

Every shelter housed the same crowd: sullen, windburnt, middle-aged men who looked as if they'd lost their motorcycles in card games. Seated on bunks in a windowless dorm or standing on the sidewalk in the morning, the men talked and talked, their every pronouncement made significant with curses. They were generally reticent and dismissive about workaday topics and their current situations but quickly warmed to talk of other times, other places. The eighty dollars-a-day you could earn on a tear-out crew in Saint Paul. Fifteen dollars an hour in Cleveland for asbestos removal. Asshole cops in Texarkana. Fine sleeping on the beaches at Biloxi. Cheap hookers here and there. In Albuquerque, thirty bucks might buy a room, a bottle, a nice woman, and two channels of porn on the tv.

One night at the Salvation Army in Jackson, the dorm talk turned on the forty dollars being offered at a donor center in Atlanta for a pint of plasma and—more to the point—fourteen dollars extra if you signed up for something known as the 'rabbit vaccine thing'. The room was evenly split on the advisability of being injected with rabbit vaccine. "Might turn you into a rabbit," a young man conjectured, and everyone, to the young man's dismay, laughed for a long time.

The men wore most of their clothes at once, shouldering sun-faded packs on an endless circuit of the country, chasing work or deserting it, following weather or fleeing it. Kenny interrogated every man who would sit still, listened closely to every story, and believed utterly every word.

*

They climbed out of a pickup in a small town that consisted of a brief collection of frayed shops along the state route.

"I think we're in Louisiana, Joe."

"Why do you think?"

"There's a Cajun restaurant."

"There's a Cajun restaurant in Dayton."

"But this one looks authentic."

A posting on a telephone pole advertised shelter to the needy, and they followed the directions to a rambling white house surrounded by a white picket fence.

A cavernous porch skirted the house, a brood of white garden sheds stood in the house's shadow, and brick paths meandered over the grounds. Vines crept through moldy eaves that had been jigged into floral designs. A wrought-iron chair sat inside a bower of creeper. Kenny stepped into the bower and turned himself about.

"This is probably where the lady of the house retires with a novel," he said. "That's what I'd do, anyway."

Joe pictured a woman in hoop skirts, hair pinned up in a bun, sitting in the bower's shadow languidly turning a page.

But it wasn't that woman who answered the door with a glance at their shoes. "Yes?" she said.

"We saw some—I think we—is there any shelter still here? If not, that's okay. Sorry, ma'am. We thought—"

A man appeared at the woman's shoulder. He exuded the florid confidence of a meat-fed man and rested a large red hand on her shoulder.

"You're our very first visitors," the woman said with rediscovered cheerfulness. "Come right in."

She introduced herself and her husband as minister and wife and asked them where they were from, where they were going. Joe said they were headed to Arizona to find painting work. "We got some good tips on jobs, me and Kenny. Can't wait to get there and get started."

They were shown to a room with a hardwood floor that gleamed with urethane. Two long-legged iron-frame beds, with blankets folded at the foots, stood against the white plaster wall. The minister watched from the door as they set their bags in the corner. He directed them to wash their hands and faces and come down to dinner in half an hour, and his eyes lingered briefly on the visitors before he turned out. After he left, Kenny tested the bedsprings and giggled at the doily on the end table.

A candleholder backed by a convex mirror was mounted to the wall. They stood shoulder to shoulder before it and examined the distorted images of themselves: their giant noses and receding chins made them look brutal and sad. Kenny turned his face side to side, wiped a streak of grime from the side of his nose, touched the reflection of himself between the eyes with his fingertip.

"God I'm ugly," he said.

*

They sat at the table with six boys and girls dressed in white, who, like nesting dolls, diminished in size by age. The children chatted and laughed about everyday things; they cast surreptitious looks at the strangers but did not address them. At a signal Joe must have missed, the children fell silent and bowed their heads, closed their eyes, and folded their hands as the minister, seated at the head of the table, initiated a prayer. "Amen," the man said, a word the children construed as permission to acknowledge the visitors, which they did with spirited greetings and warm smiles. The woman introduced them as "itinerant workers." Kenny straightened in his chair, pleased to receive a legitimate title.

As the bowls of green beans and mashed potatoes and a plate of pork chops changed hands, Joe struggled to eat slowly. He counted the times he chewed and bent his face over the plate so that he could smell the food as he ate it. After dinner, he thought, I'll wash my feet and my face, and I'll be fed and clean, and I'll lie down in a nice bed. That's plenty, he decided. That's more than enough.

Not a word was spoken during the meal. Kenny chewed and kept watch, searching for a way in, his agitation gathering like weather. Joe knew that his friend mistook the silence for a failure of imagination, which he, Kenny, might supply. Maybe, Joe thought, I can bolt this food and slip away before the idiot commenced to twaddle.

With a fork in his fist and a mouthful of potatoes, Kenny leaned toward the woman. She noted the intention and attended to him, but Kenny's throat clenched and his shoulders seized as he strained at the potatoes in his throat like an ox in harness. They all watched as, with his hands flat on the table, the visitor silently and desperately choked. He held up a finger at the woman, thumped his chest, and swallowed. Flushed and perspiring, he gasped at last, "This is great food, ma'am!" Tearfully, he sought corroboration in the faces of his hosts. Then his eyes met Joe's, and Kenny's smile vanished, and the space between them thickened with the small sounds of fork tines tapping ceramic and sipping.

After dinner, they were instructed by the minister to wash up and report back within ten minutes for Bible study. In the bedroom, Kenny raked his hair with a comb, chattering about the delicious food. Joe told him to get his shit together and to quit acting like a jackass; he complained about having to put up with more "Christ crap."

"Aren't you being a little ungrateful?" Kenny asked.

"If you mention the Mother of God I'll beat the life out of you."

"Don't worry. They're real religious. They probably know all about it already."

Night pressed at the tall windows of the lamp-lit study where the family had gathered. The children were already seated on folding chairs placed in equidistant intervals around the perimeter of a moon-white carpet. A Bible rested in each lap. Two chairs stood empty, at opposite points of the circle; Bibles lay squared atop the chairs' seats. Kenny and Joe picked up the books and sat.

"Please be more punctual in the future, gentlemen." The minister regarded Kenny's hair hanging in oily flaps down the sides of his face, and the greasy thighs of his jeans. "In the morning, in return for the food and shelter that you've received, you will have your hair cut and be clean-shaven and you'll be assigned chores as a means of contribution. And so, as meat commendeth us not to God, one Corinthians chapter eight verse eight, you've been invited to share with us in the word."

"Man cannot live by bread alone!" Kenny exclaimed, startling the children. He gauged the weight of the Bible in the scale of his hand, thumbed through the text. The only sound was that of one book's pages turning. When the silence turned to suggestion, Kenny looked up and closed his book.

"Very good," said the minister.

The man spoke about the cursing of the fig tree, and said the tree was cursed because its nature was to produce figs, but it had failed to do so. It had not fulfilled its purpose in life and was damned for that reason.

"Ah. I always wondered why Jesus did that," Kenny said. "Now I know!"

The minister said, "Joseph and Kenneth," taking the measure of their names. "You seem like earnest young men to me, and I consider myself a fairly good judge of character. Are you willing, tomorrow morning, to reject Satan, receive Jesus into your hearts, and be entered into the book of life?"

Joe concentrated on the words on the page and felt betrayed. He read the words again and again—*Moses' hands were heavy, and they took a stone, and put it under him*—but made no sense of them.

Kenny said, "We'll reject Satan—I mean, obviously—but, the book of life—"

"Revelation chapter twenty verse twelve, please," the minister said. The children leafed to the proper page. Joe consulted the table of contents. Kenny cleared his throat. "It's at the end," he whispered.

"Esther," the minister said.

The youngest girl placed her finger on the page. In a small clear voice, she began to read. "And I saw the dead, small and great, stand before God, and the books were opened. And another book was opened, which is the book of life. And the dead were judged out of those things which were written in the books, according to their works. And the sea gave up the dead that were in it, and death and hell delivered up the dead which were in them. And they were judged every man according to their works. And death and hell were cast into the lake of fire. This is the second death. And whosoever was not found written in the book of life was cast into the lake of fire."

When she finished, she did not look up but remained poised over the page. With a fingertip, she smoothed a loose ribbon of hair behind her ear.

His sense of betrayal turned to anger, and Joe said, "Well, sir, we appreciate the food and everything, and we'll do chores all day long tomorrow, but we don't know if we're into all that other stuff."

"Young man." The minister's wife checked herself with a glance at her husband, who blinked once. "Young man, what is it exactly that you are in to?"

"We're on a search for Mary," Kenny said.

"Mary."

"Yes, ma'am. I had a vision of Mary. The Star of the Sea, as some call her. She has several manifestations—like Zeus does. She appeared to me and spoke to me, and I know she's in the center of the moon, which is Mexico, because the darkness told me so. So I'm going to find her and ask if she'll bind our wounds because our brokenness is making it hard for us to see one another. Esther," he continued, leaning forward on his elbows. "Do you know any airheads? I'm sort of an airhead. I have trouble organizing my thoughts sometimes, and I talk too much without thinking. But a strange thing happened to me one night. The Mother of God visited me, and her face was as plain as your mother's face is now, and her voice was as clear and lovely as your voice."

The girl sat very still with her hands folded, her eyes fixed on the man dressed in dirty clothes.

"One night, I heard a voice," Kenny continued, turning to the minister's wife. "The voice told me things that I knew were true because they touched my heart with understanding."

The room was quiet. Just as at the jail in Missouri, Joe saw once more the many ways in which strangers suffered his friend's utterances. The minister's irritation burdened his wife, and both were disconcerted. And among the children, there were other, familiar expressions: puzzled, concerned, mildly entertained.

There was another expression too, one he'd seen only once before on the face of Travis, the jailhouse grifter. Now Esther wore that expression: not a glance but a missed blink; a shadow of a smile; a recognition of shared knowledge of a peculiar, lost, and alarming sort. It was the ancient conspiracy, whose initiates have no need of pledges or shibboleths. Now, she was manifestly glad—and perhaps a little amused—to hear those things spoken out loud in the presence of the uninitiated, in the open for all to hear.

"When Mary speaks to us, our pain will end. Then all living things will be holy again, and they'll be loved again. It's hard to picture that now, but soon a great vision will break out in the world, and it'll be a true vision shared by everyone. Her voice," Kenny said, with cheerful assurance in the power of good news to win over his hosts, "was like sitting up in bed and seeing the morning sun at the window. This might seem strange, I know. Even silly. Joe here's my best friend. He's going with me even though he doesn't believe me, and that says a lot about him. We have to walk to Mexico because we got kicked off the bus in Indiana and we don't have much money. This old man on the bus, see, he was nice but he—"

"Stop, Kenny," Joe said. "I'm sorry, sir, he was dropped on his head when he was a kid. He's deranged. We're not going to Mexico. It's just—we just don't care for the whole *lake of fire* thing and that's that. We're not out to hurt anyone or steal anything. We're just trying to get somewhere. Like I said, we'll do your chores, we'll pay for our keep, we'll do them right now in fact then pack our—"

"Enough," the minister said, with a note of mild back pain. "I don't know where to begin. The Star of the Sea? The *lake of fire* thing?" He adjusted his tone, began again. "Young men, I ask you both, shall any teach God knowledge? Job chapter twenty-one verse twenty-two. Let's start with the *lake of fire* thing, then we'll discuss the nature of visions in the spiritual life, and we'll set forth the means by which a man might know whether his vision is from God or from the devil."

"Oh, I don't think it came from either, Reverend, sir," Kenny said, "let me—"

"Be patient, Kenneth, please. One thing at a time. Now, Joseph. You don't believe in hell, I assume. You're an evolutionist, a materialist, a secularist. Perhaps a skeptic. Is that true? Or maybe you don't think of such things at all. You're a product of the schools and school science—it's understandable—but the schools cannot even begin to explain the theories of Darwin."

"I don't know the first thing about Darwin and I don't really—I don't—I'm not—"

"Science seeks to attribute to man that which is God's. Consider for a moment the age of the earth. The radiocarbon dating system on which so many theories are founded is deeply flawed. It fails to account for changes in temperatures over the course of earth's history. The varying carbon levels trapped in the stone strata reveal varying and therefore unreliable data. God created man in his image, and if the remains of humans are found in higher strata than the remains of lizards, it's because humans were clever enough to seek higher ground when God flooded the earth. The simplest explanation is most often the correct one, and in fact it was a papist who pointed that out, long ago, in the fourteenth century. Why then are the simplest explanations the ones most often rejected? So I ask you once more: Shall any teach God knowledge?"

Kenny listened from the edge of his chair, ardently waiting to resubmit, in clearer terms, his vision for the healing of man's broken heart. But the minister stood and rued the book in his hand.

"It seems improper for a reading to follow so hard on such a discussion. We'll preface tomorrow's reading with a science lesson. Perhaps I'll dig up a book of Darwin's letters. I think it will be valuable for all of us to review some of the man's private thoughts concerning this subject, for they can be quite illuminating. I do thank you, gentlemen, for introducing these matters tonight. Tomorrow," he said, "I'll wake you both at five for chores. It's apparent that more instruction is required before you make any decision. Love is patient, love is kind, says Paul, and I have faith that, with the help of this family, you will not fall on the path; you will not fall among the rocks or the thorns but find the good soil because those on the good ground are they which, in an honest heart, having heard the word, keep it, and bring forth fruit with patience. Luke chapter eight. Verse twelve."

"Fifteen," his wife said.

"Fifteen?" He smiled. "I guess I'm getting old, Joseph. I hope you'll forgive my impatience. I struggle with that weakness every day, a fact to which my wife can certainly attest. Now let us stand, please, and receive the blessing." He directed Kenny and Joe to the middle of the carpet. The family clasped hands in a circle around them and lowered their heads. The minister began, "Dear Lord," and at these words each voice began a supplication, in the key of praise, loud as song, for the two young men in their midst. Joe could glean only scraps from the tumult of voices: "jaws of death," "the new lamb," "hand of God," "long, hard journey," "clutches of sin." He heard the minister's wife say, "embrace these two boys."

It ended as abruptly as it began, and the family filed out, Bibles in hands. The minister ordered everyone to bed, tomorrow being "a big day."

In the room, Kenny was happy because he liked the family. He was learning things, he said, and it might turn out to be really enjoyable. "I wonder what the heck's in Darwin's letters?" he said, and lay on the bed with his shoes on, regretting, as his eyes closed, that he had not made better account of himself at the meeting.

*

Joe shook Kenny awake.

"What?" Kenny sat up. "What time is it? Is it five?"

"No. We're getting out of here."

Kenny sat on the edge of the bed in the dark room, dumbly examined the shadow of himself in the mirror, and spoke through his faze. "But tomorrow's a big day. Joe, last night you said I was deranged. You told the family that we weren't going to Mexico."

"Get your shit together."

They padded out of the room with their shoes in their hands. At the end of the dark hall, waiting beside the door, was a small figure in white pajamas. For a silent moment, Kenny and Esther faced one another.

He knelt before her and removed his hat. She set her hands on his shoulders and kissed the crown of his bowed head. He took her hand, kissed it, stood, put his hat on, and mussed her static-frazzled hair. As Joe gently turned the knob, he heard his name spoken. Esther, in the middle of the hallway, waved once. Joe waved back.

The young men stepped out into the windy night.

The stars rocked in the branches. The treetops pitched and the boughs heaved and the leaves waved, and a howling wind swept the woodline like a searchlight.

They found a hidden place off the road, in a grove outside of town. There, they unrolled their bags and lay face up to the sky. The wind broke in fearsome combers through the tops of the trees.

"Wild night!" Kenny said.

"A materialist, a skeptic!" Joe said. "Ha! That dude don't know the half of it." The leaves grasped at the fugitive stars. "Shall any teach God knowledge, old man?"

Five

In the evening, after his shift, he returned home with a box of beer and sat beside Vera on the couch. Two kids lay on the carpet, drawing in sketch books.

The girl sat beside him and showed him the image she had traced from the cover of a faded paperback copy of *Martian Chronicles*: a faintly Byzantine metropolis of spires and onion domes rising beneath two suns: one yellow, one purple. "Whose is better?" she asked. "Mine or Jimmy's?"

"They're both wonderful, Katherine."

When he switched on the television, the girl lay down beside her brother and resumed drawing. Vera said, "We left a plate for you."

"Thank you. I'll eat in a minute. I'll clean up." On the television, a car drove inexplicably through a wheat field. He changed the channel and asked, "Jimmy, what are you drawing?"

The boy held the drawing for Joe to see. It was similar to the girl's, but his Martian city was populated with humanoid creatures, and his sky was a tangle of red and black lines. "I'm doing Martians," he said.

Katherine, belly-down at her work, spoke gravely at the page she was coloring, as if something had been on her mind for a long time, and there was the possibility the question might be discounted if not properly formulated. "Do you think there's really Martians, Joe?"

"Yes I do. It's a scientific fact. Do you know how we know there's Martians on Mars?"

Katherine propped her chin in her palm. Her hair spilled through her fingers as she peered sidelong at him.

He said, "Because you can see the canals they built through a telescope."

"Canals?"

"Yep. The Martians dug canals for their boats. Like people."
She looked at the page. "Can we have a telescope?"
"No."
"Alright, you two," Vera said. "Go brush your teeth." The children left. "Me too. I'm going to bed and read the paper."
"Reading the paper in bed is unusual."
He pulled a can from the box and handed it to her.
"Unusual, huh?" She popped the tab and took a drink. "Where did you get that from?" she asked. "I mean about the canals on Mars?"
"You know what? I was thinking. I really was, though. I was thinking we should go to college. We can get loans and you can take veterinary classes like you said or do the therapy thing you mentioned. And I'll study something too. But we gotta go together. I don't want to go alone. I don't want to be the only old person squeezed into the tiny desk."
"We can't afford it. I'd love to go to school though. Do you think we can? I help you and you help me? You better not be joking. What about your job? You just finished your second year."
"I hate my job."
"Jesus. I didn't know you hated it. You know, Joe, you have to give this strong-silent-type stuff a break. It's unproductive and just plain aggravating. That manly business is just over. Really. No one likes it anymore. Why didn't you tell me you hated it?"
"I'm a cop. Didn't I used to dislike cops? They always scared me. Now I'm a cop. What the hell happened? Anyway, I got five years left to use my GI Bill. We can split it."
"It'll be hard," she said.
"Not really."
"You didn't answer me yet. Where'd you get that? About the canals on Mars?"

"I visited his mom's house today. She wasn't there—"

"Whose mom's?"

"Kenny's. He's somewhere downtown. I thought I saw him walking down the street, but I lost him. I'm going to find him though. He's here somewhere."

"That's good news. How do you know he's here in town? Did you talk to someone?"

"No. I just know. I just know he's here, is all."

"Do you want me to help look for him?"

"Yes. I think that's a good idea. Maybe this weekend. Let's do that. We'll find him and bring him back here for a visit. Probably he needs food. I'm sure he hasn't learned how to feed himself."

He squeezed her hand and said, "I'm gonna stay up a while."

He turned the television and the lights off, opened the windows, and listened to the city at night, a clutter of horns and voices and traffic that conspired, after three beers, to harmonize. After a few more, the city night sang like a glass harp in his ears.

He walked outside and returned with a blade of grass. On the little table that stood beside the window, he set a glass of water beside the grass blade and knelt in front of them.

"Okay, Jude. This is for your horse. There's more where that came from. If you can help. Thank you." He crossed himself and walked heavily toward the bedroom and slammed his shoulder against the doorjamb as he entered.

*

The following evening, at the end of his shift, he pulled into the overlook park, sat on the bench, and drank from a paper cup half-filled with day-old coffee. In the valley below, a brace of office towers stood beneath a tapered lid of smog. He stretched his legs and saw the city compassed between the toes of his shoes as in the notch of a gun sight. He closed one eye and gauged the distance between the top deck of the bank tower and the place where he sat.

When the sun slipped free of a cloud, random windows bloomed with light, as though fires had been set in seventy offices at once. Small sounds drifted up the hillside like bubbles from the depths: a school bell, a siren, a hammer drill.

Down the hill, at the tree line, two plastic grocery sacks hung from a branch, suspended like outlandish fruit above a busted shopping cart. It occurred to Joe that people were living there, on the brief wooded slope that separated downtown from uptown. There in the green shadow, the shopping cart poised forward on its bum wheel, seeming to peer downhill at something he couldn't see. What did those people do all day, he wondered. What did they do in the winter? When it got cold, they probably headed south like birds, probably on a work train like the one that was now crossing the river, downstream from town, on the L & N trestle.

He could see, even at a distance, the livid bands of graffiti that skirted the lower halves of the gas hoppers and freight cars. The train crawled across the trestle and disappeared among the riverside cranes and the coal heaps and the depot buildings. He could feel the dim clacking of the rail joints in his ribs, and smell the sweetish mix of diesel, the sun-warmed bearing grease, the caustic odor of scorched brakes.

He heard again the welter of warning bells at some nameless crossing, and saw a young man, his friend, in greasy jeans and greasy hair, leaning from the window of the locomotive, waving cheerfully to the mystified, idling motorists.

Six

They walked up the entrance ramp and sat with their backs to the posts of a sign that itemized the things prohibited beyond that point: farm machinery, bicycles, pedestrians. Kenny raised a thumb.

The sun rose, the day warmed. Vehicles racing up the ramp toward the highway passed in waves, the minutes turned to hours, and Joe closed his eyes. The waves of cars recalled the ocean at Atlantic City, where Kenny's mom had brought them when they were seven years old. The edge of a storm had grazed New Jersey that weekend, and the three of them had stood at the window in the hotel room admiring the crashing waves, their faces mottled by green stormlight and the penny-sized shadows of raindrops streaming down the glass.

As they kept watch, Kenny's mom imparted the outrageous news that a hurricane was passing by—"way out there"—somewhere over the horizon. And though Joe was uncertain how far *way out there* was, he knew it to be a stormy place, where tin-bottomed ships filled with tiny, bewildered men clung to sheer walls of water. And when those ships capsized, the sailors sank into the depths, into the miles of monsters and cold darkness. He knew these things because Kenny had told him so.

He was thinking about Atlantic City as he fell asleep beneath the highway sign, and he dreamed he was riding in the basket of a hot-air balloon with a pilot dressed in Rickenbacker goggles and a blowing scarf. They floated many thousands of feet up, just beneath the stars that hung about the gondola like festival lighting. Far below, the entire course of the Ohio River unfurled like a serpent from the Mississippi at St. Louis to the Monongahela at Pittsburgh, and every town and every city along the river's banks was burning—so many Tokyos and Dresdens—a chain of firestorm blazes as seen through the targeting lens of a night bomber. In places, the river reflected the conflagration like scarlet foil, and in other places it bubbled like black champagne. The pilot retrieved a small bomb from the bottom of the gondola and grinned.

"Looky there, kid. Parkersburg!"

The man reached the bomb with both hands over the edge and positioned the thing minutely, sighting down its length, then let it fall. Joe peered over the rail at the blast of gold light, the spreading burn. The heat rose to his face and scorched his skin. But he couldn't look away.

When he opened his eyes, the grille of a car was sizzling a few inches from his face. In the rippling heat from the radiator, a fritter of bugparts sizzled and smoked. In a patch of chrome on the bumper, just below his chin, Joe recognized the reflection of his own face, yawed by the bumper's curve.

A man with a handlebar moustache, wearing blue jeans and boots, stepped around the front of the car. "I cut the engine and rolled up on y'all, real quiet, in neutral. Thought about hitting the horn too, just to scare you a bit—you know, just to be funny. But then I thought, *naww*. What's the good word, boys? Need a lift?"

Kenny sat in front. Joe climbed in the back and settled his feet in a pile of trash. Inside of twenty seconds, the speedometer broke seventy-five. The man huffed furiously on a cigarette. Prescription bottles littered the dash. A beer can and a mason jar filled with water were wedged into the console. An empty prescription bottle sat on the seat beside him; Joe picked it up, read a few words on the label: Lipadel. Garlicman, Jr. Lithium. William. Carbonate. He set the bottle aside.

William and Kenny introduced themselves and shook hands. William took a drink of beer, frowned, chased it with water from the jar, handed the jar to Kenny. "Here, hold this," he said, and immediately took the jar back, chiding, "You don't know how to hold it, man. That's Miss'ssippi water!"

"Really?"

"Really! We're in Loosiana right? Miss'ssippi man can't drink Loosiana water!" He peered around the jar and slalomed through traffic as he drank. He handed the jar to Kenny, cursed, took it back again as the speedometer broke eighty-five. The man held the steering wheel stiffly, elbows akimbo, like he was steering a tank. Kenny asked him where he was going.

"Want some beer?" he said. "VA. Baton Rouge."

When they both declined, William took a deep breath and held it. "Miss'ssippi man can't breathe Loosiana air," he wheezed, his face reddening.

Joe considered proper crash positions, whether to curl up in the fetal position or crouch in the footwell. His shoulders braced as the car jerked across lanes. His stomach hardened like a dollop of spilt mortar in the sun. The faces of overtaken motorists were glimpses of outrage.

"Where you headed?" William asked, leaning over the console. Kenny stared ahead, nailed to the seat.

"We're—there's—you might—"

"Speak up. Mouth too dry?"

Kenny blew a silent whistle. "No, no. Thanks, William. We're going to Mexico."

"Why."

"To find Mary."

"Why, I said." William leaned an ear at Kenny and stomped the gas pedal by way of incentive. "Explain yourself." Gravel hammered on the floor beneath Joe's feet as the car drifted briefly onto the shoulder.

"She has news. From the other world. From the real world."

"The other world or the real world? Which is it? Be specific, boy!"

"The real world that reveals itself when we see with the eyes of our heart and listen with the ears of our heart."

"What's wrong with this world? It seems okay to me. What's the problem, kid? You don't like it here? Ain't comfy enough for ya? Got a sweet tooth, is it?" The odometer reached ninety.

"It's dark. It's dark. But the heart can see in the dark because it sees with a loving eye, and love illuminates the darkness and reveals the truth."

"Ah! And what is truth, kid?"

"The truth is that we are not destroyed by death. The truth is that love does shine in the darkness and cannot be consumed by it."

"What about me, boy? This very moment, I got your whole miserable fucking world in my hands."

Kenny picked up the beer, drank half the can, belched, and said, "Everyone will be forgiven, and all our debts will be beside the point. You, too, will be forgiven, no matter what you do. Every leaf and stone will be exalted, and every hurt healed." He handed the can to William. "Mary told me so."

William laughed, backed off the gas, and the odometer needle subsided to seventy-five.

"You're a fool," William said to Kenny. "You know that, don't you?"

"Yes, I know."

"Fair enough." William finished the water and set the jar aside gently, as one would a sick bird. When they arrived at the VA clinic, he parked in the furthest space from the entrance, twenty empty spaces from the nearest car, and observed the building through a windshield trickling with rain.

"I'd give y'all some water for the road, but it seems I drank up my stash. And I still gotta get home. It's not a crisis, but it is a problem."

William pressed money on them. When they refused, he insisted with a vicious curse. Joe took the ten.

"You two be careful. People here don't take kindly to pilgrims."

When they reached the road, Joe glanced back once more at the man, who sat unmoving in the driver's seat, a shadow behind the rainy glass, two fists tight on the wheel.

*

They began to walk.

They walked for days along the shoulder of the state route, overnighting in roadside woods, until they came to Lafayette, where they couldn't find a mission, slept in a park, woke early, and kept walking. In fine weather, they entered a causeway that spanned a flooded forest alive with strange birds.

Joe's grandfather had once told him that the swallows hibernated beneath the ice of Ohio's frozen lakes and ponds. The swallows didn't flee the coming cold in autumn but only slept for a time, reemerging to new life in the spring.

Now where did that ignorant old man dig up that dumb shit? It was pleasant to discover that the man's knowledge—and the knowledge of generations of geezers before him—was comprised almost entirely of fables. What other lies masquerading as wisdom remained to be disproved? He initiated a mental list of things awaiting refutation. With such pleasant and needful tasks he beguiled the miles, which hardly needed beguiling, for the skies were warm and blue, and the breezes fragrant and mild.

Ten cyclists in white helmets—wearing yellow, blue, and red riding shirts—streamed past like a Chinese kite tail.

Coastal clouds, fixed in the powder blue sky, reminded him of an image from one of Kenny's history books—a photograph taken during the air war of barrage balloons over the Dover coast. The blue sky, bluer than any sky he'd ever seen, betrayed the proximity of open water. The damp earth and the sunshine mingled on the breeze and left an iron aftertaste of old red wine.

For long stretches as he walked, he lost all sense of traffic and of his friend too. At times, when he returned to himself and noted that the sun had changed position, he found Kenny far ahead or far behind, deep in a brown study, thumbs hitched thoughtlessly in his pack straps.

Once, he stood aside and waited for Kenny to catch up, but his friend walked right past and didn't hear his name spoken. Joe saw the pack on Kenny's shoulder and remembered the weight of his own, and he knew his friend's feet must ache like his own feet did. But it could only be a light burden and an easy pain that attended such beautiful weather. Therefore, when he saw his friend, detached and at a distance, he could see himself as others might—that is to say, as a real person bound for a real place. And though that place be far away, and though they might not reach it in this lifetime, nevertheless that place had a proper name, and anybody could find it on a map—if they had a mind to. And if some cop stopped them, they could state with confidence and in pride of purpose: *We're on our way to our destination, so stand aside, good sir! Do you not see that we have important business to attend to?*

They reached Lake Charles after a few days. They hadn't attempted to hitch. It wasn't even mentioned. When night fell, they spread their blankets beneath the trees and slept.

*

In the morning, they flattened crumpled bread slices with their palms and ate in the cool violet shade. Around them stood forked and flood-twisted trees decked in white flowers. The air was turbid with the sour scent of ferns, the still waters redolent of black earth. Insects clacked and fifed and whirred.

Mottled geese with midnight-blue necks breasted pools beneath moss-draped trees.

"There's the ibis!" Kenny whispered.

The bird stood poised in a pool, head bowed, contemplative. Its scarlet face and legs seemed painted for a consecration or a sacrifice. The bird lifted a leg from the water, stepped, stilled.

"That's the bird of good omen, the celestial bearer of good news to the pharaohs."

"It's damned lost then. Let's go."

They walked into a battered and patched-up town that seemed to have been built last week with hundred-year-old materials. The one- and two-story wooden structures that toed the sidewalk were painted in the dull palette of weather. Litter lay in the gutters; sheet metal and busted skid-boards patched the broken windows. A half-dozen faded pop cans rested on a rusty awning.

Railroad tracks ran through the town and lent the place a provisional, impermanent aspect. Little towns like this one, situated along a rail line or a river, appeared as makeshift solutions to semi-pressing problems, as if the people were hesitant to commit the time and effort to build anything lasting, having grown complacent in the knowledge that they could, on any day of their choosing, load their possessions onto the next boat or freight and make their escape.

Few people were about. "Hair Styles by Cynthia McNutt" and "Checks Cashed," declared the sun-faded signs. *Pawn. Cheap Beer. Pepsi 40 Cents A Can.* Two kids tricked their bikes around a Buick. The elderly woman standing beneath the cypress, wearing a college sweatshirt that read *Penn State University*, awaited the millennium without complaint.

The church stood in want of paint. The wood siding was warped and parted in places, as if the structure's bones had outgrown its hide.

A man sat on the stoop beneath a wooden sign stenciled with the words, *Fellowship of Zion Bapt. Church.*

"Well, well. Look who turned up," Billy said, and they laughed and shook hands and Kenny swore that this reunion was a miracle heralded by an ibis.

"I don't know about all that," Billy said. "I do know that this is the only place for miles that opens its doors to vagabonds." Three days ago, he said, his ex-wife posted bond, and now he was on the road, headed for Mexico, there to die in peace among his cousins.

"That's where we're going, Billy! Didn't I tell you that?"

"I believe you did, kid. Couple times."

"Then we'll go together!" Kenny announced, but Billy said nothing.

Inside the church, folding chairs lay stacked on card tables. A man in shirtsleeves listened to a woman praise the meal they'd enjoyed the previous evening. Joe guessed the man to be the minister because the woman spoke to him with her hand over her heart. The minister acknowledged them with a gesture to sit.

"That little Cheswick boy," the woman continued, "eating like he hadn't eaten in days, bless his little soul, *tsk tsk*. You know, Reverend, I was talking to Missus Inglewood, and she has a whole pile of curtains from the house she moved out of, and she has no need of them, and I thought if I just had some scissors and thread, why, couldn't I make some real nice table covers to replace these old things, and wouldn't it be nice if they were ready for potluck—"

"Missus Murray, we'll have to—"

"You're not having second thoughts about potluck are you, Reverend?"

"No, it's a fine idea, we—"

"You just let me know when you're ready." She hurried toward the rear of the church. The minister lingered over a thought, then remembered the visitors.

"Dinner's over, boys. You know that, Billy."

"Yes, sir," Billy said. Joe grew desperate at the smell of scorched fat coming from somewhere. "I thought if you had anything left, these boys haven't eaten—they won't eat it here—they can take it along with 'em. They're good workers. They'll be happy to cut away the weeds in the road ditch."

"I'll have Missus Murray find something," the man said on his way to the door. "Just sit tight."

Mrs. Murray appeared with cold hot dogs and cold rice and a ketchup bottle. As she slid Kenny's plate across the table, her face was cheek by cheek with Joe's, and he caught the sour scent of last night's beer and cigarettes. She talked of things he knew nothing of while Billy positioned his plate and fork minutely in front of him, squared it to his shoulders, and proceeded to break the hot dog into bits over the rice. Kenny, watching, did the same. Mrs. Murray watched as well. "I know you," she demanded cordially.

Billy didn't look up. "Huh?"

"Day before yesterday. You cleaned my toilet for me. That was you, wasn't it?"

"No," he smiled at the food, joggling ketchup onto the rice. "Not me, lady."

She leaned over the table and gently tugged his ear. "You're a goddamned liar," she said and turned away.

Billy shook his head, flushed to the collar, and parsed his food with the fork.

"Come clean, now," Joe smiled. "What's your story?"

"Shut up and eat."

Kenny looked at him with a changed recognition, as if Billy were his own child speaking its first word. "Billy," he said. "Good old Billy. The fates brought us back together."

"Never heard of them."

*

The minister consented to one night's stay in an empty back room. "There aren't any beds in there," he told Kenny and Joe, "but there's blankets to spread on the floor. Billy, did you sleep alright?"

"Like a baby, Reverend, thank you," Billy said. "We'll disappear at first light."

In the small windowless room, four metal folding chairs were arranged in front of a dead television. Joe turned the set on and perused the three working channels, one of which displayed a weather map of the nation. Garbled data bursts punctuated the haze of poor reception. A great blue arrow, like an enemy army sweeping south from Canada, was aimed at Indiana. Curvilinear red and blue lines from Wisconsin to Oklahoma revealed the opposing trenchworks of colliding weather fronts. A jumble of red nubs and blue spikes marked a running fight over the Carolinas. He observed the unfolding catastrophe with satisfaction and kept the secret to himself.

Kenny and Billy sat with their backs to the wall and spoke in undertones of the devil.

"... I open the door and there he was, twelve feet tall," Billy said. "I could look up his nostrils and see the fires burning in his brains. And he says in this voice like he's sorry to bother me: 'Why do you put all this on me, Billy? It ain't my fault your two kids are in Texas and you're in Arizona. Why should I take the blame for that?' And I never drank another drop again. Not for two whole years."

"You know, Billy," Kenny said. "I always suspected the devil wasn't all bad."

"It's true, and nobody's gonna tell me he don't exist, neither."

"Oh, I believe it. You know, it must be hard to be the devil. We have to love him too, that's all. Until we do that, this thing will remain unfinished."

As the room darkened, Joe remembered his apartment: the television that was hot to the touch at two in the morning; the chair beside the window where he was wont to sit and keep track of the tragic folk stalking up and down in the street; his chipped dishes, his magazines; his coffee-stained cups. By now, someone else inhabited those rooms. As for that old life, it was gone, forgotten, buried in a Midwestern landfill.

Funny, he thought. I am glad.

*

Late in the night came a knock at the door. Mrs. Murray stood with her hands together. "I was wondering if one of you boys could help me."

Joe looked at the two sleeping on the floor. "Sure," he said.

A fluorescent light hung by chains from the peeling yellow ceiling, and lime-colored tiles rose halfway up the walls. The tile floor was chipped and paint-spattered, and empty rectangles of unpainted plaster betrayed those places where mirrors once hung. Mold radiated from the corners. A toilet survived the renovation of the bathroom, joined now by a metal bed frame and a nightstand that held a digital clock and an RC pop can. Big Band music played from a transistor radio. The singer's voice was tinny, distant, small: *you can't beat the horses no matter what you do; you can't beat the horses no matter what you do.*

Mrs. Murray stood over the toilet and affirmed, in cheery agitation, "I've been working on this all day." The lime ring at the waterline had been partly scrubbed away. "Look here. I used detergent and scrub brushes and everything I could think of, but I'm just too weak. I'm weak but you're strong. I'll give you five dollars if you can get that lime off." She pressed his arm for an answer.

"I'll try." He flushed the toilet, picked up a brush, and scrubbed while she oversaw.

"Oh, that's great! Can you get that black stuff off the bottom?"

It came off slowly. After a few minutes he heard, from the corner of the room, the squeak of bedsprings. He eased back on the job, calculating. The work finished despite him, however, and he got to his feet. Mrs. Murray lay on the mattress, propped on her elbows.

"I don't have three dollars." Her words lived among the tile, the benign pronouncement of the resident ghost.

"It's no problem. Two dollars for a six-pack would be fine, Missus Murray. Could you tell me where an open store is?"

"I don't have two dollars," she said.

"It's okay. You can pay tomorrow," he said. "You don't mind, do you? G'night." He returned to the room and lay down.

Late in the night came another knock. Joe opened the door once more for Mrs. Murray.

"I was wondering if one of you boys—"

"Sure." He walked over to Kenny and kicked him.

"You gotta help Missus Murray with something."

Kenny stood up. "Okay," he whispered, "Okay."

From across the hall, Joe could see Mrs. Murray and Kenny standing side-by-side at the toilet, like mourners at an open grave. He couldn't hear what was said, but from her posture it was plain that the woman had grown tired of explaining simple matters over and over to woodenheaded men. She closed the door. Joe pulled up the blanket and slept.

Billy woke him late in the night. As Joe stuffed gear into his bag, he saw the blanket on the floor where Kenny had been. Billy gathered Kenny's kit and shouldered both packs. When Joe tapped on Mrs. Murray's door, Kenny padded out, shoes in hand, gently pulled the door shut, and followed them outside.

"Well? Did you fix it?" Joe asked as they walked down the unlit street. "Was the ballcock shot? Flush-valve leaking?" He was proud of the jokes. "Was the tank cracked?"

"The only sanity in this world is a quiet moment shared by two people," Kenny said. "Don't talk mean."

"You're such a self-righteous bastard, you know that?"

Kenny didn't answer. "Where we going, Billy?"

"The tracks."

"What's the tracks?"

"The tracks," Billy repeated. "How do you propose we get out of here?"

"Hitchhike?"

"Hitchhike! Not me, chicos," Billy said. "A lot of freaks out there. They'll rape you and chop your head off. No. We'll take the train. Fasten those water jugs to your belts. This ain't no bullshit no more. Time to gear up like it's the fucken army."

When they reached the railyard, they lay belly-down on the embankment, peered over the rails, and waited.

Three blasts from a horn were followed by the tremor of a rolling train. As the locomotives passed, Joe could have reached out and touched them.

Billy set off, trotted alongside the third engine, grabbed the uprights of the ladder, sprang to the bottom rung, and hauled himself up. Kenny and Joe climbed on as the train accelerated. They followed Billy down the narrow, grated walkway into the engineer's compartment.

Joe was surprised to find the control panel lit and two turntable stools empty. "Where are the drivers?"

"They're up in the first engine," Billy said. "They won't come back here."

"Aren't we supposed to ride in a box car?" Kenny asked.

Billy laughed. "That's only in the movies, baby hobo."

"Only in the movies!" Kenny said as he leaned at the window. "Did you hear that, Joe? Only in the movies!"

*

Joe sat against the wall with his eyes closed, his heart racing in the dark, his mind slurred by the bawling diesels and the tipping sway. He lay chest-down on his pack like a man hugging a broken spar and counted out the pulses of the rail joints. Now and then during the night, he emerged unmoored from monstrous dreams to hear things he could not quite believe. When the others woke him, it was San Antonio and still dark. They climbed off.

In the railyard, among the darkened dormant trains, a solitary worker's flashlight beam scribbled the black belly of a tank car.

Three locomotives on a siding gleamed like a pod of cockroaches— long streaks of exhaust sweeping the engines' flanks like black capes.

"Is that our train?" Kenny asked.

"No," Billy said. "Truth be told, I don't know. It's hard to say. We'll ask."

The worker sat on the cinders with an open switch-light box between his knees. A flashlight lay between his feet, and the beam illuminated two hands worrying the wires. A lit cigarette burned between his lips, and he squinted and cocked his head to keep the rill of smoke from his eye. On his hardhat was a decal of a Dixie flag. At the sound of their feet, he took the cigarette from his mouth.

"How goes it, brother?" Billy asked.

The man didn't answer but glanced past them to his colleagues down the line, gauging the distance to his rescuers.

"We're just passing though. Can you tell us which train goes to El Paso?" Billy said.

The man read their faces, loosened his grip on the screwdriver, plugged the cigarette back into his mouth, and said, "Well, you got your pick. These are westbound, long haul. I can't promise El Paso. Maybe Amarillo. That one there," he pointed with the screwdriver, "with the oil hoppers, Wisconsin Central written on it? See it? That one oughta pull out shortly. Like I said, it's going west, but I can't say where to." As they walked toward the neck of the yard, the worker called after them. "Bulls are out tonight. They'll be moving with the trains. Friendly warning."

The many tracks merged to two, which led through an underpass. Concrete pylons the girth of Sequoias rose into the darkness, up to the interstate bridges, where the sky blanched in the headlights of passing vehicles. They crawled into the bushes at the foot of a pylon and sat in the litter.

The train's departure was announced by pings of stress that rifled through the rails like ricocheted bullets in a gunfighter flick. The locomotive's light transfixed the bush where they waited, vaporizing the darkness, and reduced their cover to the substance of fishnet.

Joe felt ridiculous. Unwilling to face the coming train and the engineers that he knew to be watching, he inspected the graffiti on the pylon, or picked at the candy wrappers and beer cans about him, as if he were crouching there on legitimate and unrelated business, just some guy looking for his keys.

"Don't look at the light," Billy shouted, and they began to run, water jugs flapping against their thighs.

Billy pitched his pack onto the flatcar, grabbed the upright, and swung onto the ladder with a neat spring. He knelt at the edge of the car with one hand out, but Kenny stumbled and fell onto the cinders. Joe fell over him. He lifted Kenny by his jacket collar and together they ran for another flatcar, gained the ladder, and climbed up.

Through the intervening darkness they saw him, six cars ahead, a shadow akimbo, tottering on loose knees. Billy's laughter belled above the howling night.

Joe pitched their packs across the gap that separated the cars. He took three steps back, ran, jumped, and landed on his feet and hands on the decking of the next car; Kenny followed; and so they proceeded, leaping from car to car, until they found themselves, once again, standing beside Billy Bogota.

"You did good, boys; you did good!"

A truck appeared, headlights juddering, beating down the maintenance road that ran parallel to the tracks. When the truck was abreast of the flatcar, the passenger fixed them with a door-mounted spotlight. A voice came clear and calm through a megaphone fixed to the roof of the cab.

You are trespassing on private property. Get off the train now.

"What do we do, Billy?"

"Fuck me. We have to jump off I guess."

"It's going really fast, guys," Kenny said. He turned to face the spotlight and shouted, courteous but firm, "It's going really fast, sir!"

Joe peered over the edge; the sleepers reeled like film on rewind.

Get off the train.

"There's no choice. If they catch us they'll rob and cage us," Billy said. Turning his back on the cops, he dropped his pack overboard, and stepped into the void.

Kenny shouted after Billy and leapt off empty-handed.

Joe's legs shook. He threw both packs off, jumped, rolled down the cinder embankment.

Billy arrived from the dark to hand him his pack. They started uphill at a trot, Billy shouting that the "bulls were circling the train," which struck Joe as merely outrageous.

They climbed a fence and stood at the shoulder of a freeway, anticipating the moment to cross.

Billy glanced back at the two cops picking their way up the slope. "Those pricks don't quit."

With a light-footedness that verged on weightlessness, in a welter of blaring horns, Joe sprinted across the highway as the cars bore down. Laughably slow he ran, with an agonizing lack of traction, like one trapped in a dream chase, like one whose bones had been steeped in an essence of gravity.

He hopped the jersey barrier into the median, waited for a gap in the traffic, sprinted across the next four lanes, and resumed the climb. When he looked over his shoulder, he saw the two cops walking downhill toward their truck, and he felt the sudden presence of his friends at either hand, as if they'd risen out of the earth.

On the hilltop, they lay against their packs, each nailed to his own heaving lungs. Behind them was the highway, before them the sun blossomed on the horizon, gleaming like a struck coin. Billy passed a cigarette to Joe; they shared water and did not speak. The fear dissipated with the sweat, the cold air settled on the backs of Joe's hands, and the land rolled away to the sun that—for only a moment—balanced precariously on the horizon, attached by a slim trick of light to the earth.

"I'm glad I lost my glasses," Kenny said. "That might have been scary if I could see."

Joe retrieved the glasses from his shirt pocket and handed them to his friend. Kenny opened them gently with his fingers, settled the arms behind his ears, passed a dirty cuff over a lens, and blinked. "Thank you," he said.

Kenny made bologna sandwiches for everyone. "Billy's gonna take care of us. Billy's gonna get us there."

Billy sat cross-legged with eyes closed, a burning cigarette in his lips, motionless, like a spy tied to a post.

Kevin Honold

*

That night, they hopped a train pulled by four diesels and entered the compartment of the third engine. Crouched at separate windows, they peered at the passing town. The height of the compartment, added to the height of the embankment, afforded an uncustomary view over the housetops and the darkened streets.

The green dials on the control panel emitted a dusty glow and coated Kenny's glasses with lime-tinted light. Like bug's eyes, Joe thought, bug's eyes above a pale ribbon of teeth.

"This train is bound for glory, this train!" Kenny sang, "this train don't carry no con men no wheeler dealers here and gone men ..."

The town fell behind as day broke, and the land changed from woods to scrub. Now and then, the train's passage scared up jackrabbits as big as border collies.

The locomotives braked and whistled through a small town where, at a crossing gate, a file of vehicles idled in the flurry of warning bells. The semaphore, perched like a heron on its one long thin leg, wore an outlandish bowtie of crossed boards bearing the words RAIL ING CROSS ROAD, and it watched the passing train with saucer-sized eyes that flashed with alternating alarm light.

Kenny waved at the waiting drivers. A man in a pickup flashed two fingers at them, whether as a gesture of peace or victory or something else, Joe did not know.

The intervals between towns lengthened. Rain pitted the dusty windscreen. Kenny shut the window, gave over his long watch at last, and sat on the floor with the others. He retrieved a sack of bologna from his pack and sniffed it. "I think it's turning into chicken liver."

Joe made two sandwiches and divided them into three portions. "That's it for the food. Maybe we should've thought about that."

"I don't think it's a problem," Kenny said. "Look at us, doing easily thirty miles an hour. Still, maybe you have a point. What if we never stopped? What if we just kept going on and on, too slow to get anywhere, too fast to ever jump off?" He turned the thought over. "When do you think the train'll stop, Billy?"

Billy studied an apple, took a final bite, and set the core down carefully on the grime. "Let me check the timetable," he said, shut his eyes, and settled against the wall.

The compression of the engine tugged softly at Joe's lungs. Cold air whistled through the glass.

*

The door slid open. A man stood with his back to the night. Wrapped in a yellow slicker streaming water, he regarded the stowaways with a look of fierce exception. Engine noise and the smell of diesel and rain accompanied him as he entered, pulled his hood down, glanced at the control panel.

"Evening," Billy said. "We won't touch nothing."

"Don't you boys touch nothing, alright?" the man said. He ducked through the engine room hatch. A few minutes later he reemerged. "There's some water bottles in a cooler back there if you get thirsty," he said, pulling his hood up. "Just don't touch nothing else."

"Thanks. When's the train gonna stop?" Billy asked.

"No stops for awhile. We'll slow through Vandemeer. You can jump off there."

"How long to Vandemeer?"

"About two hours."

"Much obliged," Kenny said, and the man climbed out.

"Much obliged?" Joe said. "Much obliged? Where you from? Camptown, Kansas?"

"I was just being polite." Kenny was hurt, then touched. "He was so nice to us."

Wide-awake now, Joe was beset by thoughts of darkness and rain. Billy settled against the wall and weathered, with calm precision, Kenny's interrogation.

"Baton Rouge," Billy said.

"Loud and dirty," Billy said.

"Three of them," Billy said.

"Morphine," Billy said.

Kenny said, "You've had some difficult experiences, Billy."

"Not so, son. Lots of people got it much worse. Look around." He opened his eyes narrowly at Kenny. "I'm not complaining. Anyway, like they say in the army, the only place you'll find sympathy in this world is in the dictionary. Between shit and syphilis."

"Billy, will you come with us all the way?"

Billy kept his eyes shut. "How old are you boys?"

"Twenty-two."

"Shit. I got dried-up pus streaks down my left leg older than you," he said. "Remind me. What are you after?"

Joe said, "We're going to find the lost milkmaid."

"She's not lost," Kenny said. "We're lost. *We're* lost."

Billy glanced from one to another. "I'm going to Hidalgo. You probably don't know where that is. I have some relatives there."

"It's north of Mexico City. We're going the same way! We're going a bit further, to Tepeyac Hill, where Mary appeared to Juan Diego. It's real close! Come with us, Billy. I think your presence would add some needed gravitas to our embassy to the Star of the Sea."

"You should learn some Spanish."

"Yo estudio now." Kenny retrieved a phrase book from his pack and handed it to Billy.

Billy laughed as he leafed through. "Terrible! Alright, I'll get you there. But I'm not stopping for no milkmaids. I'm too old for that silly shit, kid."

"I'm glad, Billy," Kenny said. "On the way, maybe we can pick up a nice gift. God doesn't want any burnt offerings, so he says. Mary, though—she might like a little something."

*

Late in the night they woke to blasts from the horn. They followed Billy out into the rainy dark and jumped one by one off the train. Joe hit the cinders, checked his kit, and returned along the embankment; he found Kenny on his knees, casting about with his hands, lightly brushing the rocks with his fingers.

Joe stood above him. "Glasses?" Joe said. "They're between your knees."

They walked through the lifeless town and arrived at an ill-lit park. The earth was cool and soft beneath the trees. There they lay down and slept.

Joe was startled awake by a loud pop. A thin young woman in an orange jumpsuit stood over him, backlit by the rising sun. A capacious cloth sack filled with trash hanging by a strap from her shoulder sagged against her thigh. Joe's water jug, bleeding its contents, was skewered on the end of her litter poker. She raised it high for a better look. "This yours?" she asked.

"Yours now."

She shoved it into the sack. "You need a new one anyway. This one's filthy."

On the other side of the park, several people in orange jumpsuits walked abreast, carelessly probing the earth with pokers like a squad of fatalistic mine detectors.

Kevin Honold

*

All day, in the little disused park, they rested beneath the trees. Warmth from the dry ground seeped into Joe's joints like good medicine. In the afternoon, Kenny and Joe wandered the town, past machine shops and garages and a secondhand clothing store whose window bore handmade signs that read *regalos* and *tesoros*. On the display shelf was an arrangement of flatware, tea cups, a frayed doll.

"I wonder how much that doll is," Kenny said. "That would make a nice gift." He knocked at the door, cupped his hands at the glass, peered in. No one answered.

The chipped plaster facades of empty shops faced the empty street. At the Cowboy Motel, some of the doors of the rooms stood open, revealing moldy gloom within. *American-owned*, the marquee said. *$14.99 no tax*. Three pigeons perched on a sagging roof gutter.

They paused over a dead cat on the roadside, its carcass reduced by the elements to patches of fur and a skein of bones. The sharp white teeth were bared, as though the creature were reverting with an anguished cry back into the earth. A hawk fetched a gyre above the Texaco sign.

On the stoop in front of a mission, a man with a livid face sat and argued with himself, and the setting sun sealed the far end of Main Street like a stone. It was then that Kenny stopped, in the middle of the deserted street and pointed to the sky.

Over the battered shops, in the flawless violet of the desert evening, two jet contrails intersected at right angles. The figure of a cross quartered the southern sky and ascended slowly even as it faded.

"It's a message. From Mary. A sign from the Star of the Sea."

"It's smoke trails."

"A cross rising from below the horizon. From Mexico, Joe. From our destination!"

"It's moisture evaporating."

"Big enough to crucify us all, by the size of it."

"Have it your way. That gas station looks open, moron. Let's see if they got food." Kenny didn't follow but stood in the middle of the street to watch the cross of smoke ascend, crumble, and vanish in monumental silence.

*

That night they built a fire and placed three potatoes hard by the flames. The dark came early to the pines. The fire cast a shuddering light on the nearest tree trunks.

Joe walked to the edge of the little grove where they had spread their blankets. The stars, delicate as surf spray, brightened under his eye. A satellite drew slowly, smoothly across the sky, like the ballpoint of a steady pen tracing a meridian line on the dome of night. He watched the satellite and the stars and waited for these things to enlighten him, for he had learned from Kenny that the stars were emblems of significant and durable truths, and that these truths in turn would illuminate the hidden purpose planted like a seed in the heart of each human life. But the stars neither tallied among themselves, nor spoke of any remarkable thing, and they never would. His formless speculations, like sonar pinging the depths, encountered nothing up there.

All this riddling, he concluded, was in keeping with the nature of existence, which never was intended to culminate at any discernible or sensible point. Only a fool believes otherwise. Of resentment he felt only a trace, for resentment is only weak-mindedness, he knew, and time spent dwelling on mysteries is time wasted. These conclusions—constituting his final analysis of the Nature of Things—he considered no small feat of sound and mature reasoning, and he minded himself to impart them to Kenny. Yes, he would sit his friend down at the next opportunity and compel him to listen to reason. His friend's hallucinations could use a dousing of cold clear light. With this conviction in hand, he turned back, not a little proud of his own freedom from illusion.

At the fire, Billy lay propped on one elbow. He watched an ant crawl across the back of his hand and bespoke it: "Same shit," he said, slowly rotating his hand to keep the ant climbing. "Different day."

Kenny held the phrase book close to his nose; he tipped the page to the firelight and strained to read the words. "Hey, Joe," he said. "Me and Billy were wondering what gifts we should bring Mary. I said a green apple. Billy said a silver hammer. What do you think?"

"Why not bring both?"

*

In the morning, Kenny returned from town with a loaf of bread and a brace of cheap kites.

"Buck-and-a-half for the three of 'em! Pretty good, huh?"

"What a waste," Joe said. "We could've bought cheese."

"Cheese you will always have," Kenny said. "But you will not always have kites." He scolded Billy and Joe for having never flown kites and for making him attach the strings and fit the struts to the wings, which he nevertheless cheerfully did. They fanned out across the field.

Kenny played the string out as he ran, and the kite rose over his shoulder and tracked him like a specter. The others stood in the grass and pretended to control things: jigging the strings, winding the spools, hauling down when the kites turned unruly, stepping from side to side to find the angle of wind.

Joe let the spool unwind of itself, felt the string play out of his fingers. The rattly kite drifted farther and farther away, feinting and fluttering, a drunken hummingbird.

When Kenny tugged the string, the kite raced along the ground, banked skyward. It was a bit of chaff at two hundred yards when the wind wrestled it into the upper branches of a tree. He set the spool in the grass, ran to the trunk, and began to climb.

He made quick progress as the other two reeled in their kites and gathered in the tree's shade to ridicule him. They heard the branch creak as he worked his way along—himself only visible as patches of denim and flannel.

"Get ready," Billy said. "Here comes something."

Three men crossed the open space toward the tree. The short-bearded man was flanked by two companions, all three dressed in plaster-spattered overalls.

"Bad news," Billy said. "Sheetrockers."

As the men closed the distance, Joe could see the sea-blue tattoos on the short man's knuckles, and he felt sick.

"This isn't the way I wanted to spend my lunch hour," the bearded man said, his face like a fist full of grass. "Hippy motherfuckers who fall off the train in Texas *are not* allowed to fly kites in my park." He pointed at Billy's face as if his finger were a delicate tool whose weight caused his whole frame to tilt. "You haven't read the town ordinance, have you, hippy?" He stepped in front of Joe and poked his chest. "What about you?" The finger knocked him back a step.

"I guess I haven't read that."

"Don't get stupid with me."

A clash of leaves and branches was followed by a thump of bones hitting turf, and Joe knew by the surprise on the man's face that Kenny had fallen out of the tree. He turned to see his friend on his feet, a red kite in his hand. "Got it," Kenny said.

The blow that knocked him down didn't hurt. Joe lay on the

ground, curled up. As the man kicked him, he felt a touch of relief that this ridiculous affair had finally gotten underway and would soon come to an end. In his mind, he hovered above the ground, above himself, and watched from a safe elevation as he was beaten. In the following days, when he recalled the incident, he imagined another man—clearly identifiable as himself—standing over his own body and contributing a few round kicks. The image troubled and confused him. However, over the years, he would be comforted to learn that this was in fact a common experience among men and women who undergo a beating.

In the stillness that followed, the numb places began to knot, and the pain surged in small waves to the beat of his heart. He ran through numbers in his mind—his old address, his old phone number—and touched his ribs lightly. Birdsong resolved in his head, and when he took his hand from his ear, he found blood on it. He rolled the blood between his fingertips; it was neither warm nor cold, and tasted like mud. He wiggled his toes and felt glad. From this day forward, he knew life would be both a few cents cheaper and a few cents costlier. The mystery of it was marvelous.

They lay where they had last stood. Kenny said, "Billy, you don't look good. You okay?"

Blood from the upturned side of his head had run laterally across Billy's face and dried in warlike stripes. They knelt beside him, examined a contusion and a cut, determined nothing. Kenny mentioned a hospital and Billy sat up. Joe doused his handkerchief with water and handed it to Billy.

Kenny said, "I think this was good for my soul. I feel ready now. It's best if we arrive beat-up and hungry. I think if we appear before Mary with clean shirts and full bellies, she'll turn us away."

Joe's laughter was dry and mean. "Fuck all that. Didn't you hear that little prick? You broke the laws of Texas, you dumb shit. And you nearly got Billy here killed." He laughed deeply and his whole body shook in the grass. The laughter caused his ribs to ache; though he wanted to, he couldn't stop.

"Shoot. Joe's right. I'm sorry. What's so funny?"

"I don't know," he said. "I just feel fucking happy."

"I'm sorry, friends. It was my fault."

Billy said, "You know how different parts of your brain do different things?" They waited for the answer while he dabbed his face with the handkerchief. "Forget about it, Kenny."

Stiffly, gingerly, Billy took a shoe off, pulled a fold of cash from the toe, and replaced the money without counting. The others, taking the cue, patted their empty pockets and looked about in the empty grass.

Billy said, "You won't find nothing. In this life, boys, you learn the hard way. Like they say in the army, illegitimi non carborundum." Billy lay in the grass with his forearm over his eyes. "It don't do no good to hate the rest of the people in this world. Their punishment is their own fucking miserable lives."

That night they walked along the rail line and came to a gravel lot full of disused semi-trailers, found one to be unlocked, spread cardboard, and lay down. From the back of the trailer was a clear view of the tracks.

Kenny said, "Why would people make a law against flying kites? I don't like this state at all."

By the time Billy woke them, the night had grown cold. The darkness dissolved in the light of an approaching locomotive, revealing flat scrub that faded into night.

There was an odor to the emptiness of small hours that always made Joe feel hopeless, when it was so dark that clouds and trees seemed impossible, and talk was mere obscenity. The small hours smelled like turned earth.

The air shuddered. Pings of stress shot down the rails, signaling the approach of the train. They climbed out, hitched their packs, and began to run. The darkness was wearying.

*

All day the train rolled beneath powder blue skies, sounding its horn at crossings. Its passage flushed a pair of jackrabbits that were dry and dusty as the land, living composites of burr and thistle. Cliffs ringed the horizon, their brows banded with penny and tobacco and bronze-colored stone.

Kenny said, "We're nearing the western mountains" and shouldered into the same window with Joe. Two cows stood in the middle distance, and beside each cow stood her calf, and the calves leaned into the shadows of their mothers as winds traced faint paths through the creosote.

Counter-twilight limned the skyline, the lavender haze of a proximate sea.

Yucca, so many sword bouquets, numberless as stars.

*

Billy retrieved a pint of whiskey from his pack and took a drink. By the time the bottle returned to him, his face was flushed and serene. "Anyone who says they like the taste of this is a liar."

"Why do you drink it, Billy?"

"Kills hunger," he said, passing the bottle. "Burns nice. Like fire creepin' through the short grass. That's what it is. *Fire creepin' through the short grass.* That's from an old Henry Fonda movie."

Kenny took a long drink and his eyes watered. "Do you believe in God, Billy?"

"I don't know. What do I know? I'm like everybody. I was born stupid, I'll die stupid." He yawned. "Jesus and Allah and the daily llama. What do I know?" He took his ball cap off and scratched at the gray hair that flared about his ears. "Everybody just wants to live forever, I guess." He took a drink and gagged, and his words slurred. "When it's all said and done, kid, and you're up there hanging on that tree," he said, "all your friends are gonna run off and leave you."

"I don't believe that, Billy."

"Believe it. They'll all run off in the end. They might tell you otherwise. Hell, they might even believe their own bullshit sometimes." He handed the bottle up. "Do you know that, Joe? You're a smart guy. Do you know that we live and die alone?"

Joe drank and wiped his mouth with his sleeve. "Yes I do. Because God's a murderer. I wouldn't drag him out of a puddle if he was facedown drunk in it."

"Pay no attention to him, Billy. He just does that to annoy me."

All day long, the mountains had neither drawn nearer nor receded, and now the raven-haunted crags commenced to shed their shadows.

Two vultures circled a peak.

Though he watched the mountain chains for a long while, he found no point on which to rest his sight, and the watchfulness nettled the nerves behind his eyes. He tried to imagine the peaks of the Andes Mountains, or the Himalaya peaks, the tall blue blades of ice—but he could not bring the images to life.

"What if I'm wrong?" Kenny said. "What if this is stupid like everybody says? What if it was just a dream? What if we get there, Billy, just to find that it was all an illusion? What'll I do then?"

"Don't be scared, kid. Today we got us a free ride and a bottle. Tomorrow will sort itself out," Billy said, but Kenny wasn't listening, for he'd fallen suddenly asleep with his head on Billy's shoulder.

Billy removed his dentures and dropped them into his shirt pocket. "Sufficient unto the day is the evil thereof."

Now the open window framed a black field of stars. Billy and

Kenny snored in disharmony with their mouths open. Joe slipped the bottle from Kenny's fingers. As the train entered a long slow turn, the crescent moon, like a nickel ferry, set sail across the sky, and passed slowly out of view.

*

That night the door slid open and three men entered the compartment. For a moment, the six regarded one another, three on their feet and three on the floor. Billy spoke in Spanish and the men answered shortly in undertones, setting their packs aside.

"Here for work," Billy said.

The new men shared out their apples; Joe gave them cigarettes.

One man rooted through his pack, and his modest exertions were pained and slow.

"What kind of work will they look for, Billy?" Kenny asked and pulled the phrase book from his pack.

"Put that thing away now," Joe said.

In silence, one by one, with a few words among themselves, the six of them settled against their packs and shut their eyes.

The braking of the train woke them late in the night. Billy knelt at the windows and peered into the darkness; he opened the engine room hatch, spoke a few words, and the new riders climbed through. The train came to a stop in the headlights of two Suburbans.

"Border patrol. You two," Billy said. "Just open your mouths and they'll know what you are."

The door slid open and a man entered wearing a green ball cap, military web-gear, and a pistol in a holster. He aimed a flashlight at them. The disc of light shivered on Kenny's face.

"Americans," Joe said. The man stepped over their feet to the engine room. He spoke in long flat Spanish and stepped aside as the men climbed out.

The agent said to Kenny, "Ride's over. You're trespassing on federal property. You got IDs?"

Kenny reached for his back pocket and then remembered. "We don't have any. Our wallets were stolen. Are we in trouble?"

"Stand up." He patted them down and tipped Joe's pack with his boot. "Hell yes you're in trouble." He held the flashlight at chin-level and peered along the light at Billy, seated against the wall.

"What about you, pops? Got ID?"

"No."

"Citizen?"

"Yes."

"Traveling together?"

"No."

The agent waited.

Billy said, "Look at me. I'm an old man."

"Wanted anywhere?"

"No."

While the agents led Billy and the other men to the idling trucks, Kenny and Joe waited beside the train. After a few minutes, the agent returned and reached into his shirt pocket. "Here you go. Your colleague said this belongs to you." He handed some folded bills to Joe, turned back to the trucks, and said over his shoulder, "You're free to go. We don't have space for you. If I was you I'd start walking." He pointed west. "That way. Follow the tracks. Don't let us see you get back on that train, hear?"

"Why do you have to take him away?" Kenny said. "He's a good person, sir. He helps others."

"He's in violation of his conditions. You oughta choose your friends more wisely."

The diesels powered up. In the truck's headlights stood four men with their arms behind their backs. Just before he was placed into the back seat with the others, Billy shouted toward Kenny and Joe, but his words were lost in the engine noise and the wind. He was placed in the back and the agent shut the door

"What did he say, officer?" Kenny shouted to the agent. "What did he say!"

The man picked at his key ring. "He said, Buy something nice for her with that money."

The train lurched, the engines took up the slack, each car jolted taut with a clang, and the clangorous wave receded down in the line, diminishing with distance. The train began to haul.

The Suburbans wheeled away and rattled off in a storm of gold beams and dust.

Kenny watched them go. "They've taken Billy," he said.

Joe set off at a run.

*

The locomotives, pulling hard, disappeared in the darkness, taking with them the warm compartments. Running at a dead sprint, Joe caught the rail of the last flatcar and climbed aboard. Kenny, heaving, landed beside him. They lay curled behind their packs.

But the packs made poor barriers to the wind, and the cold seeped into Joe's knuckles and feet. Nests of light—brief golden clusters suspended in the night, telling of distant towns—drifted across his field of vision. He understood that people slept in those nests of light, warm and dry and hard to believe in.

The rail joints clacked through his bowels. His eyes watered, the tears froze, the stars bleared and ran. The minutes turned to hours, and he traded with declining hope in the odds of death by exposure.

The horn pierced his stupor, and the acrid stink of the brakes tinged a darkness made gaudy with police lights. He crawled to the edge of the flatcar's deck and saw, two hundred yards ahead, three cruisers parked at the edge of the track, flashers rotoring, spotlights leveled at the passing train. Black cutouts of belted and jacketed men stood in the headlights of the vehicles.

"Get up get up get up." He grabbed Kenny's pack and dropped it on his chest. "Put it on!"

Joe jarred shoulders with Kenny as they leapt off opposite sides of the car.

He scrambled into the bushes, pounded his numbed thighs with his fists, slid down a stony slope that bottomed in a concrete culvert, which he followed until he no longer heard the train or saw the police lights. Inside a fenced lot he found an unlocked semi-trailer and climbed in.

The sun was halfway up the sky when he woke and opened the door to a world he didn't recognize. He followed the rumble of diesels through acres of waste ground back to the railyard. What had been a place of dark thickets and whipping lights during the previous night was transformed into a tract of meager scrub, narrow paths threading piles of construction debris, sunshine with undertones of morning traffic, and no sign of his friend.

He sat on a slab of busted concrete and tried to think. Here beneath the interstate bridges, railroad ties were strewn like corpses across a rubble field. Litter lay evenly sifted over the place, and the tough little bushes looked neither live nor dead. Bottles and moldered clothing marked the passage of junkies and transients. Here, below the soaring bridges—like a blighted city under the sea—all was peace and oblivion.

A small white object fell in a tailspin from the sky like a shaped stone through water and resolved into a paper cup that landed near his feet. He did not know how to begin to look for his friend.

Two men stood in the shade of a pylon. The older man wore a

heavy coat and declaimed through a long gray beard that recalled the days of the Desert Fathers. The younger man nodded along, but his agreeability diminished a touch at Joe's appearance. Joe read the younger man's thoughts, for the fellow had a face that reflected his mind. These newcomers, the younger man seemed to say to himself— these newcomers think they know the ending to every story, and they always ruin it for everyone.

"Now I'm gonna tell you how I beat that sonofabitch," the old man dictated. "You ready? Now this is gonna sound hard to believe. You ready?"

"No," the younger man said, "I mean yeah." He drank and wiped his teeth with his sleeve then handed the bottle to Joe, who drank and pressed his hand to his chest to smother the burn.

The booze warmed him, refined him. *Fire creepin' through the short grass*, he thought, and imagined Billy warm and fed in some county jail, playing Scrabble with three other men he'd never met before yet had known all his life.

"You haven't seen anyone walking around here, have you?" Joe asked. "About my height, black hair, blue jeans, flannel jacket? Kinda stupid, dirty. Looks lost?"

The bearded man set his hand on Joe's shoulder. "Don't you fret, boss. You'll find your partner. It's good to have a traveling partner. Me and Jonah here, what's it been? Three weeks? My god, he's the stupidest sonofabitch I ever met! The milkman slipped his mama some curdled spunk, I betcha. You get me? Ha! What?"

The weight of the earth pressed at the bottom of Joe's shoes, and the weight of the sun rested on the back of his neck. He decided to search along the railroad tracks, where he expected to find his friend lying dead in a ditch, for that would be the correct resolution to this business, and the confirmation of the private prediction of every soul who had ever met Kenny Stegemuller.

But first he would wait his turn at the bottle.

The old man told stories, and Jonah—who'd heard them all—shed his suspicions of the stranger, who was plainly not looking for trouble, or, it seemed, for anything of value. It cost the men nothing to welcome Joe into the charmed circle, where the magic stories went like this: one time, the old man got drunk on Lysol with a bunch of Zunis and later that same night danced a war dance in the desert. Another time, he broke into a railcar full of brand-new vehicles out of Detroit. Goddamn, he was proud of this one: he'd taken the wheels off six Monte Carlos while the train was underway, pitched the wheels into the weeds, jumped off, picked up the wheels that night in a borrowed truck, and sold the rims for fifty dollars a pop. Made fifteen hundred dollars in a single day!

"Hell, I even seen the Star of the Sea, sad and lorn, lookin' for her lamb."

"A what?"

"Pitiful. In Cruces. They call her by a different name down there."

"What did you say?"

"I ain't stupid, boss. I know what I seen. Sad she was, and that poor lamb, lost for all eternity!"

Jonah said, "Tell him how long you been riding the rails!"

"Since steam, boss," the old man reflected, frowning down his terrible beard. "Since motherfuckin steam."

*

He woke up nauseous in an ill-lit tunnel, packed into a pissed-in corner of a recess in the wall. Graffiti ran the length of the tunnel, an unbroken shoulder-high script made significant by the meticulous trouble spent on it. Pains had been taken, a fevered beauty had been achieved, one that resembled the illuminated lettering in a book of psalms composed by vagabond monks.

He puzzled over the messages as moths braided the lamps at the apex of the curved roof, filling the tunnel with quick gray shadows the size of men. He tried to abstract a meaning from the wall, but the more he looked, the more of a muddle it became. His inability to divine the graffiti troubled him at first, then angered him; he spat the bitter diesel stink of the place from his mouth. Cold light glinted off the steel rails, off the spike heads that bossed the sleepers.

Some kids entered the tunnel and filed down the maintenance walk, toward the recess where he now crouched, motionless, breathing lightly. They wore jackets with hoods, shouted at the echoes of their shouts. One carried a stick.

One of the boys flicked his cigarette at the wall above Joe's shoulder. A shower of sparks fell over his hair and clothes, and he brushed the embers from his neck and collar. The movement betrayed him, and they fired questions.

"Have you seen Kenny?" Joe asked.

They laughed. One boy kicked a can at him. "Hey man fuck you man," the boys crowed as they crowded him. "You lost, hobo?" He reminded himself that he must curl up.

Gold light spread along the walls, attended by a rising rumble and three long blasts from a horn. He stood and pushed past the boys, and their bony shoulders pressed into his back and chest like the bunt ends of aluminum bats. He walked into the light with his head down in anticipation of a thrown cinder or bottle. But nothing was thrown.

The ledge between the wall and the rolling train became a vertiginous passage gusting hot air and smoke; the noise of the engines clouted his ears. The train and the wall moved contrarily along the corridors of vision and conspired to lift him, gently, to the tips of his toes, until it seemed that he drifted off the ground. And he found himself in the night air again.

Ears ringing, he walked up and down, planting his feet until his knees recalled the angle of gravity, and his mind ground at last to a halt.

Near the place where he had gotten drunk, he recovered and searched his pack, knowing it contained nothing to eat. He lay down face-up on the bare ground, at the foot of a towering pylon, and watched the highway bridges resolve against the lightening sky.

It was then he noticed a word printed in foot-high letters—a single word that reached halfway round the pylon. The letters, written in mud, had dried.

CROATOAN

He stood before the word. When he smeared the leg of the N with his thumb, the print vanished into dust. Think now, he told himself. This word has meaning. There was a ship. The ship took people across an ocean, then left them. When the ship returned, the people were gone. Isn't that the story? But what did that have to do with me? That's the part he could not remember.

*

He sat with his back to the pylon. Near noon, a figure appeared. Even at a distance, Joe could see the grin on his friend's face as he crossed the lot.

"You found the word!" Kenny knelt and hugged Joe and thumped his back. "I'm so glad it worked!"

"What worked?"

"The secret code word! Oh, you know what? We must've switched toothbrushes by mistake," he said, one hand on Joe's shoulder. He added contritely, "I'm sorry, but I used it to brush my eyebrows."

"It don't matter. I used yours to exfoliate my nuts."

Kenny leaned back to arm's length. "Where'd you learn that word?"

"Never mind. Look. I'm going home. I'm sick and tired. We ain't got a dime. I'm starving to death. Do you understand?"

"No, listen! We'll get money. We'll go to the welfare office like Billy said and apply for food stamps. And anyway," he said, pointing over the horizon, "Mexico is right over there!"

"Right over there."

"About two hundred miles to go. We've come fifteen hundred miles by my reckoning. I checked my atlas. We're almost halfway to the Hill of Tepeyac. Let's go find a shelter and get some decent food and get cleaned up and have a good night's sleep. Tomorrow we'll apply for stamps. C'mon! We got this far. We can't go back now. Mexico, Joe! We're almost there! Have you been drinking?"

That evening in the mission, they ate bowls of beans and rice, drank half-pint cartons of milk, and washed their socks and underwear as best they could in the sink. On the street at dawn, Kenny opened the atlas and spread it flat against the back of a mailbox. Against his wishes, Joe was curious; he followed Kenny's finger.

"Here we are," Kenny said.

"Where's Mexico?"

"Here."

"And where's the cave?"

"We're going to cross the border right here, at this town called Santa Teresa. Teresa's name is a good omen. She'll help us, especially if we go through her checkpoint, because she's a close friend of Mary's. Then we take a bus to this town in Chihuahua, called Medio Camino, which makes sense because it's about halfway along the journey of our life, like Dante said. *Halfway along the journey of our life, I entered a dark wood because the straight road had been lost—*"

"Try to focus."

"Then we'll hitch onward to Tepeyac. Strangers will help us if we keep south by east—just like the ravens helped Elijah. Mary will meet us there, at Tepeyac Hill. It's a ways yet, but we can do it!"

They applied for food stamps at the welfare office, collected the stamps at the post office two days later, and left town with their packs full of bread and peanut butter, apples and raisins. For two days they walked south through the desert, along unpaved ranch roads, drinking water from stock tanks, until they came to a rail line.

For two nights they rode work trains—comfortably in the engine compartments or crouched and freezing on the coupling apparatus. The sky islands of mountain chains heaved into view, then sank below the horizon again. At times, they were baffled to find the train headed north or east. One morning they came to a city.

A drunk man called from an open door offering beer. Kenny said no and Joe said yes, and they spent the day in the man's crowded house drinking at a party. No one asked them any questions. The man fed them hamburgers and gin and they passed out on the floor. Late in the night, Joe awoke to a quiet house. The old red-faced man was kneeling beside him, his arm inside the sleeping bag, reaching into Joe's pants. He stood and kicked Kenny and grabbed his bag. As they hurried away, the old man, dressed only in underwear, cursed them from the darkened porch.

A billboard lit bright by floodlights stood in the middle of an empty lot, and thick, high grass grew around the pylons. They tamped the grass down and spread their sleeping bags, screened from the view of passing vehicles. Joe wrapped himself in the familiar sour smell of the cloth. He spat the bitter taste of cheap gin, and his head spun.

"What happened?" Kenny asked.

"I had a dream."

"Yeah?"

"Yeah. I had a dream that old man was feeling me up."

"That's interesting," Kenny said. "I think I had the same dream."

"That's great, Kenny. Well, you've been waiting for a sign from Mary. How's that for a sign? Some old pervert elbow-deep in your drawers. You want any more signs? There's probably no end to signs in the world, Kenny, and not all of them are from the great beyond. Me? I'm sick to death of signs." He felt the crawl of tiny bugs and sat up. The sky was turning red. "I'm going home."

Kenny sat with his back against the post. "We're almost there," he said, in the uninflected tone of a dream.

"We're not almost there. I'm going home. We haven't got a pot to piss in. I'm dying of exposure. Don't look like you're gonna cry. Going hungry and getting the shit kicked out of us and going to jail and freezing to death: that's one thing. But when some geezer tries to handle me, I'm done. I'm going home, and you're going with me. We'll go to your dumbass college if you want or we'll start a painting business," he said, "or we'll find some work and save up for some proper gear and bus money. Anything but this godforsaken walking to Mexico. You aren't prepared. You don't know how to do anything! You're going back with me and you're gonna start acting normal like a normal idiot acts. You're gonna live under a roof, and you're gonna get a regular job—"

"I can't do it alone."

"You're not listening. You're gonna save your money and buy a car. You're gonna read newspapers and wear a goddamn watch so you don't need to read the shadows like a common idiot."

"She told me things. I was given—"

"That's the other thing. You're gonna stop looking for Jesus and Mary and you're gonna stop caring about this bullshit world that don't give a damn about you and sure as hell don't want to be saved by you. Then, once you've done all those things, you're gonna wash your greasy hair and put your pants in a washing machine and buy underwear. New underwear. From a store. Look, your mom would kill me if I went home without you, so you're going back. You don't even have a decent shirt. You can't go prancing into some strange foreign country without a nice shirt on!"

He cinched his pack and walked off, and Kenny followed.

Seven

He sat on the stoop with his elbows on his knees, hands out, palms to the sky. The first cool traces of evening fell feather-lightly over his wrists.

Across the street, kids ran shirtless in the grass. On the shallow slope of the yard, from the front porch to the sidewalk, the kids had unrolled a length of black plastic and watered it with a garden hose. Now, they slid down the plastic to the sidewalk, one after another, hollering and laughing.

The boys' father, dressed in a blue work shirt with the sleeves rolled to the elbows, strolled out from the side of the house. He stood in the shadow, unnoticed, observing. "Damien!" he yelled at last, startling all of his sons. "How do you got that plastic secured down?"

It seemed unlikely, judging by the man's tone, that Damien would come up with a satisfactory answer. It was the same tone the man used on Saturday afternoons in his driveway, when he and his sons huddled under the hood of a Toyota Corolla. The vehicle had not moved since the day a wrecker had towed it there, months before. On a recent Saturday, Joe had listened as the man tormented his sons with the finer points of enginery. "What's a car need to run, huh?" he demanded. "Huh? Air Fire Fuel. Now, how's it gonna get fuel if that valve's in backwards? Come again? How's it gonna get fuel?"

Joe had tuned in for hours. The man was plainly skilled at both parenting and engine repair. You might learn something valuable from a guy like that.

"You better back that bolt up if you're gonna turn that nut," the man had said. "You know why? Cause you're gonna bust that line if you don't. That line's not fastened to anything, see? If you bust that line, I'm gonna bust your behind."

As the day's heat subsided and the darkness gathered, he felt sorry for the boy who stood in bare feet, silently lamenting the fresh cool water running down the black plastic like spring water over slickrock.

"I'm talking to you, Damien," the man said. "How do you got that plastic secured down?"

The boy's brothers continued to slide, though without joy. "Pieces of branches," Damien said.

"That's just what I thought I saw. Now let me get this straight: you got jagged pieces of wood sticking out of the ground and you're sliding half-naked over them. Is that what you're saying?"

He paced along the top of the slope, holding forth like a sergeant drilling numbskulled recruits. "So what's gonna happen is, one of you is gonna rip your asses open and I'm gonna sit all night in some damn hospital. I was just sitting over there, having a nice telephone conversation with my good friend Tommy Owens, then I start thinking to myself: I bet somebody's got their head up their ass out there. And sure enough, look at this. This is dangerous, am I right? Am I right? Now get your thumbs outter your orifices and get a hammer and hammer those sticks down flush to the ground. Lucas! Where's Lucas?"

"He's on the phone, Dad."

"Tell him to get off the phone and get out here. It's family time now."

The city at night commenced its music, a calliope of broken keys.

The door opened and Katherine stepped out in bare feet, clutching a book. She sat beside him.

"Hey, girlie. Your mom need any help up there?"

"No I'm helping her; we're making Indian food. She said you'll be real happy when you see all the pots and pans you have to clean." She bounced her knee as she observed the raucous boys across the street.

"Indian food, huh? What do Indians eat?"

"Chickpeas and a bunch of stuff! Missus Patel gave me a recipe and some vegetables and spices, and I gave them to mom, and we made it together. So fun! It's going to be—" she leaned back and grinned ecstatically at the sky, "—deeelicious!"

"You like living on the same street with Missus Patel, don't you?"

"Yeah, today she invited me for tea, and we ate cookies, and she told me about school coming up and what we're gonna do. She's teaching science and social studies. She gave me a book to read about Galileo because we're gonna be learning him in school. She said that the class isn't gonna have to read the whole thing but she gave it to me because she said I was ready for it and I would like it. She's letting me read ahead in science too, but I have to keep it a secret."

Her knees stopped bouncing and a shadow crossed her face, for she had given away too much information—and all unbidden too. She watched him, wide-eyed through her glasses.

"I don't know," he said, and did not laugh. "I think I better tell someone."

"No!"

"I'm just joking. Would I ever rat you out?"

"No," she said uncertainly, then forgot about it. She opened the book and read in the porch light. Moths of many kinds circled the bare bulb, and their outsize shadows flitted like phantoms in the grass.

"Joe. What does po-ster-i-ty mean?"

"Posterity. Hmm. Let me think. It means—maybe, let's see—what's left after you're gone. It means, the people who come after you—after you're gone. I think. That's a tough word, girl. What's that book called again?"

She held the cover of the book to him. "Starry Messenger," she said. "It's about Galileo and the sun. Missus Patel said Galileo said the Earth went around the sun but that was not what the people in charge believed, so he got in trouble for writing about it. She said he knew he was right because he studied math and watched the stars for years."

"Hmm. That's really interesting. You know, someone told me that there was an ancient mathematician from Greece who figured out the same thing, two thousand years before Galileo did. But that idea was lost. For a long time, anyway. For centuries and centuries. Then people remembered. Like Galileo, I guess."

The sky was low and washed-out, scrubbed starless by city lights and lingering smog and the day's heat.

"How did they … How do you … What did they look for?"

"I'm not sure, but I think Galileo probably just observed the movements of the stars for a long time." He felt unaccountably guilty. "You know, when winter comes, we'll be able to see a lot more stars. I bet we'll be able to find the North Star. We'll know that one when we see it. If it's north and it's big, like I think it is, we'll find it. And the Big Dipper. We'll find that too."

She opened the book and examined a picture. "Which way's north?"

"Over there."

"How do you know?"

Give me one fixed point and I will move the earth. Who said that? Kenny told him, but the name had slipped his mind. I'll go to the library, he decided, and look it up. A Greek name. It was shameful to not know the names of people who said such important things.

"You know what?" Joe said. "I got an idea. I have a compass upstairs. You want it? It'll tell you all the directions."

"You have a compass?"

From a shelf in the bedroom closet, he retrieved a shoebox. As he picked through the contents, Katherine stood on her toes to peer inside.

"What's that?" she asked.

"Dog tags."

"Dog tags? What's dog tags?"

"Tags dogs wear."

"Don't be silly." She picked the tags out and read. "Riley. Joseph P. Roman Cath. A Pos. What's 'A Pos'?"

"That's my species."

She took a picture from the box. "What's that? Is that you?"

"Yep."

"Who's this person and what in god's name is he wearing? He looks like a giant bug!"

"Don't swear. He's wearing a gas mask."

"Why?"

"He's just being silly."

"Who is he?"

"That's my friend Kenny."

"You have a friend? Where is he?"

"I don't know."

"I didn't know you had a friend, Joe. Why don't you ever bring him here?"

"I haven't seen him in some years."

"That's not what I asked. Can I tell mom you have a friend? Mom and I both think you should have a friend to do stuff with instead of hanging around us all the time. We think you need a guy friend to do guy stuff with sometimes."

"You're probably right." He took out the compass and handed it to her. "Let's go help your mom. After we eat, I'll show you how to use it."

She ran yelling down the hall. "Mom! Joe said he has a friend!"

That night, he lay in bed and opened Katherine's Galileo book.

Vera leafed through an issue of *National Geographic*. "I want to go to Florida and see the manatees," she said. "Wouldn't it be cool to go diving and see them in the water? They have such interesting faces," she said. "They're so smart too. Look." She showed him a picture.

"We should hurry. They're endangered."

"Must not be that smart."

"They are, though. This says they've been known to guide shipwrecked boaters to shore, like dolphins do."

"If they're that smart they oughta be eradicated."

"I hate when you talk like that. What's the matter with you?"

"Nothing."

"Alright," she said, and turned her lamp off. "Night."

"Night." He opened Katherine's book to the preface.

MOST SERENE
COSIMO II DE' MEDICI
FOURTH GRAND DUKE OF TUSCANY

A most excellent and kind service has been performed by those who defend from envy the great deeds of excellent men and have taken it upon themselves to preserve from oblivion and ruin names deserving of immortality. Because of this, images sculpted in marble or cast in bronze are passed down for the memory of posterity; because of this, statues, pedestrian as well as equestrian, are erected; because of this, too, the cost of columns and pyramids, as the poet says, rises to the stars; and because of this, finally, cities are built distinguished by the names of those who grateful posterity thought should be commended to eternity. For such is the condition of the human mind that unless continuously struck by images of things rushing into it from the outside, all memories easily escape from it.

Jesus, Missus Patel, he thought as he turned the page. She's only eleven.

Eight

"I bet this is Phoenix," Joe said as they walked. "I saw a sign that said Phoenix on it. Let's head to the bus station. There might be a Traveler's Aid there."

They stopped to rest on a bus bench. Across the street, a young woman with long, loose hair stood on the sidewalk and screamed at the lunch-hour traffic. Well-dressed people hurried past, hugging the shop fronts to keep their distance. Ignored, trembling, she formed a singular point of fury in the flow of pedestrians, like a boulder in a stream. A baby—wrapped in a blanket strapped to the woman's back, asleep with its cheek against her shoulder—shook as the woman stamped and cursed. People passed wordlessly, quickly, and tried not to see.

"Let's go," Joe said, but Kenny remained seated for a time and kept watch over the woman.

Inside the crowded station, young soldiers in Class A uniforms sat on duffel bags. Small children gazed from their mothers' laps as from distant worlds. Transients dozed beside their dirty packs. A toddler, half-hidden behind a heap of baggage, sat between her sun-burnished mother and father and tracked every movement in the place.

As he followed his friend past a mirrored column, Joe saw an image of Kenny walking two steps ahead of a man whose clothes and face were black as a roughneck's. The sudden proximity of the stranger startled him, but when he turned to look, he did not see any oil-stained man. He returned to the mirror and there encountered the grimy figure once again and found himself looking into his own eyes. A smooth mix of dirt and oil covered his face and neck. The reflection, as he watched, reached up and touched its cheek with two blackened fingers. A boil flared beneath his matted beard, and the touch of a fingertip started a needling pain. His eyes were bloodshot, livid in the blurred glass.

Across the terminal, Kenny sat disconsolately on a bench, considering his boots.

"Why didn't you tell me I was so goddamn dirty?" Joe said. "No wonder everyone's staring."

Kenny's face was fairly clean, his beard smooth. "I thought you intended to look like that."

"Why would I do that? Why?"

"The cold, man!" he said. "Inuits smear bear fat on their skin in winter, don't they? I thought you were trying to be smart like them. Guess not."

"I look like a maniac," he said, rubbing his neck. "Alright. Listen. There's a Traveler's Aid office over there. I'm going to call my cousin and tell her to pretend to be somebody who's going to give us a job when we get back, then we'll go in and tell them we want tickets because we got employment back in Ohio. Then maybe they'll give us tickets. That's the plan, alright?"

"Sure it is."

"Just play along for god's sake."

They filled out the forms and waited. In the station bathroom, Joe turned the tap, changed his mind, walked among the benches, and politely hit up old people for money. A frightened woman gave him three dollars. After a few hours' wait, a voice announced their names over the intercom, and they were issued two tickets to Ohio.

On a bench outside the station, Joe double-checked the times and dates, tapped the tickets into his breast pocket, and settled back with a good-natured curse. "Two seats on a real live diesel-powered bus, boy. We're traveling in high style now."

"You lied to that woman in the Travelers' Aid office. Every word that came out of your mouth was a lie."

"She's used to it."

The bus was not scheduled to leave for three hours. Joe bought donuts and a carton of chocolate milk with the cash he'd bummed and set them on the bench. He opened the lid for his friend, pushed the food toward him, but Kenny didn't eat. Though the sun was bright and warm, Joe could see from a corner of the sky a green curtain of cloud sweeping toward the city. But the threat of rain didn't over worry him. Rain schmain, he thought. We got tickets.

A man wearing duct-taped shoes like primitive moonboots stopped in front of the bench. "You know why they call it Tucson?" the man demanded.

"I don't know," said Kenny.

"Look." The man pointed up and squinted. "Two suns."

The man walked off. Kenny said, "That can't be good."

Joe looked around for a sign. "Why's that sociopath talking about Tucson?"

"Maybe the city's name is on the tickets," Kenny said.

Joe examined one. "I'll be damned. We're not in Phoenix. We're in Tucson." He slipped the ticket into his pocket. "Might be Peking for all I care."

Rain began to fall. He nodded at a low, littered strip mall across the street. "Maybe we can hang out in one of those shops," Joe said. "Eh, maybe not. You look too suspicious."

Kenny's silence did not dampen Joe's good spirits. They would soon be home. Within a month he would have a job and an apartment. He could sleep in someone's basement till then.

"Look there," he said. "Armed Forces Recruiting Center. Let's go in and bullshit them a while. We can act interested until the weather passes."

Kenny frowned at the place through the rain.

*

They stood inside the door of a spare, orderly room, and shared a moment of silence with two men seated behind two desks. The men wore light green dress shirts with rows of ribbons above the breast pockets. On the desks were computer monitors and pencils and staplers.

"Afternoon, guys." The soldiers stood and shook their hands. "Pretty wet out, huh? Have a seat. I'm Sergeant MacKinnon and this is Sergeant Mendez. What can we do for you?" He gestured to the two padded office chairs in front of the desks. Joe set his pack aside and took a seat.

"Been traveling?"

"Yes," Joe said. "Visiting some friends."

"Great. And you came by to see what we have to offer."

"Yes."

Green rainlight filled the office. The ceiling lights and computers were off, and only the red light from a coffee maker by the wall betrayed a live current. Above the coffee maker was a poster depicting men in camouflage sitting raptly at desks in a classroom, one with a raised arm. On another poster, a soldier rappelled down a rock face.

"Well, I tell you what. Kenny, is it? Kenny, why don't you sit here with Sergeant Mendez and let him show you some information. Joe, come on back here into my office and see if anything we got interests you." He walked talking. "Be sure to break in with any questions you have. What do you know about the Army?"

"Not a whole lot," Joe said. They sat down on either side of a desk in a cubicle of low partitions. "Just movies and such." He could see but not hear Sergeant Mendez speaking in the other office. He watched his friend accept a proffered brochure and felt relief.

"Well, it isn't like the movies," MacKinnon said. "You won't spend the whole time in the mud marching up and down hills. You won't do any of that if you don't want to. There's over a hundred and fifty specialties to choose from. Soldiers get out after two, three, four years with a bundle of cash and the experience and self-discipline that's gonna make the rest of your life gravy. A lot of guys opt for the college money. Interested in college?"

"College."

"Never mind. Like I said, the Army has a specialty to match anyone's interests. The Army's getting more high-tech every day, just like the rest of the world, and the skills you acquire are immediately translatable to the civilian workforce. You'll have an edge on people when you get out. Employers like vets. There's a recession on. The way the economy is, you need every advantage you can get. Know anything about computers?" he asked, rooting through a desk drawer.

"There was one in school."

"Me neither. Let me just say this." He leaned forward and rested his elbows on the desk. "Enlistment bonuses are higher than ever because, frankly, we're trying to get quality people into the service. A two-year commitment is worth nine thousand dollars. Cash, in your hand, the minute you finish boot. Hell, I seen guys walk around San Francisco with a suitcase full of cash, having themselves a good old time, know what I mean? Three years is fifteen. Here." He slid a bubble-sheet across the desk, along with a questionnaire and a pencil. "I'll leave you alone and you can fill this out. It's an aptitude test. Then maybe we can find out what you're geared for. You seem to be in good condition. You could write your own ticket. Let me say this: if you decide to join and your buddy backs out, fine. But if you both want to, we'll get you in together. Cohort, they call it. Same unit, same duty station."

Joe glanced across the floor, where a helpless and unwashed youngster was being subjected to the lash of a worldly man's advice.

"That is," MacKinnon said, "if you want to."

Kenny and Joe sat together while the recruiters graded their tests in a separate room.

"What do you think?"

Kenny swiveled in his chair to look out the window. "It's still raining."

"No. I mean, about the Army."

"What about it."

"Joining."

"You're lying."

"Did that guy tell you about the money? There's your Mary money, dummy! You can buy a plane ticket and fly nonstop, direct to Mexico, instead of walking there like a damn fool. You can hire a cab to drop your dumb ass at the foot of her cave. Two years and out, nine thousand bucks. Maybe a translatable skill. This is free training. Think about it. Did you know there's a recession on? I bet you didn't! The way the economy is—"

"Mary doesn't live in a cave. She told me—she asked me—"

"I know what she asked, and now these sonsabitches are gonna fund it! If this isn't a sign then I don't know what is. Mary's probably looking down right now, nodding her old giant head in approval. The best part is, we can join together. Don't make that face. You can get thousands for college too. Think about it! Didn't you say you wanted to go to school—"

"Yeah I—"

"—and you wanted to learn Russian. Good. Then you learn Russian or philanthropy or whatever you want. Then you can go to Mexico like a professional person, instead of arriving like a hobo with a bag of dirty underwear and sandwiches. Me? I'm gonna buy a nice truck with a roof rack and some twenty-foot ladders and start a painting business. Heck, maybe I'll make a bunch of cash and go with you!"

Wired on nicotine and hunger, Joe relished his sudden certainty that there was, after all, a purpose and a plan to his life. He felt as though he stood on the threshold of significant and noble undertakings.

"Mary ain't going anywhere," he continued. "Here's your opportunity to get a college degree in something smart. Then you can lead an expedition of idealistic young people down there to examine her droppings or whatever it is educated people do. Tell you what," he said. "I'm doing it. Look, I came out here on your little thing, now you do this with me. Your mom won't care. She'll get used to it."

"She'll kill me."

"So what? You're a big boy now."

The recruiters returned bearing the bubble-sheets. "We got good news," Mendez said. "We just found out that you guys both qualify for an extra fifteen hundred if you go eleven bravo—that's infantry—but that doesn't mean you can't consider some of the other fields. These results—the results are good," he hastened, "but they may limit you a little."

When they were all seated again, he asked, "What do you guys think? You want some time to think it over?"

"What do we need to do to be cohorts?"

Mendez opened a desk drawer and pulled out forms. "Cohort's easiest if you're infantry. What do you guys think of the bonus? Does it interest you at all?"

Joe swiveled in his chair toward his friend.

"The big pitch," Kenny said, searching the paper for a saving clause. "The hot seat. This is scary. What if there's a war? I had a dream once I—"

"If you want more time, that's alright." MacKinnon retracted the ballpoint with his thumb, and Joe said, "I'll sign." He glanced over the paper, satisfied himself that it bore four-figure numbers next to dollar signs, and signed his name at the bottom.

Kenny sought once more for a hint of clemency in the faces around him but found none. "Which one is for college money?"

Mendez laughed. Everyone shook hands. When they stepped outside, Joe looked at the signature on the form. The euphoria of embarking on grand and profitable adventures drained away.

Kenny held the paper with the fingers of both hands, not reading but measuring the thing with his eyes, as though it were an object whose origin and disposition remained to be classified.

Joe wanted to be encouraging, but he had lost all conviction.

They folded the papers and walked down the street toward the bus station.

*

"How much money we got?" Kenny asked.

"I don't know. Three bucks. Why?"

"Give it to me." He walked toward the woman on the sidewalk, who had not stopped screaming. By now her voice was timbre-less, a whispered shout.

The baby strapped to her back was awake and watched Kenny as he crossed the street. Its attention suggested something to the woman, who quieted and turned to face him.

The young man spoke a few words as he handed her the bills. When she opened her arms, he stepped into her embrace and rested his head on her shoulder. As she spoke to him, calmly and at length, he closed his eyes and listened.

The child, laughing now, grasped a tuft of the young man's hair in its fist, and the man smiled and drew the shawl gently over the infant's head. It was still raining.

Nine

"You're up, Riley." A hand shook him awake.

Inside the tent, the Kodiak stove rumbled, mingling its warmth with the sour smell of bodies. He put on a balaclava, helmet, and gloves, picked up the rifle and stepped out into the loathsome cold. Bare trees, black against the silver snow, crowded the path to the listening post. From a black hole in the snow came a voice. "Password."

"Fuck off," he said, and climbed down.

"Oh, hi, Joe," Kenny said.

An hour passed. Neither spoke. Joe crouched against the wall of the rifle pit and peered into the dark. Moon-pale shades, sidling among the trees, marked the soldiers' presence.

"I heard a stick pop."

"It's the woods. Sticks pop," Kenny said. "Or maybe you heard a ghost."

"Don't do that shit to me."

"What's the matter, Joe? Did you have a bad dream?"

"Yeah. I dreamed I was in the snow in the army in the woods."

"Yeah? Oh."

The moon, a spider's egg in a web of black branches.

"You know, one night, after my dad died, he visited me," Kenny said. The darkness and the hour conferred a strangeness on his voice, at once near and far away. "I woke up one night and he was sitting in a chair by the side of my bed. But I didn't feel scared. I knew he was just there to check on me. To see if I was alright. So I told him I was."

"Now I feel ill," Joe said. "If your dad walked out of those woods right now, I'd put fifteen rounds in his face. Hate to say it."

"There's no need to fear ghosts," Kenny said, from the safe distance of a dream—the dream where the missing dwelt without bitterness on the other side of life, where they worried even still about the ones they left behind and came to visit us sometimes. "The dead never hurt anybody," he said. "It's the other ones you have to worry about."

The moon-pale shadows intrigued beneath the branches.

"She hasn't visited me in so long. Every day I repeat to myself the things I learned when Mary spoke to me that night, but my memory is starting to fray a little. The last time, she said that everything—every rock and leaf and bird—is sustained in a shared knowledge of love, and when this knowledge dies, the world will vanish in an instant. Forgetting—forgetting is truly the only death. Now I understand that evil is nothing more than forgetting. Evil is everything that dims and obscures and wears away that gift for remembering."

"Evil is not forgetting. Evil is time itself. Time is what takes everything away," Joe said. Then he felt his friend's hand on his shoulder, and Kenny's face appeared before his own, and his friend's eyes, beneath the brim of the helmet, were bright with tears.

"You have been listening. Now I know. Thank you," Kenny said. "So you think I'm not crazy?"

"Don't be silly. You're a menace."

"I want you to promise me something. When this is over, you'll go with me to find Mary. We're going to cross the mountains of Mexico on foot to get there, and we're going see visions and dream dreams, just like the young men of yore."

"I wouldn't miss it for the world. Meantime, we got this thing," Joe said. "We can still bail on it. You want to take off with me? I've been thinking. We can slip out of here and go to Mexico City and get jobs working on bridges. We can save up and drink in the bars after work and have visions all day long. I think they call them cantinas. I've been looking into it."

"You should've thought of that long before. It's too late now. We can't let everybody down. What would Spanky do without me? He thinks everyone wants to kill him as it is. It's tempting; it's tempting. But if we run away, someone else will have to go in our place. See, I've already thought of all that too. I even went to the chapel. Father Flores said we're going to Somalia to help people. Anyway, it's going to be interesting."

"Interesting? This ain't a goddamn field trip, Kenny. It's all about protecting the goddamn oil tanker lanes out of the Red Sea. I read about it in a magazine. Think about it. You want a recipe for trouble? How's this for a recipe: take five thousand dumbass Americans and give them rifles and drop them in a country in Africa that's run by warlords. Hear me? Warlords. What is this, medieval France? Maybe we should have pikes and swords instead of M16s."

Kenny laughed. "We could say things again like 'Well met, cousin!' and 'By God's blood!' And we could salute each other with Sieg Heils like the Romans did before the Nazis ruined it. We could wear things like greaves and beavers and bucklers again."

"What's a beaver?"

"A helmet visor. It's all in Shakespeare. You didn't pay attention. Don't you remember Henry the Fifth in Miss Martini's class? You don't remember the Saint Crispin's Day speech? *Old men forget, but he'll remember...what feats he did that day.*"

"I was sick that day."

"We spent a month on it."

The trees became trees again, and the moon the moon once more. The cold clenched his fingers and toes. "We'll call each other by our Christian names. I'll be Joe the Bold."

"I'll be Kenny the—Kenny the—"

"You'll be Kenny the Just a Little Different, That's All."

From the direction of the tents came the footsteps of their relief. "Ah, man. Why do you put up with me? All I do is give you grief."

"Because we're going to do this thing and we're going to get out and take the money and go to Mexico, where Mary will give understanding to our hearts," Kenny said. "And we're going to wander the earth sharing the good news that she shares with us. That's why. You're my best friend, and we signed up cohort. That's why too. We happy few, we band of brothers!"

"It was a rhetorical question."

"Rhetorical question. What is that? Funny. I've never understood what that meant."

Somalia

He woke in a sweat, on a cot, in a warm hangar.

Forest-green-painted Bluebird buses had taken the battalion over snowy roads from the barracks to the airfield. He wondered how many days were to pass before they disembarked on that same airstrip to board those same buses for the return trip back to the barracks, retracing the same country roads.

Who could doubt that the same buses would be waiting beside the runway, engines running until the battalion returned? The buses' headlights would remain on day and night, and the drivers would stand together through the long turns of the seasons, through sun and rain and snow, smoking as they waited, as winter changed to spring and spring to summer. Their hair and beards would grow longer; their navy-blue company shirts would fade to shades of robin's egg in the weather.

Field mice and squirrels would make homes in the corners of the engine compartments, there to raise litters of young, which would grow plump and restless in those nests, then depart some morning for the forest, never to return. One day, a thrush would land on a driver's shoulder, then fly away again, and that man would light one cigarette with another, and watch it go. Then the bird would return with a sprig in its beak, land on the driver's cap, and begin to build a nest.

Kevin Honold

*

The soldiers around him began to stir; they sat on the edges of cots with their feet on the floor, rooting through packs for shaving gear or something to eat. A few remained facedown in their sleeping bags. A white bedsheet tacked to a far wall, painted with ragged red letters reading *The Do Drop Inn*.

At the shouts of platoon leaders, the soldiers put on helmets, shouldered rifles, filed out, and fell into ranks. Here and there stood disused buildings pieced from sheet metal that had been varnished to maroon by the sun. The wheezy rattle of idling engines filled the diesel-laced air.

The First Sergeant ordered the soldiers to gather around. "Alright, guys, here we are. We need to get our minds on our business now. All that shit you left at home will take care of itself. You can't worry about it now. So listen up. Clean your weapons and keep them that way. Drink water! Drink it till you can't drink another mouthful, then drink more. You'll drink five liters a day and I want the squad leaders counting. This heat is serious shit. Don't fuck with it."

He stepped forward and looked deeper into the crowd. "I don't know how long we're going to be here. Some of you will be moving out; some of you will remain here at the airport. Those of you who're moving out will work to get the ord'nance off the streets. This is the real thing now. This is what we trained to do. Relief columns are moving again because of this operation. Starvation out in the countryside is leveling off. Now put everything I just said out of your minds. You're here to do a job. Be aware of your situations, and be focused on the task you're given—two things at once, like picking your nose and walking, right, Ruiz? I watch you do that every goddamn day. As for yourselves, assume you'll be here for a year. If it turns out to be six months, then you'll come back six months in the black. Like hedging a bet, but mental, you follow? Never mind, I lost you at the math part. That's it, boys. Platoon sergeants, take charge of your platoons."

*

In the hangar, Kenny lay in the cot with a book titled *West African Mythologies*.

"We're in East Africa, bozo," Joe said and broke his rifle down. He spread the bolt's components on a rag and cleaned and oiled each part with care. He reckoned with time zones and date lines, but time and distance did not tally.

Thomason sat cross-legged on his sleeping bag in the next row of cots. He said, "Stegemuller, do you have any other books?"

"Sure." Kenny reached into his pack. "I got Ibn Battuta's *Travels*. I got a book about Cabot's lost voyage. That's it."

"Have you ever read anything about Paul, the disciple? I know you like travel books and Paul was a serious traveler. He visited Spain and Italy and North Africa—"

"Chrissake, Thomason," Joe said. "What, you think because he reads all this weird shit he'll fall for anything, right? Why don't you give the God garbage a break. All your Jesus crap makes my ass hurt."

Thomason kept his eyes on Kenny. "A bunch of us are getting together later," he continued, politely as before, "to pray for these people and to ask God that we all get home safe. Seven o'clock, right over there." He pointed to a far corner.

"Sure, Tom. That sounds nice. I'll be there."

"I'm going to take a walk. You want to come?" Joe said. "Take a look around?"

Kenny didn't answer.

"Don't be mad. I don't trust that crowd. He's trying to sell you something that benefits him more than you. I'm just looking out for your helpless ass."

Kenny sighed, and dogeared the page.

"We're not supposed to leave this area," Kenny said as they exited the hangar.

"We're not. We could walk for a week and still be in Africa." Joe took his helmet off and hung it from the canteen on his belt. They walked among the nondescript warehouses, past open bay doors that revealed emptiness and trash. They searched for a vantage point that offered some view of the place they were in and came to a tall and narrow concrete structure that may have been a flight control tower, but there were no signs to indicate its purpose, and no people. The pitted concrete walls rose to high windows that were situated beneath the eaves of a pointed, corrugated roof, like an abandoned belltower or a neglected minaret.

A flying staircase spiraled in hard angles up to the lookout deck, and they reached the top in a sweat. The metal roof was hot to the touch, the trapped heat difficult to breathe. Air moved in brief fits through the empty window casements, which opened on a view of a white cityscape scribbled with antennae and peppered with black windows, the whole of it embellished with flourishes of slumped electric lines.

Colors resolved gradually into focus: a small red car; a blue cloth that may have been a flag; the garish advertisement of a cola company. The elemental clamor of the city, from a distance, hardly registered. Some miles away, a column of black smoke stood at an oblique angle to the horizon.

"How strange," Kenny said.

Without a word they turned to the opposite window. There was the blue sea, and the blue sky, and many shades of blue between. Four tankers idled at the horizon.

"The Indian Ocean," Kenny said. "How many idiots like us get to see the Indian Ocean?" Kenny leaned on the sill, scanning the horizon from end to end, over and over. Turning somber, he said. "You know, the old sailors believed that sunken ships left traces where they sank. A dark spot remained on the surface, and that dark spot cast a reflection that left a stain on the sky. So, as they sailed along, the sailors could read the stains on the sky, and avoid each place where a ship went down."

Joe looked to the very center of the horizon's arc, where the sea and the sky were furthest and darkest. It was a different ocean than the one at Atlantic City, the one he'd visited as a boy with Kenny and his mom.

"The dark spots," Kenny continued, "signified dangers to steer clear of. If you couldn't read the signs, you'd sail into a whirlpool."

This was not a sea of mellow breakers and beach umbrellas, Joe thought. Neither red plastic buckets nor sailboats.

"Some believed those spots generated weather," Kenny said.

This was the Indian Ocean, and out there beyond the rusty tankers were the dark spots that bred typhoons.

Kenny pulled a pocket atlas from his trouser pocket and flipped to the Map of the World. He held it in front of them so Joe could see the blue and red and yellow patchwork of nations. He touched his finger to Somalia. "Here we are." He drew a finger lightly, a few inches east-north-east. "Here's the Himalaya. The world is big, Joe. But there's a point at which far becomes near."

The map was political and betrayed no topography, only the flat pastels of Nepal, India, Pakistan, Egypt, Ethiopia. Joe, however, could discern the presence of mountains at those places Kenny indicated, where the boundary lines buckled and veered wildly. Kenny traced the difference with his fingertip, back and forth, Africa's horn to the Himalaya. "Look, Joe," he said. "It's not so far to Kathmandu."

The ripple of waves breaking along the shore were the tremors of the sea's sunken machines.

"This is going to suck," Kenny said.

As those words echoed in his mind, Joe was seized with a convulsion of laughter that caused him to slump over the sill. He slid wheezing down the wall until he lay on his side, and his cleaned rifle scraped against the concrete. Kenny watched, perplexed, then he too began to laugh, and they both sat, laughing, until Joe felt ill, the laughter an affliction he could only endure. Several minutes passed before he recouped the strength to stand.

Pausing now and again on the way down the steps to lean against the walls, they staggered, wheezing and wiping tears, out into the sunlight.

*

"Where the hell have you two been? You don't ever leave this area without my permission, is that understood? You two need to get your shit straight, or I'm going to come down on you like a house." The sour mix of tobacco and instant coffee on Sergeant Perry's breath filled the space between. "There's been a change of plan. Hawkins' group is going to join Pacheco—"

"No, wait a minute, Jim," Joe said. "You can't split us up—"

"Riley, can it," Sergeant Perry said. "Stegemuller, get your gear and report to Sergeant Magill now."

"We joined cohort, Jim. We—"

"That shit don't matter here. Move it."

"C'mon, Joe," Kenny said as they walked to the hangar. "Don't worry about it. Don't make a stink. You know Perry's just doing what he's told to do."

"That wasn't the deal. That's not what we signed up for. We got signed papers. I gotta go talk to somebody."

"Forget about it, will you? Forget it."

It had not entered Joe's mind that he would be split from his friend. Now that moment had arrived unexpectedly and had afforded him no time to prepare. He found the First Sergeant alone in a tent, asked permission to bring up a personal issue. The man nodded impatiently as if he already knew every word that was going to be spoken; nevertheless, he permitted the young man to state his business.

"Riley," he said, "I don't give a damn about your personal problems. Get your shit in order cause it's gonna be sun-up to sun-down on this perimeter, picks and shovels, ass-deep in a hole, and things gotta happen fast, you hear? There's still ord'nance lying around: Do you understand what I'm saying to you? By the way, Private, you violated chain of command by coming in here. Next time I'll take your money and make you burn shit all day." The man returned his attention to the papers on the table. "I was walking out there today, and there's some bigass snake and spider holes too, and that's neither here nor there, except that I really hate spiders. See, son, we all got our fucking problems."

"Yes, First Sergeant. I'm sorry."

"Beat it."

Outside the hangar in the early evening, he found his friend seated on the ground with two dozen other soldiers. When Joe sat beside him, Kenny looked up from his book. "Guess I'll get to see some of the country."

"Yeah."

Three five-ton trucks arrived in a haze of dust and blue smoke. The soldiers stood and gathered kit.

"Too dark to read now anyway," he grinned. "Here we go!"

"Yep."

In the open beds of the trucks, rows of soldiers sat facing each other on wooden benches. A few talked; most were quiet, their rifle butts planted between their feet. In the failing light, the soldiers sat, each to his thoughts.

Kevin Honold

Kenny shook hands with Joe, shouldered his rifle, and climbed into the bed of the truck where the others were waiting side by side, looking at the floorboards, looking at the sky.

*

He pulled his rotating guard shifts day and night in a sandbagged bunker at the airport's perimeter. There was little to see from the aperture: wiry bushes and sand, nondescript buildings pieced together from sheet metal, the low buildings of the city outskirts. From the bunker that was planted three feet deep in the ground, he watched the heat shimmer at an eye-level expanse of earth and listened to helicopters.

One hundred and thirty-nine days to go. At the end of the month, there would be one hundred twenty-seven days. By Thanksgiving, one hundred and one days. He thought of going home, getting an apartment, living on his accumulated leave pay for a while. He would buy a case of cold beer and draw the blinds and turn the AC on and watch television all day long. Or maybe get a library card and check out a book. *Huckleberry Finn*, that's the one. His only happy memory of school was reading *Huckleberry Finn*. How vividly he saw then, in his mind's eye, the raft drifting down the wide water. He could still see it.

The soldiers settled into restless rounds of reading, playing cards, griping. Bursts of gunfire in the distance, the tremor of a detonation, the flog of helicopter blades. Red clouds of dust and trash periodically rose above the airfield. He thought of his friend, somewhere out there.

Weeks passed in this manner. Months.

*

The tent was stifling and Joe avoided it. He spent his down hours resting in the shade of a broken-down pickup, a white truck with black UN letters stenciled on both doors. A Malaysian APC had towed it in with chains a month earlier, but no one had ever come to claim it or bothered to fix it, and now expired and neglected, it gathered dust by the fence. He often wondered what was wrong with the truck. He popped the hood several times and peered in, but he had no hand for enginery.

One day, seated with his back to the tire, he dozed off. Someone kicked his foot.

"Riley Joseph. Mail," the voice said, and dropped the package in his lap. The box was wrapped in brown grocery bag paper. Inside were wet wipes, chocolate, cigarettes, and a note on a sheet of yellow stationery.

> Dear Joseph,
>
> I hope everything is well with all of you. We are all thinking of you and hoping for your safe return. Summer is here already. The hawthorn trees along the street have blossomed already. It is hard to believe how fast the time is going by. I spoke with Kenny's mother. I think he is fine. His lieutenant is tough on him, she says, but that's good. That's his job and we are grateful. Write and let us know how you are doing. Be tough and do the right thing always. The time will be over before you know it. We pray for you and for all of the poor suffering people and think of you each day.
>
> Mom

He folded the note, slipped it into his tunic pocket, and leaned against the truck tire. The air carried the smells of trash fires and burning plastic, dung and scorched vegetables, and all of these combined into something like a state of mind. Smoke lifted over the roofs, a mile away, and smudged the white sky. He retrieved a notepad and pencil from his gear.

Dear Vera,

I hope you are well. I hope your job is not too much of a pain in the you know what. I can't wait to have a cold beer and hear about all the stuff I have been missing. Thanks for your letter. It's different here I'll tell you all about it. I would tell Kenny you said hi but I don't see him because they sent him somewhere else. If he writes to you please let me know. I think he's ok and there's nothing to worry about but you know him. This is going to end soon. Snakes = the worst part. He'll be ok. I hope you're well and the little ones are doing what they're told.
Write when you get a chance.

Joe

*

"Alright guys, you've heard all the rumors," the First Sergeant said to the assembled soldiers. "Now I'm gonna confirm one of them. We're gonna get our shit together and redeploy back to the world in about eight days. That's the good news. The bad news is that there's gonna be inspectors from the Agriculture Department at the port to make sure we're not shipping any dirt back to the States. Parasites and crops, okay, scientific stuff, nothing you need to worry your tiny brains about. All you gotta know is this: if there is even one speck of Somalian dust on a vehicle, it will not get approved to be loaded onto the ship, and if that vehicle happens to be yours, you'll stay here with it after the rest of us go home. Maybe you can get a job at the Mogadishu McDonald's flipping burgers. Then you can marry a nice local girl and start a big dumb family. Maybe they'll let you shovel shit at their Independence Day parades. Harkin, you'd like that, wouldn't you? Look at him smiling. He loves this shit. Now listen up! This cleanup goes for your persons and your gear as well. Everything has to sparkle like a motherfucker. So, the sooner those vehicles are as clean as the day the factory shit em out, the sooner you get on that plane. Is anyone still confused?"

On the walk back to his tent, Joe came across three soldiers standing beside an oil drum, peering at something on the ground. The black scorpion's pincers and tail were raised like a dog's hackles as it made its mechanical way somewhere, anywhere. Joe tilted the empty drum and rolled it into position over the scorpion and rammed the drum down so that the lip caught the animal across the back. But the scorpion stood up and lifted its pincers and commenced to walk again. He smashed the drum down twice, three times, but the thing lived and writhed. He smashed it again and again until the animal lay crushed in the dust. Like a machine, it didn't splatter. It simply quit working.

"Damn, killer," said one of the soldiers. They walked away. Alone, standing in the presence of the lifeless little creature, he wondered what in God's name had come over him.

*

He retrieved his rifle and cleaning kit and climbed into the cab of his UN truck. This is the end. Maybe today the others would return from the countryside, and he would see his friend again. No doubt, Kenny had learned a lot, just as he had threatened to do. He probably won't stop talking for days. Joe sat in the truck bed and looked forward to listening to his friend's stories. Maybe today they'll return, he thought.

An elderly woman pushed a wooden handcart up to the perimeter wire. She lifted a hand at the soldiers in the sandbagged guard post, who suffered her to approach. In the woman's cart were a few brown bananas, as usual, and some roots that looked like outsize muddy dolls. No one ever bought anything from her, but every day she approached the compound with her few tormented vegetables, and every day the soldiers wondered if this time there might be something different in the cart, something worthwhile—a candy bar, perhaps, or an apple. But there never was any candy bar, and every day she turned away, cheerful and empty-handed.

Joe climbed out of the truck, approached the wire with a greeting. She placed a banana in his hand and raised four fingers; he put the coins in her palm, and she tucked them beneath her shawl, talking the while. The woman's speech was airy, high and uncertain, with a tone of genial exasperation, as if she'd just woken from a good nap.

Joe fancied that he finally understood what it was the woman was saying.

"Yes," he nodded. "You're right about that, ma'am. People are awful."

The woman picked up the cart handles and started down the road, turning her face back twice to recite the same phrase, over and over, which may have been a parting, or a blessing, or something else entirely.

*

Over the course of the next day, the stray units returned from the countryside, and the reunited battalion was once more assembled at the airport. Soldiers in olive undershirts moved among the rows of parked vehicles, or gathered with buckets at the water truck's spigots, chatting like fishwives at the village fountain.

Joe found some members of Kenny's squad, but none of them knew where he was.

Nolan said, "He caught some kind of bug, I think," and pointed to the last of a long row of tents. "He's probably in there sweating it out, whatever it is. Damn, man, people are dying of the plague out there. I don't think he liked that. I'm not saying he has cholera, but he caught something. Might be food poisoning. He made friends with some woman in a village and ate her tamales. I'm not being funny. I used to teach earth science to fifth graders, Riley. Did I ever tell you that?"

Joe turned toward the tent and Nolan called after him. "We've returned to the Dark Ages. That's what he told me. Actually, what he said was, the Dark Ages have returned to us. But what do I know, Riley? I'm just a grade-school teacher."

Joe paused inside the tent as his eyes adjusted. Two rows of cots lined the tent walls. The air was still and close and smelled of sun-scorched canvas, gun oil, bug spray, sweat. A body lay in the farthest cot. Kenny was thin. The sunburn on his face, like a poorly applied cosmetic, hardly concealed a pallor. The sleeping bag was unzipped and he held it clutched tightly around his shoulders like a man freezing. His hair was plastered with sweat to his temples.

Joe squatted beside him. "Hey." He pressed Kenny's shoulder.

Kenny's eyes opened, his throat contracted, but he made no sound. He tried twice to swallow. Joe put his canteen to his friend's mouth. Kenny choked and spoke the way people speak in a high wind.

"Hey, Joe! Did I just see you? I tried to get up. Jesus."

"You're sick, dummy."

"Yeah. A few days now. Everybody's really busy." He closed his eyes and breathed shallowly. "Make sure someone tells me when it's time. When it's time to go back, I mean. Everybody's real busy right now. They might leave me here."

"If only. Let's go see the medics."

The T-shirt and the liner of the sleeping bag were drenched with sweat. An odor of urine bloomed when Joe pulled him to a sitting position, and Kenny retched briny air. Joe helped him to his feet and ducked his head under Kenny's arm.

"Jesus it's bright," Kenny said, out in the sunlight. "People in that town were hungry. They hadn't seen food in a long time, I think. We gave them what we had but—"

"Shh."

He led Kenny through the tent flap of the medic station. Eight soldiers sat waiting on a wooden plank. One cradled his arm. Two had thickly bandaged hands. One sat beside a pair of propped crutches. A few wore nauseated expressions. A medic gingerly turned up the bandage from a soldier's nose and peered at the damage while the rest of the soldiers observed the new arrivals who stood waiting at the entry. Their attentiveness suggested something to the medic. He glanced up at Kenny, then at Joe. "Bring him back," he said.

The man led the way through a partition to a treatment room. An orderly appeared at his call, and the three of them laid Kenny on the exam table, which was a wooden door laid across sawhorses and covered with a plastic sheet.

The medic put a thermometer in Kenny's mouth. "He looks like shit," he said to Joe. "How long has he been like this?"

"I don't know, Sergeant. I just found him. He's not my unit."

"You don't know him? Whose unit is he, Private?"

The man took Kenny's pulse while he read the thermometer. "Christ. Get a bucket of ice from the chow truck, quick," he said to the orderly, "and do not take no for an answer."

"Take his boots off," the medic said to Joe and chided Kenny in a loud voice as he worked the T-shirt over his head. "You got a hundred five fever, soldier. Sampling the local cuisine, huh? I swear I don't know what y'all been crawling around in. Something wicked's making its rounds."

Kenny was in and out. "They must have heard the vehicles, from a long way off," he said, with a startling clarity and precision to his words. "The women already lined the road when we arrived. They held their hands out, the way hungry people do. The kids all hidden away. We gave them what we had but—"

"I understand," said the medic as he hung a saline bag, cut and fitted the tubes, ran the needle into Kenny's arm.

When the orderly returned with the bucket, the medic grabbed two handfuls of ice and pressed them to Kenny's chest. His body stiffened at the shock; his eyes clenched. He didn't breathe for a time, and then in chopped drafts. He spoke without breathing, from high in the throat.

"We were out of water, later on. Then I saw the well. Did you know if you look into a well at noon you can see the stars? And then she was there, standing beside me."

The three of them rubbed his chest and thighs with ice. The medic joked with Kenny, told him how lucky he was in this heat and all, what with the premium on ice. He started a second saline bag. Kenny shuddered.

The medic put the thermometer in. "Guess what, soldier. If your temp doesn't go down this time, you're getting an ice bath. You think this is fun. Just wait. It gets much better." He read the thermometer. "Damn. Hundred and four. You missed your chance, Private."

They rubbed his skin with ice. The orderly hung another saline bag. "Well? What did she say, brother?"

Kenny trembled as he looked at each of the young men standing over him. "It was her."

The orderly leaned over the table. "Of course it was her. Now tell us what she said."

"If I told you what she said, you would leave me here to die."

Ten

He drove the uptown streets. The sky was blank at noon, and no wind arrived to sweep away the heat. He drank water from a plastic bottle and avoided looking at people. His head was numb, insensible as a toenail. Stopped at a red light, he heard a voice—disembodied, raging—carry around the corner of a building. The voice echoed from the blank facades of the buildings.

A woman rounded the corner, then, dressed in a black Pittsburgh Steelers sweatshirt, held her head back as she shouted, and her voice scorched the air like a dragon. A small girl trailed a few yards behind, watching the woman's feet. The light changed; he hit the gas.

He found quiet streets and drove them. Three shirtless teens with buzz-cuts stood in front of a diner, blocking traffic and cursing into the windshields of cars that lurched and braked in their attempts to pass. The teens laughed, threw their fists in the air, took giant steps back and forth.   He drove on.

He stopped to buy a bottle of iced tea at a shop. As he sat in his car drinking the tea, a man approached his window. "What's the news, chief? Hear about that shooting on Miami this morning?" The ammoniac stench of dried urine drifted off the man's coat like a pollen cloud. A thin trace of dried blood ran from behind his ear, down his neck, beneath his collar. "They thought the social worker was a cop and ended up shootin' the retarded kid! It's gettin' bad as Dayton up in here, don't you think?"

Joe drank the tea and scrutinized the birdshit on the hood of his cruiser.

The man said, "I done five years in the pen, and the day I got out they shot me in the head!"

"That's some bad luck."

The man snorted. "Luck, hell! Somebody was waitin' for me, you better believe it. Luck, hell! See that chicken tied to that car antenna? Ha! See that chicken?"

Joe backed out and drove off.

On the sidewalk in front of an apartment complex, a man stood waving his arms. He continued to wave his arms as Joe pulled to a stop along the curb.

"I see you, you stupid prick," he said to the rearview mirror as he shifted into park. The man was mid-sentence as Joe opened the door.

"—agent with the Housing Department I got a woman here who won't vacate—" The man's shirt was unbuttoned at his sweating neck. "—got all her shit in there still. It's in boxes—I can't—you need—not my—"

Joe followed the yammering agent up the staircase. An orange sheet of paper, a city notice, was taped to a closed door. The man threw the door open and let himself in, talking loudly, waving his arms about the place. Beside a window, a thin, elderly woman sat quite still on a metal folding chair. Hands folded, she kept a silent watch over the street below.

Around her feet lay a few boxes packed carefully with dishes, books, ceramic figurines of raccoons.

A lamp, a transistor radio, a globe.

Joe squatted and considered the globe while the man berated the woman for her stubbornness. On the globe, he found Europe, then turned the sphere left and found Pakistan, labeled *E. Pakistan*. On India's left shoulder he found West Pakistan. There's East Germany, Yugoslavia, Burma. It was a dated earth. Kenny would love this, Joe thought.

"Grab a few of these boxes, will you. I got six places to go today." The agent stood over him now. The smeared toes of the man's low quarters violated Joe's field of vision. He suppressed a surge of fury, gave the globe a final turn with his finger, and stood. The man placed a cardboard box in his arms.

He followed the agent down the stairs, out into the heat, across the blasted lawn to where several other cardboard boxes were stacked beside a concrete bus bench.

The bench cast no shadow beneath the yellow sky. Small chunks of concrete lay beneath the corner of the bench, where it had been hit by a car or a city bus.

Joe set the box down, walked back in, picked up another. The woman had not stirred from her vigil.

For the second time, he carried a box out to the curb, and there he paused.

The man's angry complaints followed him to the cruiser.

What are you doing, Joe said to himself as he opened the door and climbed behind the wheel. He turned his radio off and removed his hat. He barely recognized the face in the mirror as his own, with its glazed eyes and the lines trailing down, deeper now from dehydration.

Now, at last, dressed in slippers and a sweater, the woman emerged from the building. As she walked the sidewalk, she did not look to either side but came directly to the bench. She brushed the slats lightly with her fingers and took a seat, ignoring the boxes of her belongings that were stacked about her knees. She reached behind her neck and gathered her long silver hair gently in her slender fingers, drew the hair over her shoulder, laid it against her breast, and smoothed the hair into place. Satisfied, the hand alighted in her lap and quieted there with the other.

The agent walked down the street to a gray sedan. The car rocked on its struts as he threw himself into the driver's seat.

Joe put the cruiser into drive and pulled into traffic hoping that the woman would not see him as he passed. Maybe if I make myself small, he thought, and look straight ahead, she won't see me.

Our Lady of Good Voyage

*

Seated at the end of the diner counter, he slid the plate forward, set the coffee cup in its place, and opened the newspaper. On page 14, he learned that a group of Japanese and American archaeologists working a riverbed in China's Ningxia Province had begun to unearth what could prove to be the oldest specimen of its kind ever discovered. He read the scientist's comment twice.

> This one is an Iguanadon from the Orinthopod group. As the names suggest, it bears the qualities of birds and lizards. That is, it's an herbivore, but it has a beak, it's big, and it's mean. This one, I'd say, may prove to be ten meters, but they grow as long as fifteen meters, or forty-five feet. It has a long, stiff tail and thumb spikes for stabbing attackers.

He sipped his coffee.

The usual afternoon shower arrived. The place darkened; the ceiling lights tripped on. A peal of thunder rattled the windows; the spoon shivered on the countertop.

The pavement smoked. The gutters quickened with streams of black water bearing scraps of trash.

He asked the waitress for a pair of scissors to cut out the article about the Iguanadon. He'd tell Vera's kids what the scientists had discovered, and he would try to describe the creature to them. What the hell, he thought, they knew more about dinosaurs than he did. Their friendship with dinosaurs, their love for dinosaurs, was without conditions. But such faith was far from him.

He considered taking a trip with Vera in October. To North Carolina, maybe the Gulf of Mexico. He pictured a shirtless figure sitting on a beach by an ocean, a book about dinosaurs in his hand, a cold beverage beside the chair. He pictured himself regaling the girl and boy with stories and their eager faces looking up as they sat cross-legged in the sand. He saw their faces clearly, but his own face was indistinct, and he had no words to put into its mouth.

At a crack of thunder, the lights cut off and cast the diner into green twilight. The people seated here and there seemed to have lost their voices, and they turned inward until they became part of the place, so many fixtures gathering dust.

*

The next day, Vera and Joe took the two kids to the levee. When he stopped to buy kites, Vera informed him that there was no wind, but he bought them anyway. In the meadow grass, he assembled the kites and handed them to Katherine and Jimmy. They sprinted back and forth, strings over their shoulders, dragging the kites through the dead grass. Their spirited efforts faded soon, and they set the kites aside and took turns hitting a tennis ball with a plastic bat. Vera sat cross-legged and chewed a No. 2 pencil as she examined a catalog from the city college.

The absence of barges on the water was a disappointment. He would have liked to watch a limestone or a coal barge push by. But the low water was empty, the trees wilted, and the buildings across the river appeared deserted.

Katherine pointed at the binoculars hanging around his neck. "What are you doing with those?"

He slipped them off and handed them to her. "I'm giving them to you. They're yours and Jimmy's. Did you know you can use them to see far things and near things?"

On hands and knees, he searched the grass till he found a proper subject. He instructed her to hold the binoculars in reverse and aim them at the spot that he indicated. She peered down as though she were peering deep into the earth. "Mom! It's like a microscope when you hold it backwards! Oh, look at that grasshopper! It's huge! It has eyes!"

Joe held the grasshopper in his palm and spoke to it, "Autumn's coming." He tipped the grasshopper into the girl's hand. "Don't hurt him."

The creature quieted in her palm and withstood her scrutiny with ancient patience. The girl asked, "What are you going to do when you quit, Joe?"

"There's a guy named Fergus I know. He's a friend of mine. He's got a job for me. Me and him'll paint houses."

"Mom said you're looking for somebody."

"I am. My old friend."

"I hope you find him."

"I'll find him. Then I'll bring him to our place so you can meet him. He's weird. You'll like him. He's probably hungry."

"Will you? I'll make some cookies for him!" She set the grasshopper gently in the grass. The creature marched off, its dignity restored. "Can I go with him, Mom? Can I go help Joe find his friend?"

"Come here and sit down. You gotta help me get ready for school. I start in two weeks. I need notebooks and pencils and stuff, and so do you. Will you help me? We'll buy our school supplies at the same time. Then we'll eat ice cream."

Katherine said, "That'll be fun!"

"You're a good kid," he said. "Today's my last day. A few more minutes, then let's head back."

The trees exuded a clear light that was not the unclean, heavy light of summer. And though it was a warm day—high summer yet—some aspect of the clouds betokened the coming change. They retained a brightness even as the sun began its long decline. Trimmed with blue, far-off-seeming, remoter somehow, the clouds refused to fade above the fading afternoon.

*

He stood at the rear of a car and wrote on a notepad, then checked the words he'd written against the bullet holes in the rear windshield of the car. He wrote some more while the woman talked.

"And last week they shot the Jones girl's dog! Now whatta you up and do a thing like that for? Shoot a little girl's dog! There's its blood still. Look here." She shook her head and presented the sidewalk to him with a sweep of her hand. The cracked pad bore a mud-colored spot.

"I was standing there—right there next to where that dog laid—and I watched it quiver and pant while its lifeblood run out, and that little girl was crying! And that poor dog thank-the-lord finally give a shudder and give up."

Apartment buildings ringed the cul-de-sac. Broomsticks or boxfans propped the windows open. A woman in lilac scrubs walked toward the bus stop. Some kids idled on their bikes, sweat dewing their thoughtful faces.

"I wish I could be more help, ma'am, but there's just too many doors to knock on without some description or something. Just keep your eyes skinned is all I can say. Call us with anything you got. Here's the number."

"I know who's doing it and I know y'all can't do nothing till—" She leaned forward and peered into his face. "You alright? Is the heat getting to you? Sit right there for a second and I'll get you a glass of tea."

He didn't protest. He was thirsty; she was kind. She was a talker. It would be nice to hear someone talk. But a call came and he couldn't wait for the tea. As he drove the circuit of the cul-de-sac, the woman stood on the stoop of her building with a glass in her hand. He waved an apology to her as he passed, but she did not respond. Soon he was speeding over the viaduct—cars peeling away before him—past a line of brake lights on the shoulder.

Beneath the viaduct, down in the railyard, files of flatcars and coal hoppers waited among the cranes and towers. Powerlines sagged over the many converging rails, over the dormant signal lights. He glimpsed a figure stepping with long strides over the tracks. When he looked again, the figure had disappeared.

A pair of bicycle cops had detained a man, who sat cuffed on the curb in the alley that separated Fourth and Third. The man wore an angry and nauseated expression. The red-ink tattoos on his back and stomach resembled cartoon wounds.

"Tried to yank a purse off some fifteen-year-old girls," said one cop as he placed the man in the back of Joe's cruiser. He shut the door and said to Joe, "Then one of them girls pulls a knife. They chased him off, gave a good description. So there's a happy ending."

Joe pulled away with the man in the back seat. "What a day, huh?" he said in the mirror as they crossed the viaduct.

"What?"

They entered the industrial district west of the railhead, factories and trashed lots and cannibalized cars docked at crumbled curbs.

"Where you taking me?"

Joe pulled into a wide, empty street between two disused factories and parked beside a brick wall. A long series of windows spanned the wall, each window busted to a different pitch. Below the row of broken windows, a shoulder-high band of graffiti stretched the length of the block, corner to corner—an unbroken course of illuminated script.

Joe spoke through the mesh. "Look. I'm going to ask you a question and I'd like you to answer it. All you gotta do is answer the question.

Ready?" He pointed at the wall just beyond the man's window, to a word in green iridescent letters. "Look there. What's that say?"

"What's what say."

"You don't lose nothing by answering a single simple question. I can't read that but maybe you can. Now what's it say. Just answer me. Please."

"I don't know. It says *west end time*. What's this bullshit about?"

"That's three words? That's a W? Are you sure?"

"I don't know. Just take me in. I'm tired of you."

"Have you ever seen a word on a wall, spray-painted on a wall somewhere, the word *Croatoan*? C-R-O-A-T-O-A-N. *Croatoan*. Ever see it?"

"I don't have no idea what—"

"Have you ever seen it? Just answer the question, for Christ's sake! This ain't hard. Have you seen it?"

"I'm done with questions. I'm done with you."

Joe flipped the gear into park and got out. He opened the trunk of the cruiser, took out a can of spray-paint, shook it as he paced, paused at an auspicious stretch of brick, and—in plain tall unadorned Latin letters—sprayed the word CROATOAN on the wall.

Epilogue

"Are you deaf?"

Kenny's mom, a grim shade blocking the sun, stood behind the two boys who were seated on the curb. Hands on hips, a ring of keys looped on her finger, she said, "I've called to you three times now. What the hell are you doing? You didn't do anything I asked you. The kitchen is still a mess. Go get some decent clothes on. You're going with me to Mister Hugelmeyer's today."

Kenny stood with his arms at his sides and protested. "Why do I have to go to Mister Hugelmeyer's, Mom? I don't like going there. I'll stay home and clean the kitchen!"

"Too late. Get your ass inside and get dressed."

Kenny trotted toward the door. Joe leaned away from the woman and considered running off, but he didn't know where to go. There was no one home at the moment, everyone was away or at work. Only the resident ghost remained—a ghost no less real for having only been seen only by Kenny, who evaded questions concerning the ghost's appearance, leaving Joe to his own unruly visions of a dark and restless modulation in the air or some gloomy, ticking vapor. When he looked across the street at his empty house, he believed he saw something drift past the window on a pair of green wings.

Kenny's mom sighed. "You can come along if you like, Joseph, but you gotta run home and change. Quickly, now. Go go go."

He ran across the street without looking and opened the door. In some disused corner of the house, a thirsty specter shook itself awake and commenced to home in on him as he rifled the drawer for socks and a shirt. Shod and clothed, he burst from the front door heaving for breath, like a sailor surfacing from a stricken vessel.

Kevin Honold

*

Joe sat in the back seat of the Cordoba. The air inside the car was a cloying mix of sun-scorched vinyl and spilt pop, and he breathed the heat in shallow drafts. Kenny's mom set a cold plastic container of soup between his knees and ordered him to be careful with it. They drove to an apartment building shaped like a tipped shoe box.

She let herself in. "How you doing today, Henry?" she asked and carried the soup to the kitchen. "I'll put some soup in the fridge, alright? Boy is it hot out there. You're lucky to be nice and cool in here, Henry."

The boys stood inside the door awaiting instructions in a warm twilight that smelled like a bear's cave. Mister Hugelmeyer, dressed only in underwear, sat frowning at the far end of a meager couch. A pair of trousers lay like a collapsed cake in the middle of the room, damp and sour-seeming.

Kenny and Mister Hugelmeyer regarded one another with similar expressions, with the same looks that people in cars and dogs on medians exchange when the people are driving past on the highway. His mom caught him in that trance, pulled his shorthairs, pushed him into the kitchen and set him to work cleaning dishes. As she made defeated jokes about work and weather to the old man, she wordlessly introduced a vacuum cleaner to Joe and pointed at a receptacle.

Taking a stand, then, in the middle of the room, hands on hips, she held forth for Henry's benefit, bemoaning the laziness of boys generally, and condemning her two charges as fair specimens of all boys everywhere. She departed the room with the man's soiled trousers and returned with a glass of water and a bologna sandwich and placed these on the end table. Finally, she set a clean pair of pants in Mister Hugelmeyer's lap.

The old man spoke angry words that the boys didn't understand but would always remember. He leaned forward with his blue hands on his knees and peered at Kenny. "A cuckoo lays its eggs in other birds' nests," he said, "so other birds raise the baby cuckoos. And these birds, according to the jackass on the tv, get tricked by the cuckoo that way. Tricked! Tricked, you hear?"

The boys stood before the couch like a pair of shoeless barbarians before the emperor, who had resolved, after all his fainthearted senators had fled, to confront the untutored brutes with the dignity befitting his status.

"What a load a shit that is. Are you going to stand there and tell me," Mister Hugelmeyer continued, "that a creature that has the ability *to fly through the godforsaken air*—you follow me?—that can *build a nest with its mouth*, can't recognize its own goddamn eggs? No, sir. I will not have it. No, sir."

Kenny's mom returned from the bedroom with a plastic garbage bag full of clothes that smelled, handed it to Kenny, told them to say good-bye, promised Mister Hugelmeyer that she would return in two days, and shooed the boys out.

On the ride home, Joe sat in the back and closed his eyes to the hot gusting air. When he looked again, he saw Kenny's face in the passenger door mirror. The reflected face was small and dark like a stranger's, and the brow was shadowed with a stubborn reckoning. When Kenny finally spoke, his words were tentative, as if he'd been arranging them for days. "Mom, why is Mister Hugelmeyer so mad? Is it because he poos his pants?"

His mother checked both mirrors. "Well, partly." She checked them again and said, "He's suffering. He's senile, Kenny. Do you know what that means? It means you're old and tired. He's in a lot of pain. Hopefully God'll end that for him soon."

"How's he gonna do that?"

"He'll either make Mister Hugelmeyer better or let him go so he doesn't suffer anymore."

Kenny twisted the tuning knob of the dead radio back and forth between his thumb and finger.

"What's that in your pocket, Kenny? Is that a book? Where did you get that?"

"Mister Hugelmeyer gave it to me."

"When?"

"Just now. He told me I could have it, Mom. I swear I didn't steal it!"

She held it up and examined it as she drove. Joe could see that the book was an old pocket edition with a sailing ship stamped in gold on the cover, and tiny print on ice-colored pages.

Kenny explained, "Mister Hugelmeyer said it's about a voyage to the Arctic Sea."

She set the book on the dash. "You're gonna give that back."

"But—okay."

A man in a blue shirt walked out of a gas station garage and took a seat on a metal folding chair in the shade of a vacant repair bay. Two pumps stood in empty sunlight, in a tract of oil-stained concrete. As they drove past, Joe watched the man, wondering what decision God was going to make concerning Mister Hugelmeyer. He had a bad feeling about that.

Kenny said, "Why do you go there, Mom? Why doesn't his family clean up for him?"

"I don't think he's got a family. So me and some other people, we help him a little. Like me and you and Joey did today. A lot of people don't have anybody who loves them like you two have. A lot of people don't have anyone in the world." At these words, an image resolved in Joe's mind, an image of so many people, hundreds, maybe a thousand, waiting on an empty tarmac, suitcases at their feet, coats folded over their forearms.

When they pulled into the driveway, Kenny said, "I'll go clean up the kitchen."

His mother pushed the shifter into park. "No. Go on and play with Joey."

She squeezed his knee and smiled at him and told him to *git*, and the boys climbed out and ran away, their bafflement forgotten in an instant.

*

They pedaled up and down streets lined with houses. The entrance to the maintenance road was screened with overhanging branches, like the entrance to a bootleggers' camp. They pushed the branches away with their free hands and rode the brakes down a steep hill to the electrical power plant that stood like the skeleton of a spider, high on spindly legs, its joints knobby with bushings and insulators. For a time, the boys idled on their bikes and listened to the drone that slackened and surged and seemed to come up from the earth. The vibration traveled through Joe's sneakers and up his shin bones.

"Flying saucers come here at night to recharge," Kenny said.

Even in the heat of July, it was cool and dark down there, where a small creek ran beside the plant's chain-link fence. Houses and four-family apartment buildings, barely visible through the intervening leaves, lined the high ground all around. The buildings stood with their backs turned, watching out over sunlit streets and traffic. The people who lived in those houses, Joe was certain, never visited this place or cared about what happened down here beyond their back doors, where the power plant hummed day and night, every day, without pause or inflection, as it had since the beginning of time. He imagined flying saucers hovering above the place, paying out electrical cords like anchor chains, siphoning power from the plant under cover of darkness.

They ditched the bikes in the weeds and walked beside the creek into the green shade of the woods. Kenny jumped the stones across the water, searched the far bank, and retrieved a metal gas can from a root hole.

Joe walked down the trail to look at the snapping turtle whose shell was the width of a manhole cover. Some older kids had beaten it to death with sticks. It still lay in that gloomy and littered place where a heavy scent of rot lingered. The turtle lay on its back, its stomach caved. Around the carcass was a frenzy of sneaker prints and, casually flung aside in the nearby weeds, the sticks that had served as the instruments of its destruction. The sticks were thick as bats and as tall as he was, and their presence profaned the place and implicated him as he stood there, for he was present when the crime was committed, and he recalled how the turtle's legs pawed the air as it was dragged by the tail across the mud. He recalled the laughing boys who stood over it, who wore baseball caps pulled down so low you couldn't see their eyes.

The shadow of vice had fallen over that unremarkable little bend in the trail. Something drew him back to the place, sometimes with Kenny, sometimes alone.

It appalled him now, as he stood there looking at the turtle, that he would grow up and be compelled, some day, to kill a thing that big. He wondered what kind of animal he would kill. If he stuck with Kenny, he reasoned, perhaps he would not be made to kill turtles. For his friend would doubtless refuse to commit any such act. Kenny would undergo horrible tortures; he would refuse unto his last breath to hurt any animal.

Joe considered burying the dead turtle or dragging it back into the water. But he decided against those ideas and walked back to his friend.

*

They spent hours contriving little ships from bark and twigs, binding the planks and timbers with long green grasses. Kenny bored holes in the hulls with his buck knife and inserted cane masts. Joe fashioned sails from some moldered red fabric he'd found. They chewed the gum of the cane as they worked. Indian gum, Kenny called it.

Once in a while, they would admire without envy an especially fine example of shipcraft or a novel lashing technique. Joe formed sailors out of clayey mud and placed them at their battle stations as the sun went down behind the enormous trees.

They stood in their shoes in the ankle-deep water as Kenny gently soaked the fleet with gasoline, inadvertently splashing Joe's fingers as he did so. They stepped back, Kenny tossed a wooden match, and the ships burst into flames that cast green shadows on the water. They followed the burning vessels as the fires died and the scorched sailors toppled overboard. After drifting twenty feet, the ships ran aground on a pebbly shoal. The sails, as they disintegrated, smoked blackly.

The boys dropped flat rocks on the stricken craft, and there was an end to it.

"Fireships," Kenny said. "Just like Drake at Gravelines."

*

When they returned home, Kenny's mom was reading a paperback at the kitchen table.

"Hungry?" She frowned. "Why do you smell like gasoline?"

Kenny poured water into a pot and dropped three hot dogs in. As his mom prepared macaroni and cheese, she listened to her son's thrilled account of the recent action, in which he and Joe had discomfited the Spanish galleons. Kenny recalled to her the tree that he'd climbed and the mud puppies he'd seen. He asked if Joe could sleep over.

They washed the dishes and sat on the couch watching television until Kenny's mom stood and turned the set off. She put an album on the turntable and sat back in the recliner with a bottle of beer and sang along to make them laugh.

> I'm gonna be a wheel some day
> I'm gonna be somebody
> everything gonna go my way
> then I won't wantchyou.

The boys laughed as she sang, so she turned the volume higher, and the careless joy in the singer's voice quieted them and carried them away on a riot of quick, light keys.

She turned the volume down, sat with her head back in the chair, recalled dance halls where the young men had waited turns to dance with her. Joe pictured an antiseptic royal court where fancy people didn't smile, where couples in crisp black suits and ruffled white dresses spun like tops in rigid pairs under impending chandeliers.

"Were you old then?" Kenny asked. "Did dad dance?"

She affirmed that he did dance, and danced well too. Riveted, Kenny listened to her talk about the Mashed Potato and the Watusi, the flasks of bourbon in her purse, his father's good-natured fistfights out in the parking lot. It was beyond belief, and he said so.

Joe grew sleepy, the voices drifted, and he had a dim sense of being carried upstairs and laid in bed beside Kenny.

A woman arranged the sheet around them in the dark. He felt the warm hair on his face as she drew the blanket over his shoulder, and he fell asleep.

*

When Joe opened his eyes, the room had resolved to gray. Cool morning air, tinctured with birdsong, fell through the open window and spilled over his forehead. On the walls above the bed were pictures of sailing ships cut from magazines and images his friend had traced from library books. Slips of paper taped beneath the pictures recorded, in Kenny's stylized script, the classes and names of the ships as well as the seas of their demise. Phoenician merchantmen and Greek triremes, stout Roman galleys with ranks of long oars spreading from amidships. English seventy-fours hammering away at the French flagship at Trafalgar. The *Bonhomme Richard* and the *Serapis* locked in a pall of fiery smoke, sails slack, masts splintered, sailors desperately treading water. Those pictures constituted a sort of arcana, the paraphernalia of an obscure cult whose sole initiate was Kenny Stegemuller.

Looking at the pictures, it occurred to Joe that the ocean is rounded, like an eye. That's what an ocean was, a great livid eye staring back at God, flecked with the black motes of drowned men, a cruel place where nothing good ever happened. He hoped he would never have to set out across one.

Kenny woke, and within a few minutes they were pedaling through the empty streets toward the big woods, where they rode their Huffys down the creekside trail, butts off the seats, legs and arms juddering over the rough, packed mud. The air in the trees was river-green, cool and damp, and the sun, cheerless and small as a hunter's fire, flared between the trunks.

They shouldered their bikes through the concrete pipe that carried the stream beneath the road. Their voices resounded as they splashed through the littered slimy water.

Kenny pushed the bike uphill. The sound of bike pedals shredding sumac accompanied them as they made their way through the undergrowth. They arrived at a muddy shelf of level ground, where a low enclosure of logs—the depth and width of a tool shed—was situated.

They walked the perimeter of the works, inspecting corner posts, making businesslike remarks. The posts had arrived in the spring, fortuitously shorn and broken to specification, delivered by rains that had flooded the stream valley. The stream's bends were still choked with great tangles of logs and brush, ready lumber for a palisaded camp.

After the flood receded, they had cleared a path with switches and chopped steps in the hillside mud with axes. For days they had dragged trunks to the terrace, a site chosen by Kenny after much consideration of avenues of approach and supply routes and other mysterious factors. They set to work digging postholes with Uncle Darryl's collapsible GI trenching tool.

On that far-off day when the camp was finally finished, Joe thought he and Kenny would move in, and no one would ever find them. They would conduct foraging parties every few days to steal food from businesses or gardens. That idea had been tested on a recent Saturday when they had knocked on the glass door of Rizzi's Bakery before dawn and told the woman who answered that they were hungry and had no homes. She'd spoken in a language that they didn't understand and given them each a pint carton of chocolate milk and a cruller, which they devoured behind a strip mall.

That's how things would be, life on a shoestring, catch-as-catch-can. They would live in the woods, and their names would be anathematized by the school authorities for their transgressions, and the kids in Sister Benedicta's sixth-grade class would whisper their names—Stegemuller, Riley—like watchwords to inspirit one another when things got tough.

There was much work to do today. They retrieved two hand axes—fashioned imperfectly from creek stone under Kenny's tutelage—from a hollow trunk and set about mortising logs. All efforts to sharpen the stones had been defeated, as the stones invariably broke against the grain, but the things served their purposes well enough. The work, for these reasons, progressed slowly and was often interrupted to discuss a wood spider or a colony of ant flies. No matter. Neither deadlines nor schedules constrained them, for the world's troubles were not their troubles, and the long days led away, in gratuitous succession, to the very vanishing point of time, which was inexhaustible as air, and warranted as little concern.

A shadow that crossed their hands, as they mortised the logs, belonged to a great horned owl. The trees held their breath as the bird threaded the trunks, its wings taut as dragon's wings. In the morning stillness, the wing feathers cut through the air with a wispy, burring sound. The owl backstroked once and lit on a high branch, lost to green leaves.

"That thing was bigger than me," Kenny said.

When they were bored with the work, they squatted behind the walls and kept watch against enemies whose duplicity was known well enough.

The trees creaked in a rising breeze. Birds sang. Squirrels chacked. Mayflies drifted among the canted columns of sunlight, and white clouds drifted in silence.

The hours passed; the woods drowsed in the rising warmth.

Kenny said, "I have to get back and go to mass."

His mom was waiting, dressed nicely, in the driveway.

"Where the hell have you been? Get those muddy things off and get dressed. Joseph, you can go with us if you want. Go home and change, and tell your mother you're with me."

*

The priest and servers marched up the aisle to organ music. A boy in a white cassock belted like a friar led the procession, clutching a tall crucifix at port-arms. The priest climbed the three steps to the altar and stretched out his hands.

The stained-glass windows depicted David as a boy with his flock, and Simon carrying Christ's cross. Each scene was shot through with sunlight that Joe wanted desperately to return to.

Kenny folded his hands and sang. During the second reading he closed his eyes and bowed his head. His hands gripped the beveled rail of the next pew.

And it shall come to pass in the last days, the lector read, *I will pour out my spirit on all people.*

As the closing hymn played, the priest and the altar boys and the parishioners departed, but Kenny and his mother waited. When the place was nearly deserted, they walked to the rear of the church where votive candles were arrayed on a rack of tiered shelves. A plaster statue of Mary in bare feet stood on the top shelf looking down and away. Light from the candles cast her shadow severally against the wall.

Kenny picked up the matchbox and looked at his mother. "Let me light it this time," he said.

She assented with a nod, and he picked out a match, struck it, and reached the flame to a candle near Mary's foot. As the glass bloomed with light, he looked to his mother, and they both folded their hands, crossed themselves, closed their eyes.

Joe stood aside, nettled by a sense of omission.

The quiet warmth of a summer Sunday morning greeted them as they walked out.

On the empty sidewalk, Kenny bounded around them, beside himself, and could not suppress a shout. At last, and with no other way to articulate his happiness, he broke into a run, headlong down the block, waving his arms at his mother's worried calls.

ABOUT THE AUTHOR

Kevin Honold is the author of a novel, *Molly* (winner of The 2020 Autumn House Book Prize), an essay collection, *The Rock Cycle* (winner of The 2019 River Teeth Book Prize), and a poetry collection, *Men as Trees Walking* (winner of The 2009 OSU Press/*The Journal* Book Award). Honold is a graduate of the University of Cincinnati, and is currently a History and Special Education teacher in Santa Fe, New Mexico.

ABOUT ORISON BOOKS

Orison Books is a 501(c)3 non-profit literary press focused on the life of the spirit from a broad and inclusive range of perspectives. We seek to publish books of exceptional poetry, fiction, and non-fiction from perspectives spanning the spectrum of spiritual and religious thought, ethnicity, gender identity, and sexual orientation.

As a non-profit literary press, Orison Books depends on the support of donors. To find out more about our mission and our books, or to make a donation, please visit www.orisonbooks.com.

Orison Books is deeply grateful to our recurring annual donors for sustaining our important work. If you'd like to make a recurring or one-time contribution, please visit www.orisonbooks.com/support-us.

Sustainers' Circle

Carol Dines
Michele Laub
Laura & Barry Rand
Bruce Spang
Lee Stockdale
Anonymous

Advocates' Circle

David Ebenbach
Anonymous

Supporters' Circle

Nickole Brown
Richard Chess

Friends' Circle

Paige Gilchrist
Laurel Haavik
Alida Woods

Printed in the USA
CPSIA information can be obtained
at www.ICGtesting.com
LVHW090547250424
778371LV00001B/6